CHELSEA BLUES

by

RODERICK COOPER

Published in 1986 by
Academy Chicago Publishers
425 North Michigan Avenue
Chicago, IL 60611

Copyright © Roderick Cooper 1984

Printed and bound in the USA

Library of Congress Cataloging-in-Publication Data

Cooper, Roderick.
  Chelsea blues.

  I. Title.
PR6053.0594C5   1986   823'.914   86-22147
ISBN 0-89733-239-3
ISBN 0-89733-228-8 (pbk.)

ONE

Giles Buildings were exactly 100 years old. Not that anyone was celebrating the centenary, although the inscription "Giles Buildings, erected 1880 by the Cornworthy Trust" was marked clearly enough on the block nearest the street, too high to be seen by pedestrians, but at eye-level from the nearby flyover carrying traffic from the airport over the Edgware Road and into the heart of London. If Dave and Myra Dilley from East Lansing, Michigan, or Hal and Sherry Carpenter from Toledo, Ohio, spotted it from their seats on the flight coach speeding to the air terminal in Kensington, they would have given it no more than a casual glance, like those at the hoardings which told them that Britain, too, was Marlboro country and there was a welcome at Macdonald's here as well.

Possibly, eager for their first glimpse of British living conditions after the drab approach to the city from Heathrow, they might have noticed the depressing grime and ugliness of the four apartment blocks beside the flyover. They might have noticed Mrs Elsie Dunn hanging out her washing on the flat roof of the second block, but then they would have been over the Edgware Road and heading for the terminal with no thought or knowledge of the inhabitants of Giles Buildings, which would really have been just as well because Dave and Hal and a good many others would be dead within the week and Giles Buildings would have a great deal to do with that fact.

So Elsie Dunn hung up her last pair of knickers unobserved, looked up at the long line of washing already flapping in the stiff breeze and hurried to the flight of concrete steps leading down to her open landing on the top floor before her bacon burned to a crisp.

Sidney Dunn heard the roof door slam overhead. He opened his eyes reluctantly and waited for his mother to call him. The brown, diamond-shaped damp patch on the ceiling over the bed was spreading. If it reached the wall behind him he would have to move his

5

Buddy Holly poster from above the bedhead to beside the wardrobe on the facing wall. Still, he could see it from where he lay then.

Sidney was a Stamford Bridge Shed boy. For ten years, more than half his life, he had spent every other Saturday afternoon from August to May packed tight in the great metal barn behind the Fulham Road end, roaring his allegiance to Chelsea Football Club. But the best part of it all was like now, waking up and realizing it was match day and the Blues were at home.

"Sidney! Are you getting up? Your breakfast's on the table."

His mum. Even Saturdays ran to a timetable, however sluggish. He swung his legs out of bed, shuffled into his slippers and tugged an old sweater over his head. He yawned again, combed his thick hair carefully in front of the old dressing-table mirror and wandered out to the living-room.

His mother, laying the table busily, tutted. "I don't know why you can't wash and shave before your breakfast, like your dad," she said.

He slumped into a chair and reached for the paper, slightly crumpled and grease-stained beside his father's long since congealed plate of bacon rinds and toast crusts. "Yes you do," he said morosely. "Because we haven't got a bathroom, that's why. How could I wash while you were rinsing out clothes or cooking breakfast? You couldn't swing a cat in that kitchen."

"We're getting a bathroom, you know that," she said. "Although heaven knows what Mrs Franks will do to the rent when it's finished. Then there'll be no hall space left for your crash hat and your dad's uniform great coat and I don't know what else."

He sighed as he poured milk on his cornflakes. He should not have started her off. Now she was in one of her I don't know why we still live in this dreadful place moods. Well, it was no good asking him. She knew the answer well enough. It was because his dad would never move to the council blocks over the other side of Lissom Grove. Would not budge. Not living on no council estate and that's flat. They had heard that often enough and however much his mum grumbled, she felt the same way. Neither of them would move until the place came down about their ears. They had both been born in Giles Buildings and they would probably die there. But at least the council flats down by the canal had real people in them. Giles Buildings had lost all its old regular tenants, apart from his parents and three old couples in the block. And now there was talk of Mrs Franks doing up the flats as they fell empty, tarting up the kitchens with cheapo pine, adding a shower room and letting them as West End holiday flats at two hundred nicker a week.

"These cornflakes are all bendy," he said. "They should be crisp."

"Fat chance anything's got of being crisp in this place," said his mother, returning from the kitchen with his bacon and egg. "There's damp everywhere."

"Including my bedroom," he said through the last mouthful of his cornflakes. "That damp patch on the ceiling is spreading."

She tutted again. "I'll get your father to have another go at Mrs Franks. They'll put some more of that shiny stuff on the roof, I suppose. It's getting like a skating-rink up there. I nearly broke my neck hanging out the washing this morning. Get that breakfast down and then stir yourself. I got all the shopping to do and then Mrs Blakey's coming to tea this afternoon. You remember Mrs Blakey— used to live in Bell Street. They got a council place over in Hillingdon. I want this place looking nice, if that's possible, so the sooner you're off out of it, the better."

"Oh ta," he said. "Charming."

He ate the rest of his breakfast in five minutes, glancing through the sports pages of the *Sun*. There was nothing about Chelsea in it. He would be glad when they got back into the first division where they belonged. You got more publicity up there, specially when you were playing Liverpool or Manchester United. He flipped back to page three and gazed at the topless beauty. "Seventeen-year-old Suzie lives in Kensington and is busy decorating her new home." And to prove it, Suzie was clutching a paint brush between her generous breasts which had burst through the front of her dungarees. What a pair.

"And don't sit there slobbering over that baggage," said his mother, emerging from the kitchen again.

"All right, all right, I'll be off in a second," he said, licking egg yolk from his thick lower lip as he rose.

"You coming back for a bite of lunch or having something on the way to the match?" she said. "I need to know because I'm not having your dirty boots all over the floor just as I've finished cleaning."

"No, I'll have something out. Where's my scarf?"

"Airing on the heater. It needed a good wash."

"Blimey, Mum, it's not meant to be clean!" he said. "I like it sort of grey."

"It was in a disgusting state. You see any of your friends' mums

7

down the market and they'd think I never washed your clothes."

"But clean ones are for beginners, and I been going down the Shed for ten years now."

"What about this evening?" said his mother wearily. "Will you be in for supper?"

"Depends. I don't know," he said. "Probably be back about seven."

"You can leave your money on the table before you go out and all," she said, taking his plate to the kitchen sink. "I'm not having you spend it all on records down the market. And you owe me two pounds from last week."

"I hadn't forgotten." He wandered out to the hall.

"Sidney!"

He groaned and slouched back.

"You can't go out in that state! You haven't washed or shaved."

"My spots is bad," he said. "You know the doctor said not to shave when my spots is bad."

"You can go on down the baths and have a good soak," she said. "Here's a clean towel and there's a carrier-bag on the hook in the hall by the lavvy door. Leave the towel in the carrier with Mrs Mountjoy down the market and I'll pick it up when I'm shopping."

He grunted.

"Off out of my way then, and just keep out of trouble at the match."

He slammed the front door behind him. Out on the open landing he hesitated for a second and then slipped quietly up the steps to the roof door. He liked it up on the roof. He looked across to the flyover with its speeding traffic and then over to the West End skyline dominated by the Post Office Tower. The cinema opposite was showing a new double bill, *Nuns in Scarlet* and *Hot Pussy*. He might be glad of that tomorrow night.

He reached for the nearest of his mother's sheets flapping in the breeze and wrapped one corner round the bath towel in his hand to dampen it. Then he slipped it back in the carrier-bag and set off at a gallop down the nine flights of stairs. There were no lifts in Giles Buildings. Down in the yard he made sure his motor bike was securely covered and locked before strolling through the Buildings towards Church Street.

The market was in full cry. Fruit and veg, jellied eels and cockles, meat and cheese, fabrics and furniture, children's clothes and blue denim everywhere, china, pictures, books, bric-à-brac—and the

8

stores and antique arcades behind the stalls were thriving, too.

"Hullo, Sidney. I been looking out for you," said Les Ford, behind his record stall in the centre of the market. "Something special come up—*Holly in the Hills,* issued '65. Mint condition, you've not got that!"

"Reissued later as *Washing* and that I have got," said Sid. "You know me, Les. I collect them to play, not to take out and stroke like some of them Elvis freaks. I just like Buddy's sounds."

"Not interested then?" said Les shortly.

"Now, Les, I didn't say that," said Sid. "And mine's getting scratched. Only I'm not paying collector's prices to replace a few tracks. That's my point."

He felt important talking to Les. The other kids, riffling through the punk rock, the reggae, the heavy metal and the new wave romantic albums stacked in boxes on the stall could hear a real connoisseur discussing the business with Les Ford who was generally too edgy about his stock being stuffed under blousons and jumpers to keep a civil tongue in his head for long. He snatched the record back from Sid's grasp. "Right then," he said. "I'll put that out on display until you make your mind up. I brought that back from Brum specially for you, Sidney lad. You don't want it, that's all right. I'll find someone who does."

"OK, Les," he said easily. "See you later." He sauntered on down the crowded street. He wanted it all right, but he was not paying over the odds. He would leave it for a couple of weeks. He had stumbled on his first Holly albums years ago in a job lot at a jumble sale and the first two really early ones he had picked up from Les were for peanuts. Then the hustler realized Sid was a keen collector and the prices started to rise. So he would leave it for a couple of weeks. Then they could start negotiating. They had been playing the game long enough.

"Sidney!" The screech was all too familiar. His mother pushed her way through the crowds, shopping trolley rattling along behind her. "Have you been down for your bath yet?"

"Yes, course," he muttered. "You have to tell the world we got no bathroom?"

She grabbed the towel from under his arm and thrust one hand into it suspiciously. "Well, you were quick then," she said grudgingly. She dropped it into the trolley. "You wouldn't fancy pulling your poor old Mum's trolley round the market for half an hour, I suppose?"

9

"Have a heart, Ma," he said. "I got to meet the lads."

"Oh well," she said. "Keep out of trouble."

"Don't I always?" he said, injured.

"There's always a first time," she said darkly. "Have a nice afternoon, son."

He escaped thankfully and dived through a gap in the shoppers as he spotted Wayne and Kenny standing listlessly on the far pavement. They brightened up as they saw him approaching.

"All right then, Sid?" said Wayne, a tall, close-cropped youth with Sidney's pimples and tombstone teeth. Like the smaller, less spotty Kenny beside him, he had knotted his blue and white striped scarf round his right wrist from which it dangled down to the pavement. Sidney tugged his own scarf from his denim jacket pocket and knotted it in the same fashion round his wrist. Two Japanese tourists stared at the three of them. Sidney made a rude gesture with right fist and forearm. They turned away. He grinned.

"We seen you talking to Les Ford just now," said Kenny. "Then we lost you in the crowd."

The three of them drifted slowly through the market. "The secret of getting on with geezers like Les Ford comes from being a collector," said Sid, picking up an argument where it had been dropped a week ago. "Like he knows I'm into Buddy Holly. You're not a collector of anything, Wayne. That's why he don't fancy your custom."

"Only scalps," said Wayne darkly. "I got Fulham and Tottenham scalps, Arsenal, Orient and West Ham scalps."

"Scarves!" said Sid scornfully. "You got scarves. What can you do with bleedings scarves? You can't play 'em. I mean, put 'em on a turntable and you wouldn't get much of a tune out of them. Hang about, Les is waving."

"Oh strewth, not again," Wayne grumbled. "We want to get going."

"You don't want to carry a record down the match, Sid," said Kenny. "I mean, you can't clap or wave or do nothing holding an album all afternoon."

"Suppose we got some aggro," said Wayne. "How you going to smash someone in the teeth if you're trying to protect your record?"

"Aggro! When did you get into any of that?" scoffed Sidney. "You're all mouth, you."

"Then how come I got all them scarves, big bum. Tell me that,"

10

said Wayne triumphantly.

"Oh well, anyone can nick a guy's scarf when he's outnumbered ten to one," said Sidney. "Now hold up. I'll just see what Les wants and then we can push off. Only him and me's in the middle of some tricky negotiations over a Holly album I'd particularly fancy—not that he knows that. You have to box clever.

"All right, Les?" shouted Sid.

"I certainly am, old son," said Les smugly, cigarette twitching triumphantly. "I just sold that Holly album."

"You never! Just like that? In a few minutes?"

"Just like that. And it was more like a few seconds. Moment I put it out. American girl. Tourist. Holly fan like yourself. You don't want to hang about when I come back from my travels with a gem for you, Sidney boy."

Sid grunted and pushed his way back to the other two, scowling.

"Well, only Buddy bleeding Holly," said Wayne. "I don't see what you get from that plink plonk stuff anyway. It's about as prehistoric as ballroom dancing. I mean, you're a couple of years older than me and Kenny but that stuff goes back before you were born."

"That's not the point," said Sid loftily. "You wouldn't understand."

"It was an album you wanted real bad, Sid?" said Kenny.

"No, that's not the point neither," said Sid. "I got all the tracks under another title. Not in bad condition and I taped it for safety anyway. I just don't like naffing tourists poking in everywhere and pissing up the prices by paying over the odds. I could have got a real handsome clasp-knife in Bell Street the other Saturday morning and some bleeding Yank went up another quid. Marked price on the table too. I mean, that's not on. And there was a real storm brewing nicely at Charlie's stall this morning and some nosy peace-making bugger of a tourist ruined it for everyone just as it was getting good. Tourists—I hate 'em. You can't get a bleeding hamburger round here for less than eighty."

"That's not their fault," said Kenny mildly. "It's the greedy sods who charge 'em."

"Yes, well, they're not British either, are they?" said Sidney.

Wayne groaned. "Not all that again," he said.

They turned left out of Church Street into the Edgware Road and wandered slowly back towards the distant flyover, pausing every now and then to inspect the music centres and hi-fi equipment in the shop

11

windows. "I want to get one of them personal stereos with the headphones," said Sid. "You can have full blast stereo all night, lying in bed, and no one could complain."

There was a queue inside the chip shop near the flyover. They walked through to the back and joined it. Heads were craned up to a television set on the wall over the door. It was football preview time although the sound commentary could hardly be heard above the sizzling fat in the frier as golden portions of heavily battered cod and coley hissed and spat. One of the three Greek Cypriots behind the counter shook another mountain of chips into the drainer. Lurid-looking pies shone bright orange under the lights, steak and kidney, chicken and mushroom and minced beef standing beside fat sausages and saveloys.

The three edged forward with the queue, necks craning up at the television over the door.

"That's Man United and Forest last year," said Wayne. "They'll not give much second division coverage. Cripes, I'll be glad when we're back in the first. I mean after your Liverpool, your Everton, your Arsenal, who gets worked up over your Oldham, Cambridge or Shrewsbury? And there's no good aggro any more."

"Aggro!" Sid scoffed again. "Oh, sorry, chief. Cod and chips once."

"Here, look, this is a second division game," said Kenny. "Charlton and Leicester."

"It's on BBC, though," said Wayne. "They never show Chelsea."

Sid collected his change from the Cypriot.

"Cod and chips, ta," said Kenny. "Once."

The man glared at him. "You three together?"

"Yes," said Kenny.

"And what you having?" said the Cypriot to Wayne.

"Cod and chips," said Wayne.

"Then why you not ask for cod and chips three times?" said the Cypriot to Sid who was generously salting his chips from a large shaker on the counter and still looking up at the television screen. "Why you make me go that way and this three times, eh? Get the fish, get the chips, wrap up, take the money, get the change, give the change—all three times. You three together, all have cod and chips, you say three cod and chips. That makes sense?"

"Christ, don't take on so, Pedro," said Sid. "Hey up, lads, Blues are on!"

He jabbed a chip at the screen as he reached for the vinegar bottle.

"Two cod and chips," said the man, slamming them angrily down on the counter in front of Kenny.

"I'm not paying for his," said Kenny. "Can't you take separate money?"

"He pay you for his," said the Cypriot. "One more pound."

Wayne pushed a grubby pound note across the counter, muttering.

"You say something?" said the Cypriot.

"Keep your hair on, Makarios," said Wayne. "Christ Almighty, you'll need a driving-licence and references to buy fish and chips soon."

"There is change of forty pence," said the Cypriot. "Twenty for you and twenty for him. I work it out for you in case you cannot do it."

"Cheeky peasant," said Sid as they stood gazing up at the screen. "Come on you Blues!"

"It's that Clive Walker goal against Cambridge!" said Kenny.

"You lot—out!" called another of the fish friers.

"Hang about, there's one more good goal coming up," said Wayne.

"Out!" said the Cypriot, starting to climb over the counter.

They ambled out, Wayne blowing a loud raspberry as they went.

"Cheeky bleeding Dago," said Sid angrily.

"He's not a Dago," said Kenny. "Strictly speaking."

"Strictly speaking, he wants his cobblers kicking in," said Sid through a mouthful of battered cod. "And he'll bleeding get it and all, one night. Bleeding wops, coming over here and telling us what to do."

"He's not a wop, neither," said Kenny.

"At least he's not a tourist, Sid," said Wayne with a grin.

"He's not a Londoner neither," said Sid. "And living here twenty years don't make him one. Can't even speak English proper. Ignorant greaseball."

They wandered slowly down the steps into the subway running under the flyover where the central chamber echoed to the footfalls and polyglot chatter of tourists from the nearby Metropole Hotel, all gazing perplexed at the labyrinth of tunnels.

"Say, son," said an elderly American in a light check overcoat, "which way to the Marble Arch?"

Sid jabbed a vague thumb in the opposite direction, towards Kilburn and the three of them moved on up the stairs towards the

13

tube station, sniggering. "With a little bit of luck he'll end up in Watford," said Sid. "Oh bloody hell, look at this queue!"

The line at the booking office wound round the corner of the hall and back again. Sid screwed his greasy wrapping-paper into a ball and kicked it across the pavement. He sucked the vinegar and oil from his fingers as they joined the long line of families and young couples with heavy backpacks.

The booking clerk was making heavy weather of his morning, patiently redirecting tourists to the Bakerloo line station on the other side of the flyover for Oxford Circus and the West End, sending others on their way to the Tower complete with tube maps and colourful London Transport pamphlets.

"Day return Fulham Broadway," said Sid abruptly when he finally reached the little window.

"How about behaving yourselves for once when you get there?" said the booking clerk.

"And how about . . ."

"Leave it out, Sid," said Wayne impatiently. "I'm pissed off with hanging around here."

"Hurry up, Wayne," said Kenny from the rear. "Train just in."

They waited for him and then the three of them rushed for the stairs down to the platform, scattering outgoing passengers on their way up.

The West Indian ticket-collector on the barrier grabbed Sid by the wrist. "You know de train turns round here. Ain't no rush. It just come in. You seen it. None of your mischief in this station, boy. No call to go stamping on people all over de place. You hear me good."

The other two were watching, grinning, from the foot of the stairs.

"Not your day, is it, Siddo?" said Wayne, laughing. "First a wop and now a coon takes you to the cleaner's."

"Interfering sod," said Sid bitterly. "No law against running down-stairs, is there? Here, I'll have that last bit of cod."

He grabbed the crisp brown titbit that Wayne had been saving until last and swallowed it with a gulp. Wayne shouted angrily and chased him in and out of the empty carriages as they made their way down to the rear of the train. They swung the last few yards by the hanging straps overhead and finally sprawled out, feet across the gangway, in the middle of the final car.

"Isn't it bloody marvellous, though?" said Sid. "There's hardly a sodding Londoner left round here."

14

"Leave it out, Sid," said Wayne. "We heard that record more often than your boring old Buddy Holly period pieces."

"Here comes Agger and the boys," said Kenny, peering over his shoulder and up the platform towards a distant clamour of guttural shouts and chanting. The noise grew louder and the gently humming train rocked and swayed as the latest arrivals swung their way in and out of the carriages until they burst in to join them. Agger Harris, Poncho Gale and Terry Barnes, home and away Chelsea Boys.

Every away trip provided fresh tales of triumph to which Wayne and Kenny listened with envy, however much they scoffed. Their parents would never allow them to make the long trips north on the soccer specials. Sid did not care for other towns and cities anyway. London was his patch and he preferred to spend his alternate Saturdays working on his motor bike and prowling the city on his own while Wayne and Kenny settled for second best at Fulham or Queen's Park Rangers.

The doors slid shut and the train changed pitch and jerked forward into the tunnel as Agger and Poncho bragged of their battles with Cardiff City fans at Ninian Park the previous week.

"Kids' stuff," said Sid loftily.

"Kids?" said Agger. "This git had his scalp cut from one side to the other. Ask him if it was kids' stuff."

On the platform at Notting Hill Gate older passengers stood aside in alarm as several dozen close-cropped teenagers piled into the train. The coaches rocked again.

"All right, Agger?" yelled one tall youth with a Chelsea crest tattooed on his left forearm.

"You ask him then," said Agger. "Dangler! That's right we done over three dozen Welshies last week, innit?"

"They was mincemeat when we finished with 'em," yelled Dangler over the swaying heads as the train gathered speed again.

At Earls Court a small group of away fans in red scarves kept nervously to themselves at the far end of the car. The crush grew heavier as more fans piled in, squeezing even more tightly together as the doors finally shut behind them at the third attempt. Then they were rattling on through West Brompton and on towards Fulham Broadway.

"All I'm saying is," said Sid, "I got better things to do with my time than beat up a few kids in the street. I mean, it's different for you, Agger, working in an office all day under some snooty bugger who

15

keeps you in late if you miss the bus in the morning. Only natural you need to run about a bit at weekends. I did at your age."

"Cobblers," said Agger weakly. It was a sore point. He worked as a tea boy and messenger in a large office block in the city and was terrorized from Monday morning to Friday evening by a small, bald, bespectacled chief clerk who made his life a misery with his carping criticisms, his insistence on punctuality, cleanliness and silence and his passionate conviction that persons under the age of twenty-one should not answer back their elders.

Agger had worked off many a week's frustrations with a kick or a belt in the ribs on a Saturday away day. The rampaging, train wrecking, shop looting and general mayhem in towns and cities up and down the country went some way to making up for the misery of his week.

But there was no denying that Sid had the superior job with the freedom to ride the streets on his much envied motor-bike. And however much they might brag over wounds received and beatings handed out in battle, their own injuries were sadly unimpressive a week later when the tales were told. A long since faded black eye or a grazed knuckle soon washed smooth could hardly compare with Sid's spectacular scars and scrapes after skirmishes in heavy London traffic with cabs and buses. To date, Sid had broken both wrists and one ankle in three years and had them in plaster to prove it the following Saturday. Ridden on in them, too.

Sid was all too well aware that his freedom was an illusion. His boss harassed him as mercilessly as Agger's bullied him, urging him on from one delivery to the next with oaths and threats.

But that was all forgotten now as they arrived at Fulham Broadway on a Saturday afternoon, spilling out on to the platform and then surging up the stairs to the booking-hall where the first frisking searches began as waiting police spotted a suspicious bulge in a jeans pocket here, a dangerously metal-capped boot there and the transport men grabbed the fare dodgers who protested loudly that they only got on at Earls Court, honest guv.

Thousands thronged the Fulham Road already, pressing the rosette sellers back against the railings of the Oswald Stoll Foundation to protect their colourful boards of badges, pennants, posters, team pictures, caps, scarves, bobble hats and balloons. Percy Dalton's original fresh-roasted peanuts were selling well and programme sellers, peak-capped and blue-coated, expertly flicked

16

precise piles of change into outstretched grubby paws as the younger fans eagerly scanned the pages for mentions of their particular favourites.

Sid and his mates drifted on down the road towards the great floodlight pylons. It was not yet two, but they liked to claim their positions early. When Sid had first come as a nine-year-old with his father they would wander down to the main entrance for half an hour, watching the camel-hair-coated, cigar-toting punters who emerged from fat Jaguars and then stood chatting in groups as they in turn waited to greet by Christian names the players who swept in through the gates in their own sportier motors, or walked importantly from the club offices in their Chelsea blazers to collect or leave tickets for friends, relations or hangers-on.

But all that was years behind Sid as they turned into the entrance gate to the Shed, running another gauntlet of gimlet-eyed police as they shoved their way forward.

"All right, stop that barging," said a large sergeant fiercely. "You lot, stand aside."

"Not us!" whispered Terry. "That's done it."

"Why?" said Kenny.

"Agger's carrying a blade," said Terry. "He nicked it last week on the train back from Cardiff."

They stood quietly to one side as first Wayne, then Dangler and finally Poncho were searched with a swift patting of jeans and socks, a stooped inspection of boots. Agger lolled beside them, hands on hips, moving off with them to rejoin Sid, Wayne and Kenny.

"Not you," said one constable. "I haven't done you." Agger sighed and drifted back. The constable patted his pockets and ran a thumb along the waistband of his trousers.

"Oh that's nice, sweetie," said Agger. "Do it again."

"All the same to me if you watch the match or not, sunshine," said the constable pleasantly. "One more word and you can sit in a van till kick-off and then be on the first train out of here. That what you want?"

"No, sir," said Agger meekly. He rolled his eyes at the others as the constable bent to inspect his socks and boots.

"And wash your feet more often," said the PC, straightening up. "And don't wear those heavy boots next time or we'll have them off you and you can watch in your socks. See what that would do to your mates. Shed'd be empty in five minutes flat, I reckon. On your way."

Agger sauntered over to them, grinning.

"Blimey, Agger," breathed Poncho as they swarmed up the steps behind the Shed. "How'd you get away with that then?"

"I got rid, didn't I?" said Agger. "Dumped it on some moon-faced mug when I seen that one with the droopy moustache giving us a close gander as we come in. Hey, some saucy bastard's standing in my spot. Come on."

The Shed stood high above the Fulham Road goal, a vast metal barn over the steep terracing that fell away swiftly, broken only by crash barriers, to the track behind the goal posts. Sid and his mates liked being good and high in the heart of the swaying mass which would roar and chant loyal hymns of support one moment and bitter obscenities to the opposition the next. There was still room for thousands now, but however thin the eventual attendance throughout the stadium, the heart of the Shed would be packed as tight as possible to the final whistle. There was never any space in the Shed.

There was plenty of room at the far end of the ground where the small group of away supporters who had made the long journey south stood in a defiant splash of red behind the opposite goal, their chants thin and distant.

The two grandstands at either side stood relatively empty at this early hour, the wings filling slowly as the cheaper seats went first in the West Stand, the centre sections of the new East Stand bare, as they would remain until the last moment before kick-off when wealthy season ticket holders would emerge from the bars to take their regular seats. But now was the Shed's hour.

They sang and roared and scuffled and swayed, reinforced by hundreds and then thousands more as the minutes passed. A thin blue line of policemen watched them impassively through the heavy metal cage mesh at the bottom of the terrace.

"Telly's here. ITV," yelled Kenny in Sid's ear.

"They always play rubbish when the telly's here," yelled Wayne on the other side.

A storm of booing swept through the Shed as the Sunderland team strolled out through the players' tunnel and on to the pitch in their expensive three-piece suits and elaborate coiffures, gently prodding the turf in their hand-made Italian shoes to decide on the length of boot stud needed but above all to enjoy the importance of this pre-match inspection ritual and loftily ignore the abuse that swirled over their heads.

"What a bunch of wankers!" roared the Shed.

The tension was mounting nicely. Middle-class families were filtering through into the grandstands now in rosettes and bobble hats and bright blue scarves. Sid, having twice ground his own scarf in the dust of the terrace at his feet, held it at full arms' length over his head as he swayed with the rest of the Shed, a sea of blue and dirty grey.

Then at long last it was almost time. The away team ran on to greet their own fans in the dim distance as the Shed whistled and jeered and then the roof nearly blew off the ramshackle cavern as the Chelsea team followed their ballboys on to the pitch and ran down to the Shed end in their all-blue strip and white socks. This was the greatest moment in Sid's fortnight. The excitement, the sound, the match about to begin. Great. Bloody magic.

The game itself was a poor one, as even the most loyal of Shed boys would have agreed if really hard-pressed in a torture chamber. Not that there was a moment's respite or silence in the Shed during the first forty-five minutes of ear-splitting clamour. There was little chance of communication between friends over the din. Occasionally Sid or Wayne would exchange hoarse exclamations as the ranks surged forward from the rear at the climax of a rare exciting attack, leaving ankles and shins kicked and bruised, but the only other contact attempted was the exchange of cigarettes or sweets in mime. And when the half-time whistle blew the entire Shed was grateful to pause briefly for breath as records blared out over the loudspeakers.

"Never the same at home," said Agger dismissively. "Different team away from the Bridge."

Sid snorted.

"Bloody are!" said Agger. "And how would you know different?"

Actually none of them had seen much of the game. The scarves and outstretched arms, the bobbing in unison, the shoving and swaying all demanded intense concentration as the great mass rolled like waves to break against the crash barriers. Action on the field was seen in short snatches in between.

But the racket soon resumed as the teams ran out for the second half. The floodlights were on now, creating a great bowl of bright white glare over the gathering gloom of the late autumn afternoon. The rain started to fleck down, clear and glittering in the brilliant blaze. Sid clenched his fists. Just forty-five minutes left. Christ, he would give anything for a couple of goals, specially now the Blues were kicking towards the Shed end.

Neither side looked remotely like scoring in a second half which depressed and bored the marginally less committed in the stands, but passed all too swiftly in the Shed where they roared and sang themselves hoarse in the closing minutes. The final whistle as the rain fell more steadily against a dark violet sky came as a relief to everyone.

Then there was just time for a final burst of wild optimism with chants of "Champions!" and "We're gonna win the league!" and the teams had disappeared down the tunnel, the punters in the stands were stretching thankfully and the Shed was already spilling away down the steps and terracing and into the road outside.

Sid, Wayne and Kenny found themselves on their own, hoarse and curiously deflated. "Where's Agger and the others?" said Kenny, kicking an empty Coke can down the road towards the station.

"They'll be hanging around to catch the Sunderland lads when they come out," said Wayne.

"Some chance," said Sid. "The Old Bill wait till the Shed's empty and escort the away lot to the tube now. Have done since that West Ham rumble. Anyway, who wants to see Agger? Always going on about those away games. Boring sod."

"You can be just as boring about your bike, or Buddy Holly," said Wayne, catching up with the Coke can and giving it a hefty punt.

"Ah, piss off," said Sid disagreeably. He had a headache and his throat was sore from shouting. "Look at the length of that tube queue! Gets worse every season."

The four-deep queue already stretched a full four hundred yards back from the station as police shepherded fans into straggly lines on the pavement. There was a weary, jaded look about the fans now as they shifted weight from foot to foot, argued half-heartedly about the action or lack of it and occasionally danced in alarm out of the way of the skittish police horses which side-stepped and clattered between pavement and kerb, noisily and heavily relieving themselves whenever they felt inclined.

"I'm definitely not waiting in that queue," said Sid. "I'm going up Parsons Green. Trains come through there practically empty."

"No, hang about," said Kenny. "Here comes Agger and the others."

They looked back. Agger, Poncho, Terry and Dangler were being ushered forward by another pair of police horses as a long thin line of away spectators was led through to the station by a column of special constables.

20

"They'll get them on the train, though," said Kenny. "Old Agger'll get his bother."

"He's welcome," said Sid. "You coming, Wayne?"

"We're all going up Dangler's tonight," said Wayne. "His folks are away for the weekend. We'll pick up some Carlsberg Specials at the off-licence near his place. Come on, Sid. He'll have some birds coming round later. His sister's mates."

"Right little scrubbers," Sid sneered. Talk of parties and girls made him uincomfortable. He hated sodding parties. Your mates were all right for the first hour or so before the birds arrived, or while they were still in a giggling group on the other side of the room. But just when you were getting tanked up your mates paired off with the birds and left you in the lurch. "Anyway I got things to do later tonight."

"Like what?" said Agger, joining them and cuffing Kenny playfully over the ear.

"Like I wasn't talking to you," said Sid.

"Back into line," said a large bearded sergeant. The others grumbled and shuffled back behind the police horses in the glistening gutter.

"And you, spotty," said the sergeant.

"I'm not even going to the bloody station," said Sid angrily.

"See you tomorrow then, Sid," said Wayne.

"After lunch," said Kenny. "My gran's coming round to Sunday lunch. I shan't get away till mid-afternoon."

Sid grunted and crossed the road, allowing the passing throng to carry him beyond the old Town Hall and the station to the crowded fish and chip shops and hamburger bars where hungry fans were making up for the deprivations of the past two hours. As the road curved to the left and then divided the crowds grew thinner and he turned into a chip shop to wait patiently in a small queue as the fans in front listened to the final football scores on their radios.

He bought a meat pie with chips, sprinkled both with brown sauce from a bottle on the end of the counter and drifted back out.

The pastry was like warm, wet cardboard and the meat curiously tasteless, despite the rich-looking gravy that oozed, thick and dark, from the pie as he bit into it, but he had had worse after a match.

By the time he had reached the quiet road of Victorian villas that led down to the next station up the line the crowds had almost dispersed. He swallowed the last corner of pie crust, crammed the

21

final four greasy chips into his mouth and hurled the paper into the gutter, belching loudly. Parsons Green station stood quiet in the early evening gloom. A few handfuls of supporters, who had made the same walk through the glistening streets of Fulham, stood chatting and drinking from cans of Coke and beer on the platform.

An Edgware Road District Line train rumbled in almost at once and he climbed into the last coach. There was time now to study the crumpled match programme at leisure—the pictures of last week's match, the team news, letters from old buffers who remembered Chelsea sides of fifty years ago, details of away trips by coach for fully paid-up and accredited members of Chelsea Supporters Club carrying identity cards complete with passport photos in colour. Not for the Aggers of this world.

He was sorry Agger had not been nicked before the game. He looked up to see an elderly couple move forward from the end of the carriage as the train rolled into Fulham Broadway station. There were still enough fans five deep at the front of the platform to burst into the car in a stampeding scrum, pinning the terrified old couple against the rear connecting door. Sid sniggered. Fancy trying to get out at Fulham Broadway less than an hour after a big match! Tourists, all right. You could see from the cut of the old geezer's overcoat. They would not forget London in a hurry.

The doors shuddered together behind the last of the fans and the train rumbled on through West Brompton. It was Earls Court before the old couple were able to make their escape while half the crowd shoved out to change to the Piccadilly Line. The man looked back angrily at the grinning louts behind him in the coach as he stepped off the train, one protective arm round his shaking wife.

"You guys need a good whipping," he said, white with rage. "Animals!"

The animals cheered as the doors slid shut behind him.

Sid got out at Edgware Road and slouched moodily out through the booking-hall, programme rolled tight in his fist. In the old days he had waited for the classified football editions of the two London evening papers, complete with match reports, photos of the early action, and up-to-date league tables. Now there were not even papers on a Saturday evening. No shortage of tourists, though, he noticed, as he cut down through the subway opposite the hotel. He hated London now. No, that was not right. He hated the buggers who ruined it.

22

Back at the buildings he took the stairs slowly and heavily. The flat would be hot and stuffy, walls running with condensation. His parents would be glued to the telly. Usual crummy Saturday evening programmes and nearly all of them American. He slammed the front door behind him.

"Mind that door!" shouted his father as usual.

"Have you eaten?" asked his mother, knitting in one sagging armchair. "There's fish fingers in the fridge."

"I had pie and chips on the way home," he said.

"Rubbish match according to the sports round-up," said his father. "On the ITV tomorrow then."

He grunted and walked through to the bedroom.

"And don't play those records loud enough to wake the dead!" shouted his father as he started to shut the door. He closed it with exaggerated care and waved two fingers at it before slinging his jacket on the chair in the corner and reached for a record from the rack under the dressing-table. It was one of his favourites. *Remember*. Late '71. He spun it over to the B side, lowered the pick-up and sat on the bed to pull off his heavy boots as the music swirled over him.

"And don't throw those boots in the corner," yelled his father, a split second too late, as always. He waved the two fingers at the closed door again and sang along softly with the record.

> There comes a time for everybody
> When true love will come your way.
> There comes a time for everybody
> That's what they tell me.
> That's what they say.
> I didn't hear them say a word
> Of when that time would be.
> I only know that what they say
> Has not come true for me.

"I just like them" had been his lame explanation when his well-meaning Auntie Glad had asked him why he collected Buddy Holly records. He knew he liked the way they were true for him. Not just moon and June songs and true love in the end. Because nobody seemed to get anybody. Or at least the hero never did. The girls got married to other guys. And he certainly never got a bird. That was why he was sitting in the middle of the West End of London on a Saturday evening, playing records in his bedroom while horrible

Agger was probably already touching up some under-age chick in tight jeans and no bra, or would be before the evening was very much older.

He lay back on the bed and picked up John J. Goldrosen's *Buddy Holly, His Life and Music* from the small pile of paperbacks on his bedside table. It was one of his gospels, together with the *News of the World Football Annual* and the *Biker's Year Book*.

The evening passed slowly. "Mum!" he yelled. "We got any Coke?"

"There's a six-pack in the fridge," his mother called back.

He grabbed the rolled-up programme from the table and padded through to the living-room. His parents were watching *Dallas*, his mother raptly over her knitting, counting stitches as she gazed, his father reflectively over his pipe. He looked bored.

"Here you are, Dad. Programme."

"Oh, ta, son." He unrolled it. "No bother this afternoon?"

"No. Well, I keep out of it. You know that."

"I hope so."

"Fair's fair, Jim. He's never been in trouble," said his mother. "Make yourself a hamburger if you fancy one, duck. There's buns and burgers in the fridge, too."

"No, ta. Just Coke. Can I take a couple?"

"Well, we shan't be drinking them. You can depend on that," said his father with a shudder.

He took three cans and wandered back to his bedroom. He drank the first third of a can in a thirsty gulp, placed it with the other two on the bedside table and rummaged deep in the bottom of his wardrobe for his motor-bike tool-box. He found it and opened the lid cautiously. Under the first layer of tools was a new bottle of Haig, bought with his wages the previous evening and smuggled in under his jacket. His dad did not mind him drinking beer in the flat or having a pint down the pub with the lads, but he drew the line at spirits.

Working rapidly now, he opened the other cans, again drank the top third off each, belched very loudly indeed and tossed the ring pulls into the waste bin. Then he filled each can to the top with long, gurgling measures of Scotch, tucking two into the recess of his bedside table and taking a deep pull from the third. Christ, that was better! He topped it up again, set it down carefully and returned the bottle to its hiding-place, shutting the wardrobe door.

24

He carefully chose a stack of records and loaded the player before settling on the bed again and reaching for his drink. The first can would take him through to *Match of the Day* without getting pissed enough for his father to notice anything through his clouds of pipe smoke. For his own part, he found he always got on better with the old man after a stiff drink or two.

Soon after ten he heard his mother putting her knitting away in the sideboard cupboard. He switched off the record-player and wandered back into the living-room.

"Good-night then, dear," she said. "Mrs Blakey was asking after you this afternoon, by the way."

He grunted. Interfering old sow. Probably amazed he hadn't killed anyone with his bike yet or landed up in Borstal. Probably disappointed, too. He'd heard one of her ten-minute sermons on football hooligans and motor-cycle louts. Still, she'd moved from the Buildings now.

"Sleep well, Mum," he said gruffly.

"I'll be in after the match, Else," said his father as she fetched her nightie from the bedroom and took it through to the kitchen with her tooth-mug, shutting the door as the familiar strident music of the football show started.

"Liverpool or Man United, you can bet," said his dad gloomily.

He was right. They watched the highlights of two matches complete with slow-motion replay of all goals three times from different angles and at different speeds with analysis from the bearded pundit in the studio. Sid didn't got a bundle on telly football, unless it was Chelsea and even then it wasn't the same. You could even see the beads of sweat on the players' faces. It was nothing like being in the Shed.

Anxious he might slur his words after more Scotch than he had intended at this stage of the evening, he was more ingratiating than usual. "There's not the players around like there was when you first used to take me, is there, Dad?" he said.

"You're right there, son," said his father solemnly, tapping out his pipe on the ashtray. "And going back a few years before that, too. Jimmy Greaves. What an artist! Not just in his Tottenham days like you seen on the telly. I mean when he was a Chelsea player. Younger than you are, Sidney. Forty goals a season, no trouble. Run the length of the pitch and stick it past the keeper time and again. Pick that one out, my son, he'd tell the poor blighter."

Sid nodded wisely.

His father rose and stretched with a sigh. "You want this on?"

Sid shook his head. "I'll get an early night, too."

His dad patted him on the back. "You don't have to stay in of a Saturday night, you know, boy," he said. "I mean, you're a good lad. We've no complaints—well, you could smarten yourself up a bit, but apart from that you keep out of trouble. You want to get off out with your mates more Saturday nights, we'd understand."

"No, it's all right, ta," he said, embarrassed by the rare burst of intimacy. "The others went to some crummy party tonight, but I just didn't fancy it after the match."

His father nodded. "Up to you, boy. You know that. I'm going fishing down the canal early tomorrow if you want to come?"

"I've got to give the bike a good check-over for the week."

His father nodded. "You do look after that bike, I'll always give you that," he said. "I'll say good-night then. You want to do your teeth first?"

"No, I'll have a Coke in bed first. Write up my Chelsea diary." He crossed to his bedroom door. "Good luck with the fish in the morning."

His father laughed. "I don't catch a lot, do I? Never mind. Keeps me out of your mother's way while she's doing the Sunday grub." He winked unexpectedly.

Sid shut his bedroom door and sank back on the bed under the cover. The second drink went down a treat, quicker than the first can now there was no need for caution. He started on another and jumped convulsively as his father opened the door and stuck his head round, face wrinkled and sunken like an old prune without his teeth. "You still drinking that fizzy stuff? See you remember to clean those teeth."

"Yes, I said I would, Dad."

"And no more music tonight, son."

"No," he said patiently. "I wasn't going to. I'm going to get some proper headphones at Christmas, then I'll never disturb you."

His father gave a toothless grin. "No need to wait till Christmas for that, son," he said. "I'll stake you for those next weekend and that's a promise."

"Oh, ta, Dad," he said, pleased.

"I'll say good-night again then." The door shut.

He sipped thoughtfully from his third can of whisky and Coke.

Free headphones. Great. Old man wasn't bad at all really. Nor was life right now. His head sang and he felt good. He tiptoed to the wardrobe and pulled the bottle out of his tool-box again, topping up the drink in his can.

He flopped back on the bed. He wished he could always feel the way he did when he was suddenly getting pissed. It had happened in the five minutes since his dad had gone to bed. He felt cocky, confident, high. It would last for an hour, maybe two. He would drift off to sleep to wake at four with a mouth like a caked-up sewer pipe and lurch out to the kitchen for glass after glass of cold water before stumbling back to change into his pyjamas, to wake again at six with a blinding headache and a grumbling gut. But it was all worth it for the way he felt now. Confident, yeah, like he did for the hour or two he was out with the lads at Chelsea. Funny how booze never worked like that at parties, though. When you felt confident enough to say anything to anyone, you were always too pissed to say it. Still, in your own room you could hold your own with imaginary anyone in the world.

The Scotch was going down more smoothly than ever now. Before he put the bottle away he poured a final long slug into his almost empty can. The last mouthful burnt his throat and set his eyes streaming as the neat liquor went down. Why not a final stroll? He had too much energy to go to bed. In half an hour he'd be ready to crash out, all right. But once round the block first.

He opened the bedroom door quietly and tiptoed across the living-room to the hall, letting himself silently out of the flat, then winding his scarf round his neck and stealthily making his way across the outside landing.

The night was still young when he got down to the bright lights of Edgware Road. The chippy on the corner was doing brisk Saturday night business, the Cypriots sweating profusely as they worked flat out in the neon lights and blue smoke haze to cope with the drinkers, ready to mop up some of that beer swilling in their stomachs with pie and chips or a piece of cod before swaying their way home to last trains to bed-sits.

He wandered down towards Marble Arch, although his legs seemed curiously reluctant to take him there, or anywhere. For all the bright lights and the closeness of Oxford Street and the West End it was a dispiriting street late in the evening, only the occasional small restaurant providing any colour and warmth among the endless

27

succession of hi-fi shops, jewellers, gents' outfitters and wholesale toy suppliers.

A cold wind swept down from Marble Arch. He knotted the scarf tighter round his throat before stepping into the shelter of a doorway to light a cigarette from the battered pack of ten left over in his pocket from the match. No matches. He swore and fumbled in the same pocket. A middle-aged pair of tourists sauntering back towards the hotel at the flyover stopped to peer into the shop window. Sodding tourists. They wouldn't give him a light. They never smoked. No use to anyone. And they were everywhere. He hated the buggers. Look at this one's wife. Great fat legs like an old sideboard. What would it look like in the buff! Sagging tits, bulging belly ... He suddenly realized he was talking aloud. Shouting it out. Christ, he was pissed!

The tourist stepped into the doorway. He was in his fifties, neat grey hair, light raincoat, smart. Sid could smell the keen scent of aftershave as a well-manicured hand came out and seized the collar of Sid's coat, turned up to the scarf against the bitter wind.

"No drunken bum of a kid talks to my wife like that, buddy," said the man softly.

Sid's left hand was still thrust in his pocket, wedged against the window. As he jerked it out he saw the long blade between his fingers, felt it in his palm. Agger's blade. Got rid, Agger said. On some moon-faced mug. The bastard had got rid of it on him. He could have been nicked.

"You listening to me, sonny?" said the tourist.

In a twisting surge of hatred he thrust the blade deep through the front of the man's raincoat. It went in surprisingly easy. The man let go of him, staggered back and looked at him wonderingly. He half turned to his wife on the pavement behind him.

"By Christ, Myra, the young creep stabbed me," he said. Then he slumped to the ground as the woman pitched forward to him with a low moan of terror.

Sidney leaped past her and ran away towards Marble Arch. He hesitated, swung left and raced away down the nearest side-street. Behind him there were no screams or shouts, no sounds of running feet. Nothing at all. He ran on, doubling back in the direction of home through the back streets. On across Sussex Gardens and down towards Praed Street, alive with sightseers drifting between restaurants, clubs, sex shops and all-night stores. Tourists everywhere. He giggled crazily as he raced across the road, narrowly missing a

28

honking taxi-cab. There was one less tourist now.

Breathless, he eventually slowed to a walk as he approached the flyover and, controlling his heaving chest with difficulty, strolled down the subway to climb up the other side to the silence of slumbering Bell Street and the Buildings. He passed no one. He climbed the stairs quietly and went on past his parents' front door on the fourth landing to the final flight up to the roof. It was a cold, clear night up there. The cinema lights still flickered opposite and down on the right was the blue lamp of Paddington Common police station. He wondered if they had heard yet. A stabbing in Edgware Road. A tourist.

The traffic droned on over the flyover, but otherwise it was peaceful. The blinding headache that had suddenly built up as he stood in the shop doorway had gone. And he could breath easily again. He felt great. But suddenly very tired. He couldn't remember ever feeling so tired. He pulled the blade from his pocket. In the darkness he could see no blood. He should have dropped it as he ran. That would have put Agger in it! He giggled. No, that would have been stupid. As it was, he was safe. He shut the roof door and went quietly down to the flat. He bolted the front door silently, twisting the bolt upwards as his father always did, and went through to the kitchen to clean his teeth.

In two minutes he was in his pyjamas and tucked up snugly between the sheets. From the wall Buddy Holly looked down blandly at him through thick black-rimmed spectacles.

"Nobody talks to me like that, buddy," he murmured and with a contented smile he drifted gently off to sleep.

In the street below the police car siren wailed its urgency as it sped past.

TWO

Tom Baxter was ten minutes behind the patrol car. He drove fast down Edgware Road in his unmarked Triumph towards the distant blue flashing light. Most of the traffic was heading away from Marble Arch and Oxford Street and out to the suburbs after Saturday nights out in cinemas, theatres, clubs, pubs and restaurants. He swung hard across the flow of cars and parked outside the Lotus Blossom Chinese restaurant. As he opened his door an ambulance clanged noisily away towards St Mary's Hospital in Praed Street.

He pushed through the small group of people gathered on the pavement and recognized the patrol car driver hurrying towards him.

"Wife's gone to the hospital with him, guv."

"He's dead."

"Oh yes. Small wound, but through the heart by the look of it. Lynn Craig's gone in the ambulance, too. Your skip's sent out a first description."

"Which is?"

The constable flicked open his notebook. "Youth in late teens, jacket and jeans, both dark and possibly navy. Blue and white football supporter's scarf, by the sound of it. Broad stripes, she said. Sounds as if he was pissed. There was a brief struggle in the doorway and he stabbed the old guy. American tourist, we think. Wife's from the States, anyway. I've only been here two minutes."

"Here comes forensic. Get back to the street search anyway. I'll be over when I've had a word with Armstrong."

"He's through that little lot, sir. Just getting things sorted."

" 'Evening sir," said the middle-aged sergeant from forensic. "Body gone?"

"St Mary's. The foot boys have chalked and staked out. See if you can find me something for starters. I must have a word with Frank Armstrong." They pushed their way through the small crowd of

31

curious onlookers to the pavement, protected by two foot-patrol constables. A uniformed sergeant was guarding the doorway.

"Get your chaps to sort out any possible witnesses from this lot and then clear them right away," said Baxter crisply to the sergeant. "Four more on their way to you in the van. They can try premises in the immediate vicinity."

"Hullo, sir, that was quick," said his sergeant, Frank Armstrong.

"I'd just got back to the nick. What did the wife say?"

"Not a lot. They were strolling back to their hotel from Oxford Street, stopped to look in a shop window. This one. There was a kid in the doorway. Insulted her, she said. Sounded drunk. Husband had a go, verbally. Kid stabbed him. She never saw his face. He was hidden in the dark of the doorway and her husband obscured him, falling back in her arms as the kid made off down Connaught Street. Jacket, dark, possibly reefer type, collar turned up. All she could be certain of was the blue and white scarf."

"Nothing on voice or accent?"

"She's American. They'd just arrived this morning. No way she could have sorted out an accent. Just thought he sounded very drunk. Lynn Craig went with her in the ambulance. May get something at the hospital. In shock, of course."

"Weapon?"

"No sign yet. They're fanning out down Connaught Street. Might have chucked it as he bolted."

"And a small wound?"

"Puncture. Must have caught the heart."

"We must find that weapon. Doesn't sound as if we'll get a positive ID on this one, but drunken yobbos don't wear gloves so that blade's going to be our main hope."

A police van screeched to a halt in the gutter beside them and three young constables piled out. The uniformed sergeant hurried over from the doorway and helped them to unload the barriers from the back.

"Sergeant Billington?"

"Sir?"

"You find anyone who saw anything I want them ferried straight back to the nick in the van. Don't take statements. I shall want to see them personally. No witnesses yet among that little lot?"

"No, sir. One heard the wife screaming, but no sign of the attacker. Sharp was on patrol three hundred yards up Edgware Road and he was here in a couple of minutes to call the ambulance."

"Where is he?"

"Helping with the questioning. Sharp!"

The young constable hurried over, slipping his notebook into his top pocket and fidgeting nervously with the button as he joined them.

"I did have a quick word when I got here," Armstrong muttered out of the side of his mouth. "Go easy, guv. It's his first week."

"Sir?" The young PC licked his lips and looked worried.

"You were the first man on the scene?"

"Yes, sir. Like I told Sergeant Armstrong, I didn't know whether to give chase up Connaught Street or look to the man on the pavement. Only I figured he had a good two- to three-minute start on me and could have taken any turning. Whereas the man on the pavement, I didn't know if he was dead or dying, sir." He looked as if he might cry, Baxter noticed with alarm. "So I thought best get on the radio first."

"That was quite right," he said evenly. "What were the wife's first words?"

"She kept saying 'Oh God, he stabbed my husband' and 'Help him, help him'."

There was a short pause. "The man said nothing?"

"Just a horrible gurgling in the throat, sir."

"Get on with your questioning, Sharp," said Baxter after another brief pause. "You were quite right to stay with the man. And a prompt radio call did more to cover the surrounding area than you could have managed pounding down Connaught Street in your boots on your own. Where's the man who heard the wife scream?"

"Over there, sir. I was just taking a statement. He saw nothing, though. Thought the husband had had a heart attack and that was why the woman was screaming. Being as how it's all offices and shops round here he just set off up the road to flag down a car when he saw me. You want a word with him, sir?"

"No, you take your statement. That'll do," said Baxter. "You seem to know what you're doing."

The young constable straightened his shoulders, saluted and hurried back to the pavement.

"Who's on your car radio, Frank?" said Baxter.

"Arthur Bailey. It's up here." He led the way. They climbed into the back of the car.

" 'Evening, guv," said the driver, half turning in his seat.

"Anything?"

"Youth seen running across Praed Street in blue and white scarf. Alpha Four following that one up. And two held at the Edgware Road tube, Circle Line. Blue and white scarves again, but no real sus. Claimed they'd just come from the chippy and it checks out."

"Blue and white. It's going to be a bugger. Bloody hell, everyone wears blue and white round here. Chelsea, Rangers—and weren't Everton at Arsenal today? That's a third then. Always supposing he was a football fan. No law says you have to be to wear one of those. She was sure about the blue?"

"About the only thing she was sure about, guv," said Armstrong. "But in that lighting—it could have been black or navy."

"Which could give us Spurs or Fulham for good measure."

"You reckon he'll dump it?"

"Wouldn't you?"

"Depends what sort of state he's in, I suppose."

"Anyway, get these uniformed boys sorted. You got a map, Arthur? Ta. We might get lucky with the blade or scarf, but we'll have to sweep every street from Bayswater Road down to Praed Street. Confine them to that area, all night if necessary, then the day shift can carry it on. The London Transport boys are on full alert?"

"Yes, guv," said Bailey. "Both Edgware Road stations, Marylebone, Paddington and up the Central Line from Bond Street to Oxford Circus."

"Right, I'll tie that in when I get back. We don't want every bugger in a blue and white scarf brought in on a Saturday night. The nick wouldn't be big enough. Full search, movements and name and address will do for now."

"Clean kill. There'll be no blood," said Armstrong dolefully.

"I know, makes a needle in a haystack look child's play," said Baxter. "When you've got them sorted here you'd better get down to St Mary's, Frank. I know Lynn Craig's a capable girl, but that description is just going to have to be better. We want a photofit from her. The lads should be through with their questioning over there, Arthur. Take a bunch and try all the boozers in the immediate area. Knock up the guv'nors if you have to. She seems clear he was drunk, anyway. I'm getting back to the nick. This is all going to be about foot-slogging, gutter-gazing and door-knocking and it's time I was pulling the strings. I'll want to see the wife later, though, whatever her

34

condition. I'll come over to her hotel if I have to. Where were they staying?"

"Metropole."

"Just over the road. That's handy, anyway. Make sure they'd had no brush with any football hooligans earlier in the evening. They might have been followed."

"Don't think so, guv. They'd had a nap, jet lag and all that. Just popped out for a half-hour stroll."

"You can drop me off on the way to St Mary's. You've got five minutes to get these boys organized properly. You can be on your way, too, Arthur. You'll have two more CID along in the hour. Restaurants as well as pubs, I think."

The radio crackled as they slammed their doors. He reached over the driving seat and answered his call sign.

"We've found this cabbie saw a guy running down Praed Street," said a Scots voice from Alpha Four through the static. "Heavy build, donkey jacket, blue and white scarf, panting hard. And he was laughing fit to bust, the cabbie says. He's following us to the nick now. Over."

He acknowledged the call and sat back to consider for a precious two minutes. He started as a fist tapped at his window. He wound it down. The forensic sergeant looked in. His breath smelt of strong peppermints.

"Going to be a right bugger," he said heavily. "Enough prints for an army in the doorway, all over both windows and sod all else. No blood. I'm taking dust. There's two new paving stones just laid ten yards back so there's plenty of sand, but it's my guess you'll get nothing from us on this one without the weapon. I'll see you back at the nick."

Baxter grunted and the macintoshed figure moved off with a nod to the returning Armstrong who slipped into the driving seat. "Billington's done it all a hundred times before," he said, starting the engine. "Bastard job, though. Mad impulse killing by a drunken football fan on a Saturday night in town. You got a murder room sorted, guv?"

"Mason's doing it," he said. "Yes, if we don't pick him up tonight it can only get worse."

Young Mason had cleared his office as efficiently as could be expected in twenty minutes. There were already eight entries in the murder log. He ran an eye swiftly down the page. There was nothing he did not already know. He sighed. It had been a long, hard day and the night promised no better.

Nor did it deliver. The cabbie was the most helpful sort. Earnest, middle-aged, Jewish, but he could add little to the description they already had from the widow. "Only wish I could help you more, chief," he said. "But you know how it is, driving in this traffic at night. Some lunatic runs across the street right in front of you. By the time you've braked to miss the silly sod and slammed the window down to give him a bollocking, you're more worried about the bloke up your backside than clocking his dial. But he was laughing like crazy, I do know that."

"You saw the laugh—the lips, the mouth. Think about it," urged Baxter.

"The lips," said the cabbie, pondering again. "Yeah, now you mention it, I can see the lips. They was thick. Not, you know, like a negro's, but that way. And the laugh, that was odd. I mean, you get these stupid bastards run across the road deliberate to impress a mate on the pavement, like playing chicken. But this bloke wasn't laughing like that, at causing the aggravation. He was laughing to himself more. Real crazy. But the rest of the face—collar turned up, scarf and all, no, I can't help you there."

"Blue and white scarf, you said."

"No doubt about that. Chelsea, I reckon. Could have been QPR, the Rangers, like. But I had him down as a Chelsea hooligan. They're the worst."

"And you're positive about the plimsolls?"

"Oh yeah, no doubt at all, dirty white plimsolls. How he came to be moving so fast, I guess. I mean they wear these heavy bovver boots normally, don't they?"

"Think again about the hair," he said. "Close-cropped like a Shed lad? Shaved off like a skinhead? Wild and spiky like a punk rocker? Think about it hard. You remembered the lips just now."

"I don't think he was no skinhead," said the cabbie. "But I really couldn't say. It was drizzling. You get the lights reflected back off the streets. Only I'm thinking if I'd sort of noticed, subconscious like, that he was a skinhead, I'd have called him one to your lads. Only I didn't, did I?"

"You didn't notice anything about the hair so maybe it was plastered down by the rain?" said Baxter. "Was it long and shaggy, over his ears—or shortish back and sides, like mine?"

The cabbie shook his head. "You'd have me guessing, chief," he said.

He plugged away for another ten minutes, but to little avail. At ten past two in the morning Armstrong arrived from the hospital with the widow. He took her into the least cheerless interview room and left her with the young policewoman while he reported to Baxter.

"I offered to take her back to the hotel, but she insisted on coming," he said.

"In shock?"

"Could be worse, I suppose, but she's taken it bravely. Wants to do anything she can to help, she says."

"No progress on the description since you rang in?"

"No. God knows, she'd tell us if she could, but there doesn't seem much hope there. I'll put a call through to her sister in the States when you've done. I offered earlier, but she didn't think she could locate her till now."

"I'll have a word," he said. "Then she can talk to the sister on her own. You grab something to eat."

He walked slowly down the corridor and into the interview room. The WPC nodded and slipped out. Myra Dilley was a heavily built woman in her early fifties. Her hair was still well groomed, her clothes immaculate, but the grief was heavy as she looked up.

"I'm so sorry to have to pester you with more questions at a time like this, Mrs Dilley," he said.

Her fingers were tearing at a handkerchief held between her large knees. She smiled faintly. "I understand," she said. "Mr Baxter?"

He nodded and took the chair opposite her. Her coffee stood untouched on the table between them. "You must be tired," he said gently.

She shook her head. "Not really. They were very kind at the hospital. And they let me sit with him awhile. The doctor offered to give me something, but I guess I'd gotten my hysteria over by then. I feel kind of ashamed of that. I mean if I could have stayed calmer at the time maybe I could have helped you more."

"Nobody stays calm at a time like that. Can you try and take me through your evening again. I know it's for the third time."

"Sure. I understand. We arrived and checked in at the hotel mid-morning. The flight was tiring. We'd come stand-by and we had a long wait at Kennedy. We'd stayed with my sister and her brother in New York for a couple of days before we flew over. We didn't feel like any lunch so we went to bed and slept most of the afternoon. We had tea in the hotel and went upstairs to plan tomorrow with a London guide we bought in the lobby. We were going to Westminster Abbey and St Paul's Cathedral."

For the first time she looked as if she might break down, but she struggled on.

"We had dinner and chatter with a real nice couple from Yugoslavia in the lounge over coffee afterwards. Then we went out for a short stroll. I guess we were still feeling pretty tired and we knew we had a heavy day ahead." She faltered again. "At least we thought so. We walked down to Marble Arch, is it? Then along Oxford Street as far as Bond Street, just looking in the store windows and trying to convert your pounds into dollars. We walked back to Edgware Road and headed back towards the hotel. Then was when it happened.

"I know how terrible it must be for you, but I do have to take you through those last minutes again," he said. "Up to that point, you'd had no trouble, seen no yobs, sorry, young hooligans or drunks on the pavements anywhere?"

She shook her head firmly. "I thought the sidewalks were surprisingly quiet for a Saturday night," she said. "New York is busier. I guess the crowds head on farther up the West End to the shows and bars and things?"

She took a deep breath and launched into the final yards of the walk again.

She could tell him no more than he knew. No, she had seen nothing of the face. Only a burly figure in the shop doorway, crouched to light a cigarette out of the cutting wind. The steady scream of obscene abuse had startled them for a second.

"Would you know one English voice from another?" he said. "A London accent, for example."

She thought for a second and shuddered. "He said quite a bit in those seconds before Dave went for him," she said. "Horrible things—about my legs, my body. I'm not gross." She collected herself and went on. "Yes, I would say it was maybe a London voice as far as I'd know one. Tommy Steele, Michael Caine, Twiggy. Stanley Holloway as the dustman in the *My Fair Lady* movie." She bit her lip.

"That could be a great help," he said eagerly. "If you're really sure . . ."

She nodded her head more certainly. "I'm sure," she said. "I guess

38

I should have realized that much earlier."

"You're doing fine," he said. "And the voice sounded young, you told my sergeant earlier."

"Yeah, kind of young. I just got the feeling he was young when we first saw him. And he was dressed like young—sneakers on his feet, tight jeans."

He leaned forward. "Sneakers? Light canvas shoes? Plimsolls, we call them."

She frowned. "Yes, I spotted them straight away. They were white, but dirty. I didn't tell your sergeant that either, did I?"

"That's why we have to keep going over this," he said. "But it really is important that you're sure each time."

"I'm sure of the sneakers," she said. "He was dressed pretty much like kids at home really, the lower half of him, anyway. But the jacket was heavy and long, like a construction worker might wear in the winter. And he had this blue and white scarf on. I saw that clearly as Dave went for him. Then it was all over in a second. They just kind of pushed at each other and Dave fell back. Then he said, 'The little creep stabbed me, Myra.' Those were his last words. His dying words. He closed his eyes as he fell into my arms."

"And the youth?"

"As I caught Dave—he's . . . he was a big guy—his weight took me back with him, but I just saw the animal run off round the corner and away. And then I guess I started to scream. I held Dave to me and screamed again and a minute later this man came running across the street to help."

Enough was enough. He led the sobbing woman out of the room to the waiting policewoman in the corridor outside. "Sergeant Armstrong will help Mrs Dilley get through to her sister on the phone," he said. "Take her through to him and go back to the hotel with her afterwards.

He rubbed his bristly chin thoughtfully as the two women went up the corridor, arms round each other. No witnesses, no motive, no forensic help, no weapon yet. But at least the canvas shoes seemed a clear link with the youth described by the cabbie. And he was no skinhead. That eliminated a good few thousand football fans. Probably a Londoner, heavy-featured. It could have been worse. But it still meant weeks of encouragement to the team, keeping spirits up, urging scrupulous attention to every tiny detail, spot checks and questions at every football ground in West London. Unless they could come up with a clear lead like the weapon or the scarf in the next twenty-four hours. He glanced at his watch. Correction. In the next ten hours before his report to the chief at noon.

And so the painstaking checking went on throughout the night and beyond into daylight and the next morning.

Fresh squads of detectives and uniformed constables continued to comb the side-streets between Bayswater Road and Praed Street and to tour the restaurants and hotels, tube stations and cafés, questioning, thanking politely and questioning again, encountering perplexed Italians, bewildered Austrians, inscrutable Japanese, with language difficulties prolonging an already almost impossible task.

By nine the incident book was eleven pages longer but hardly more informative. Five other tourists at the Metropole had taken the same walk back to the hotel from Oxford Street within an hour either side of the murder. Eight others had made the same journey by taxi or bus. None had seen the Dilleys or the drunken youth, separately or together. Countless youths in blue and white scarves had been stopped, searched and questioned at tube stations, all-night bus-stops and main-line railway stations. Searches had revealed a surprising number of blunt instruments, lengths of chain, suspiciously long-bladed penknives for sharpening pencils, and had resulted in seventeen charges of being in possession of offensive weapons, three of being in possession of house- or office-breaking implements.

Those with the knives had been brought into Paddington Common nick but the intensive questioning always led to a clear alibi and no lack of friends to back it up. Few football fans, it appeared, found much source of amusement in the Edgware Road area of London on a Saturday night and why indeed should they, thought Baxter dismally as he leafed through the book one more time. It was a bleak sprawl of radio and electronics shops, restaurants, offices and the occasional clothing retailer. But in that very bleakness, he thought as he closed the book, might lie the answer. What would take a youth to such an area—unless, of course, he had strayed drunken and unwitting from the bright lights of the West End—except his normal journey home? For behind the luxury tower flats, the shuttered offices, the expensive hotels and restaurants and the cheaper boarding-houses and eating-joints, lay a sprawling council estate a mile to the north, hard by the Grand Union Canal at Lissom Grove. And it was here and in the meaner older terraces and tenements around the estate that Baxter's team were despatched in a general call five minutes later.

It was 9.05 a.m., Sunday, 12 November.

THREE

One hundred yards away on the other side of the Edgware Road Sidney Dunn was waking slowly from a deep and dreamless sleep. He stretched and yawned loudly. He felt good. Chelsea had dropped a home point and the reports would not be good, but he had no Sunday morning hangover. He climbed out of bed and was slipping into his jeans when the previous evening swept over him with a sudden clarity that made him gasp. He was a murderer. A killer who struck in the shadows. Beat that, Agger, with your nicking bog rolls off the trains and duffing up fifteen-year-old bovver boys, ten to one.

"There comes a time for everybody," Buddy had sung. Well, that American geezer's time had come all right. He picked up his shirt and sauntered through to the living-room. No hangover at all. Amazing.

"You slept well," said his mother from the kitchen where the last of the weekend's half pound of bacon was sizzling in the pan. "You're usually out here waiting for the sports pages at eight of a Sunday morning."

"I was tired," he said. "Must have had a good eleven hours."

"Yes, your dad said you turned in when he did. He was up at seven to go fishing. He's not seen those papers yet so don't you get bacon grease all over them. Two eggs?"

"Ta. I'm starving." He picked up the papers from the settee and scanned the front page of the *News of the World*. By Christ, he was on the front page of the *News of the World*! Agger would never make that either. It was only one paragraph, but black and bold, down at the bottom.

"An American tourist was stabbed to death in Edgware Road, London NW late last night. His name has not yet been released."

Bloody hell, though, that wasn't much, was it?

"There was a murder down the road last night," said his mother, bringing in his breakfast."

43

"I just seen it in the paper," he said, moving to the table. "It don't say much."

"What a terrible thing," said his mother. "I wonder whereabouts it was. Just imagine, as we lay sleeping some poor soul was breathing his last, done to death just a few hundred yards out there."

"I expect they'll get them," he said, cutting his bacon.

"I certainly hope they do. They should have kept the death penalty. There was that poor man stabbed to death on the Circle Line last year, too. I'd have them hanged, really I would."

He could find nothing in the *Sunday Mirror*. He turned to the sports pages for the Chelsea match reports. They were harsh, but he read them slowly with enjoyment. And this afternoon he could see the game again on the telly. This time he fancied the sideways views with close-ups after the distant and obscured glimpses from the Shed, even with the old man tutting away beside him.

He washed down his eggs and bacon with two cups of tea and added a large slice of bread and marmalade before wiping his hands on the front of his shirt and stretching. His mother was making her bed next door. He ripped off the shirt and tossed it into the dirty-clothes bag in the corner of the kitchen and ran some hot water for a shave and wash. He didn't always shave on Sundays, generally felt too lazy and hung-over for it. But this morning he felt good, really good. He decided to wash his hair while he was at it and reached for the shampoo bottle under the sink, singing loudly over the splashing of the taps into the deep plastic washing bowl.

> Blue is the colour
> Football is the game.
> We're all together
> And winning is our aim.

He plunged his head into the bowl, reached out for the shampoo bottle on the draining board and poured a generous measure over his greasy head. He gurgled and gargled in the foaming water as he came up for breath.

> So cheer us on in the wind and rain
> Cos Chelsea, Chelsea is our name.

His mother surveyed him with astonishment when he emerged from the kitchen ten minutes later, shaved, shiny and with dripping head. "You are improving and no mistake," she said. "All clean and tidy on a Sunday morning. Aren't you going to work on your bike?"

"Yeah and if I get dirty I'll have to have another wash, won't I?" he said. "I just felt good this morning. I slept so well. And I noticed when I was shaving—my spots is clearing up."

She stared at him again. "Yes, they are too. That rash on your cheek is much less angry. It was quite livid yesterday morning down the market."

"I'll bring the carburettor up and work on it on the landing," he said, towelling his hair briskly. "I'll be going down in a minute. You want any rubbish dumping?"

She looked startled. "What? Yes please, dear. Thank you. It's in the bin. There's a good boy."

He pulled a clean T-shirt over his head, collected the plastic bag of rubbish from the pedal bin in the kitchen and strode, whistling cheerfully, from the flat. His mother shook her head wonderingly and rummaged in the cupboard for a clean rubbish bag.

Mrs Roberts from the flat below was brushing the third-floor landing with as much vigour as her arthritis and seventy-odd years would allow. She looked up in alarm as he came clattering down the concrete stairs. He usually grunted an ungracious acknowledgement, but this morning wished her a hearty "Good-morning, Mrs Roberts."

"Hullo, Sidney," she said.

"Did you see in the paper there was a man killed down the road last night?" he said.

"No! Never!" she said.

"Yes, it's in the paper all right," he said, gratified at her shock. "Terrible, isn't it? Mum says they should hang them. Can I take any rubbish down the bin for you?"

"That would be kind, Sidney," she said, shuffling back through her front door and reappearing a few seconds later with a carrier-bag brimming with empty tins of cat food, scrapings and soggy tea-bags.

"So they should," the old lady screeched after him as he galloped down the next flight. "String 'em up, the murdering swine!"

Out in the yard he hurled the bags into the high communal rubbish bin that stood on wheels in the far corner and returned to the front of the flats. He groped in his jeans pocket for a small key and unlocked the cover on his motor-bike. He stripped it back, dropped to a comfortable crouch and, fishing an old rag from the box on the back, started lovingly to stroke clean the gleaming chromework. He had wiped away the worst of London's grime and oil when he arrived home on Friday evening. But he never tired of polishing and tinkering. It was a four-stroke twin, a Kawasaki Z250.

"A bleeding Jap bike?" Wayne had said when he first saw it. "And you always going on about Jap tourists all over the place. I would have thought you'd at least have got yourself a Triumph."

"Nothing wrong with Jap bikes," he said. "They're the best. And me record player's Jap and me records are all American. I'm not bothered by that. I just hate bloody tourists ruining our own patch."

He loved the bike all right. It was economical, quiet and clean to run and the roadholding and braking were tremendous. He needed all five qualities on his eight-hour days among the heavy London traffic and if some of the other lads on the run game could get a few extra miles out of their two-stroke twins, he could certainly hold them in mid-range acceleration and burn the backside off them on top gear throttle roll-on below sixty.

The bike was surprisingly light for a four-stroke twin and it had the Honda and Yamaha beat every time in Sid's book. And being on a bike all day, as he explained to an elaborately uninterested Wayne, you needed good protection from engine vibration at anything over idling revs. The overhead camshaft unit was mounted in rubber brushes to take care of that.

"I bet you go to bed with that bike," Wayne said. "You can't keep your hands off it."

There was certainly nothing he would have changed about it. From half eight on a Monday morning to six on a Friday night he purred and throbbed through the London traffic, from Stoke Newington to Dulwich, from Hackney to Shepherd's Bush, ferrying artwork from cramped studios in partitioned-off dockside warehouses to smart Mayfair advertising agencies, X-ray plates and blood samples from clinics and surgeries to hospitals and research laboratories, press photographs from fashion shows and royal openings to Fleet Street, messages and parcels, gifts of flowers and wine packs from city office blocks to clients on light industrial estates in the suburbs, his radio between the speedo and tachometer over the bars crackling and blaring as he rode—not that he could hear it until he stopped. But it all added to the importance and urgency of his missions.

All the same, by Friday night he'd had enough. There were no other bike owners in the buildings and anyway burn-ups down the motorway and easy-riding trips to the coast really needed a sexy passenger in tight leathers on the pillion. And he couldn't get one of those. So five days of battling through the heavy traffic, choked up the worse, in his opinion, by tourists' coaches and over-laden buses stopping every fifty yards, was his limit, apart from the odd road test.

He'd paid off half the £900 plus interest and all the cash he had borrowed from his dad for the deposit. And soon it would be his very own.

Carefully he checked over the ball and roller bearings and needle roller big ends supporting the crankshaft and then set to work dismantling the two 32mm choke constant velocity carbs. The light drizzle increased to a steady downpour and he set the carbs aside and hastily draped the cover back over the machine before collecting the bits and pieces he needed for his work on the top landing.

He had been cleaning, scraping and smoothing for half an hour outside the family flat when weary footfalls on the steps signalled the return home of his father who puffed on up the last flight, laden with fishing tackle.

"That's it, boy," he wheezed appreciatively. "Look after it. I'll bring you a beer out."

"Ta," he said.

"You made a bit of a conquest," said his father, chuckling.

"You what?"

"Old Mrs Roberts downstairs. 'Your Sidney's growing up into a nice boy,' she said."

"Oh, her," he said, embarrassed. "I only took some rubbish down."

"She appreciated it. She finds those stairs murder and I'm beginning to see her point," said his father, still breathing heavily. "I'll fetch you that beer."

"I was just telling your mum," he said when he emerged five minutes later with the promised can, "there's police all over the place down the estate. I seen them from the canal bank. Knocking from door to door. This murder last night—they reckon it was a local feller done it, on account of his blue and white scarf."

"Bloody hell!" he said scornfully, not looking up from his task. "That's a great lead, isn't it? I mean we all wear blue and white scarves of a Saturday—Chelsea fans, Rangers loonies and Everton was in town yesterday and all." He stretched and reached thankfully for the can of beer. "They reckon it was just one done it, do they? I mean, didn't anyone see him?"

47

His dad shook his head, wiping the froth from his moustache. "Not from what I heard. This feller fishing along from me said they didn't hardly have no sort of description proper."

"What time did it happen?" he asked, wiping the oil from his stubby fingers. "Do they know that much?"

"About half eleven, they seem to think."

"Oh well, that leaves me out then," he said with a laugh.

"No joking matter, boy," said his father sternly. "Stabbing like that. Stranger to our country too. He was an American tourist out with his wife. Terrible thing."

There was some sort of commotion in the yard far below. His father looked out over the balcony. "Anyway, they've reached the buildings now by the look of it."

Sid joined him at the balcony and looked down on the helmets of four policemen spreading out, each heading for a block doorway. "Well, that shouldn't take them long," he said. "There's precious few football fans left in this place, I'd say. Only me. And you," he said with a sly grin.

"I told you, it's not funny," said his father. "Hullo, sounds as if they're starting at the top and working their way down."

A heavy pair of boots could be heard tramping slowly on up the stairs beneath them. The helmet appeared briefly at the balcony of Mrs Roberts's flat below.

His mother appeared excitedly at the doorway. "The police are here. They're in the buildings," she said.

"We saw," said Sid laconically. He drained his beer can and placed his tools carefully on a piece of oilskin in the corner of the landing. "That ought to do it. I'll fit her up when the rain stops."

"Yes, I want a good dry-off and a change," said his father. "I hope this doesn't take long."

The constable turned the last corner and came towards them. He touched his helmet courteously to Mrs Dunn.

"You've come about the murder?" she said excitedly. "We saw it in the paper. My husband, he was fishing down the canal this morning. They said you were going round the flats there."

"That's right, missus," said the constable wearily, removing the clipboard from under his right arm and suddenly looking down at Sid who was still crouched over his tools. "This your son?"

"Tha's right," said Sid's father.

"This is all routine," said the constable reassuringly. "We're

48

asking you all for help. The more places and people we can eliminate straight away, the more chance we've got of catching the killer. What's your name, son?"

He stood and stretched. "Sidney Dunn."

"Date of birth?" said the constable, starting to write laboriously.

"October 18, 1962," said Sid. "Is it right you think it was a Shed boy or a Rangers fan? I mean, you know Everton was in town yesterday?"

"Oh yes," said the constable heavily. "We realize that. This flat is number what?"

He copied the number from the open front door.

"Would you like a cup of tea, love?" said Mrs Dunn.

"No, thanks very much," he said, still writing. "I got two more hours of this and then I'm off. Ever been in any bother, son?"

"Never," said Mr Dunn sharply. "No trouble of any sort."

"Only asking," said the constable easily. "No harm in that. Of course we check all names off afterwards as a matter of routine. You a football fan, son?"

"Chelsea," said Sid proudly.

"Look," said his mother, anxious.

The constable held up his free arm. "I've asked these questions a hundred times this morning and I'm likely going to ask them a hundred times more before I'm finished. It's elimination, like I said. We've got to catch this kid and you can help us do it."

"Yes, I understand," she said. "I'm sorry."

"Now then, son. You go to Chelsea?"

"Yes, all the home games anyway," said Sid.

"Not away," said his mother eagerly. "We don't let him go to away games. Too much trouble, fighting on trains and then bother with the other fans when they get there. We don't allow him to go to away games, ever."

"You have a Chelsea scarf of course," said the officer, still gazing steadily at Sid.

"Of course," he said. "You want to see it?"

"Yes, please."

"I'll fetch it," said his mother.

"No, let the boy go," said the policeman. Sid squeezed past his mother in the doorway and went through to his room. He heard the murmur of voices behind him as he went. He wondered what they were saying. He grinned to himself. Nothing damaging from Mum and

49

Dad anyway. He tugged the scarf off the back of the chair where he had thrown it the previous evening, and came back through the tiny hall.

The constable took it and inspected it rapidly. "Cleaner than most I've seen this morning," he said. "New, is it?"

"No, I washed it during the week," said his mother. "It had got disgusting, all dirty and grey."

"And you like it that way," said the constable with a wink to Sid.

"Well, you don't want it looking new," said Sid.

The constable nodded and made a brief note. "Your parents were just saying you were in early last night," he said.

"About seven, I guess," said Sid. "Stayed in me room playing records, watched *Match of the Day* with Dad and went to bed just before him, about eleven."

"That's right," said his father. "We had a little chat in his bedroom. And I locked up and turned in last."

"And he didn't wake up until late this morning because we commented on what a good night he had, didn't we, Siddie?" said his mother.

He scowled. He hated being called Siddie. She hadn't called him that in years.

"The sleep of the righteous, hey?" said the constable, making a final note and pushing the cap back on his pen. "And the three of you heard nothing after you went to bed. No yobs around, no shouting, anything at all?"

They shook their heads.

"Oh, one final thing, who do you go to the games with, son?" he asked casually. "A group of mates?"

"Yes, three local lads. We meet some of the other mob on the train or in the Shed, of course."

"What about these three?"

"Two live down the Grove—you'll likely have talked to them this morning. The other one lives in the council flats over Balcombe Street."

"You came home after the game together?"

"No, I left them outside Fulham Broadway tube. I always walk up to Parsons Green, beat the train queues. They was all going on to a party over Balham way."

"I'll have their names and addresses," said the constable, un-capping his pen again.

50

"Christ, do I have to, Dad?" said Sid.

"This is a murder inquiry," said the officer, suddenly severe. "I'll say it again—the more we eliminate, the closer we'll get to solving it. Look, you write them on my board for me, Sid. Addresses and names. I've got writer's cramp.

"I'll be leaving you to your Sunday roast then," he said as Sid accepted the board reluctantly and started writing. "Roast beef and Yorkshire, is it? Thought so. Smells grand."

"Is that all?" said his mother, disappointed. "No photofit descriptions or nothing?"

"Nothing clear enough to give the public," said the constable. "And the description we have got so far would fit your Sidney and a thousand more like him. You'll likely see posters around soon and a picture on the telly once my guv'nors have decided to release one. Thanks, son. Any other soccer fans in the buildings?"

"No chance," said Sid promptly. "Mostly nurses from St Mary's, a few students and some old couples."

"And one or two are being fitted out as holiday flats for tourists, would you believe," said Mrs Dunn. "Lord alone knows who'd want to spend their holidays in one of these, though."

"Ah well, central, see," said the policeman. "Let them at a hundred a week and they'd be cheap compared to those hotels."

"Hundred a week. Fancy!" she said. "And I thought our rent was steep!"

"Even tourists got to stay somewhere," said Sid. "Stands to reason."

His father looked at him curiously.

"Well so long as they don't force our rent up to a hundred a week they're very welcome, I'm sure," said his mother.

"I must get on," said the officer. "You all go and have that roast beef." He turned and knocked at the door opposite.

"You'll have to bang harder than that," said Mr Dunn. "That's the Prices. Both eighty-odd and deaf as posts. Come on you two, we must leave the officer to get on with his work."

They followed him indoors as the policeman pounded on the faded blue front door opposite with his fist.

Sid wandered into the kitchen behind his mother and slipped behind her to the sink to wash his grimy hands. That was that then. Not exactly the third degree. Easy peasy. The man with the cast-iron alibi. All the same, it could have been nasty if someone had bumped

51

into him and got a good look at him. And next time he wouldn't wear the scarf.

Over the road, Baxter's lunch was a cheese sandwich and a coffee. He continued to flick through the report sheets brought in by the young DCs. The door-to-doors had certainly flushed out plenty of young football supporters with blue and white scarves, but they seemed to go everywhere in numbers. He had never seen so many tight alibis. He said so to his sergeant.

"Still, all to the good, really, guv," said Frank Armstrong. "I mean the fact that they go everywhere in threes and fours makes it easier to check out and eliminate. I reckon our man's a loner."

"You've been watching too many late-night westerns, Frank," he said. "Still, he ought to stand out, I agree. Solitary drinkers are rare in the West End on a Saturday night and they tend to be older. A kid of maybe eighteen, drinking on his own—you wouldn't see that very often. But we can't even assume he was drunk. Drugs, maybe. Just as likely in that age group. Glue-sniffer, even. They can be nasty. We can't even assume he was a loner. He was alone when he killed. That's all. He could have left his mates five minutes before, innocent as can be. Nothing in those search sheets, Mason?"

"No, guv," said a rumpled-looking detective constable at the desk opposite. "Screws, nails, one broken penknife, but nothing vaguely like the weapon we're after. Council depot want to know if they can start normal cleaning in those streets again, by the way."

"Yes. They've been checked twice now. Have someone gen them up down the depot though, just in case they spot something. The ordinary dustmen too—could have been dumped in a bin or chucked over a railing into a basement yard. Now then, Frank, how many so far with no corroboration?"

Armstrong flicked through the sheets in front of him. "Five. No, seven. Four say they went to the pictures and then home to bed-sits, one went to some heavy-metal concert and went back on the tube to his room. Scarf had a different name tag in that case, but he said he found it on the tube three weeks ago which is plausible enough. You know how football yobs horse around on the trains."

"I do," said Baxter grimly.

"Another came up to London from Liverpool for a job last week and spent the night exploring. Went to the Everton game that after-noon at Highbury—hence the scarf—then dropped into one pub

52

after another and eventually drifted back to his bed-sit around midnight."

"Where's the bed-sit?"

"Westbourne Grove."

"Is it now? That could tie in with Praed Street very nicely. What else was he wearing?"

"Donkey jacket, jeans and working boots. He's got a job on a site in Kilburn. Liverpool Irish."

"Build?"

Armstrong peered at the form before him and sighed. "Beat man's writing is worse than mine. 'Small and—what's this?—wiry'."

"Hmm," said Baxter doubtfully. "Oh well, worth someone from CID taking a shifty, I suppose. Wife could be wrong about the build. Cabby, too. Dark night and raining."

"Short hair anyway," said Armstrong.

There must be dozens like him all over London, thought Baxter. Young wanderers alone in the big city, drifting round the streets by night, perhaps a little pissed, probably not knowing where they were half the time and certainly unable to account for their movements at a precise time. "She reckoned she recognized the London accent all right," he said thoughtfully. "Fairly seized on that when I mentioned it. We've got so little positive that we're going to have to make every scrap count. We'll check out this one, but then I think we're going to have to discount away supporters. The transport boys can keep a look out at the main-line stations for another twenty-four hours, but he'll likely be home by now if he did come south for the day. My preference is a West London lad on his own doorstep."

"What about the old man?" said Armstrong. "We using the Yard?"

"If we have to," said Baxter. "I've had a word with Tinker Bell on the blower. But it's strictly our patch at the moment, after all. Tinker's got plenty on his plate anyway right now. Anyway, you've had the luxury of six hours' sleep and now I'm going to do the same. Ring me if anything comes up, of course. Otherwise, check off at nine and leave it all to Len Hanson tonight. Then we can tackle it fresh together in the morning. Any problems?"

"None. You get home, guv. Your Sunday roast might still be in the oven."

"Some chance," he said. "I'll see you."

He collected his car from the yard behind the nick and drove slowly up Edgware Road towards Marble Arch again. Within a couple of minutes he was approaching the scene of the murder. The barriers had gone. Sunday afternoon walkers, mostly tourists, were strolling disconsolately through the rain. One couple were actually looking in the same window that had so fatally drawn Dave Dilley's attention. Baxter glanced out to the nearside and spotted a young DC sheltering from the rain in an office doorway. It was worth a try anyway. It would not be the first time a killer had returned to the scene of his crime. He grinned wryly despite himself. Maybe they all watched too much television in the force these days. Kojak would have had this little lot sewn up in precisely fifty minutes, just in time for *Match of the Day*. He had missed both the football programmes this weekend, he thought idly. Chelsea on this afternoon, too. He always seemed to miss Chelsea on the telly. He headed up Oxford Street, nodding to a beat man outside Marble Arch tube. The window-shoppers were thick on the ground here. In the entrance to Bond Street tube, further up on the other side of the street, two more uniformed men were stopping at random. "Were you in this area at around eleven o'clock last night, sir, madam?" He didn't envy them. Still, he had had plenty of that twenty-five years ago and the task that confronted him now was not exactly a cheering one. He hated this sort of crime. Murders, oddly enough, were often a doddle. Ninety per cent of them were domestic tragedies in which the killer was obvious from the first inquiry. And where robbery or revenge was the motive, the trail generally led clearly enough to an early arrest. But unreasoning killings like this one left you nothing. Except a body.

He drove on through the West End, round Piccadilly Circus, the garish-coloured advertising signs flickering aimlessly on and off with no one to gaze up at them on a dull November Sunday afternoon but a group of long-haired youngsters huddled in a damp-looking cluster at the feet of Eros. Down the Haymarket and down to Trafalgar Square where there were more signs of life with two coachloads of tourists swarming up the steps of the National Gallery to his left and away in the square to his right the usual hustle of sightseers, cameras, pigeons and hustlers. He swung on round the square and headed left down Whitehall. The mounted trooper at the head of Horseguards Parade sat patiently before the clicking cameras, his horse twitching and tossing his head at the occasional flash bulb. Uniformed police stood yawning outside Government buildings. God, what a job. That was worse than the random checks and doorstepping. And then he was approaching Westminster Bridge with the first queues of the day waiting for the river buses down at the pier on his left and Parliament Square thick with more trundling coaches bringing more visitors to Westminster Abbey. Big Ben struck two. He would be home by half-past, anyway. He had promised Di a drive out to Wisley to see the roses. She was very good. Twenty-three years and never a complaint. Well, not about the job. He accelerated down Westminster Bridge Road towards the Elephant and Castle.

He was half-way down the Old Kent Road, just past the Thomas à Becket, when the rain stopped and fitful autumn sunshine filtered through the rapidly shifting clouds. He switched off his windscreen wipers and flicked the radio button, jiggling the tuner to find the local news station, London Broadcasting. There was always a news bulletin on LBC. Two minutes of jangles and programme puffs and he caught it, third item.

"Police are still combing a wide area of the West End in a search for clues after the brutal murder of an American tourist in the Edgware Road last night. Sue Jenkins reports":

"Dave and Myra Dilley had only arrived in London on their European holiday of a lifetime yesterday morning," said the girl reporter.

"After a meal and a stroll they walked back to the Metropole Hotel in Edgware Road. It was a journey they never completed. Mr Dilley was attacked from a shop doorway by a youth wearing a blue and white football supporter's scarf. The youth ran off down Connaught Street and is believed to have made away across Sussex Gardens and Praed Street. He is described as well built with heavy features, wearing a donkey jacket or similar garment, blue jeans and dirty white plimsolls. Police have so far been unable to recover the murder weapon, believed to be a long, thin stiletto-type blade or scalpel. Anyone in the vicinity of Edgware Road between Marble Arch and the Westway flyover after 10.30 yesterday evening is asked to contact the murder inquiry number at . . ."

He switched off. It might help. There would be the usual ration of nutters, of course, but leads came from the unlikeliest sources. And the best lead of all, though he would only admit it to himself in the privacy of his car, would be if the maniac struck again. And failed.

He reached into the glove compartment and pulled out a cassette. Gilbert and Sullivan time. He played little else in the car when his mind was on the job. He pressed the cassette home into its slot. The strains of *The Pirates of Penzance* overture filled the car as he drove up

Blackheath Hill.

"I thought if I grilled a couple of pork steaks with apple sauce and gravy we could pretend we were having a Sunday roast like other people," said his wife mildly, twenty minutes later on the doorstep of their brightly painted, double-glazed, three-bedroom semi in a quiet cul-de-sac on the outskirts of Sidcup where Outer London suburbia met the first tentative swathe of Kentish green belt.

He walked up the path towards her between standard roses they had loved and tended for years. He sniffed the fragrance of a pure yellow King's Ransom as he approached the neat draught-cheating porch he had built during four rare days off in early September. The mild, wet autumn had kept the frost at bay and the roses were flourishing late.

"I'm sorry, love," he said. "I was going to take you to Wisley."

"I'm too hungry," she said, stretching forward for a kiss. "And I decided I was definitely not lunching on scrambled eggs at one on a Sunday. So I had an apple and waited for you. Wisley can wait until next week. Rotten case?"

"Mmm." He followed her inside and shut the front door. "Did Shirley ring?"

"Last night. They're at Hector's people for the weekend. They'll look in for a couple of hours on their way back. About seven."

"Good. I'll enjoy that." He missed their only daughter, had done ever since she and her husband moved to the Kent coast when he got his deputy headship. For the first two years of their marriage they had lived just round the corner. She taught at the local primary and continued to sing in the amateur operatic with her mother. She was forever in and out of the house then, leaving untidy trails of sheet music everywhere, while the placid Hector repaired the garage roof, laid a new crazy paving path and generally did all the odd jobs he was never around to do himself, working an eighty-hour week as a DI. He had been able to return the compliment occasionally, on odd half-weeks off, building them a rose trellis in their tiny back garden and choosing the most reliable rambling roses for it. And then suddenly Hector got his new job and they were gone, only forty miles away, but the rare hours of relaxation were more lonely for them both now.

"Go up and change. Why don't you have a shower?" called his wife from the kitchen as he gazed ruminatively at the coatstand in the hall. "I thought we'd get on with some pruning and clear up the leaves afterwards."

56

"I could have a bonfire," he said.

She laughed. "Yes, You shall have your bonfire," she said.

He hummed a Sullivan melody as he hurried upstairs. Sunday could still be rescued then. A proper lunch, an afternoon in the garden, pleasant company in the evening, the new Glenfiddich he had won in the nick monthly raffle.

"Have we got anything for sandwiches tonight?" he yelled over the banisters.

"Ham and tongue," she shouted. "Oh, your book of the month arrived just after you left yesterday morning."

He rubbed his hands as he went into the bathroom. A good bedtime read, too. *Compost Cultivation.* Perfect end to the day. For the next eighteen hours he was going to forget about poor Dave Dilley.

Sidney Dunn had already forgotten as he rose from the television set with a yawn and a stretch. He belched loudly. His mother's Yorkshire pudding had been as tasty as ever and the Chelsea match even worse under the close scrutiny of the television cameras than he had seen or remembered from the day before. He decided to go out for some air before his father wandered down Memory Lane with Jimmy Greaves and Roy Bentley again. In one armchair his mother snored gently, worn out after the washing up. His father was frowning at a TV commercial for a new under-arm deodorant.

"I'm off out for a bit. Just give the bike a check-over on the road for tomorrow," he said.

"Have a care, son," his father murmured.

"I always am," he said. "You know that." Out in the hall he put on his bike gear, dropped his tools and cleaned parts into his helmet and fished his gauntlets out from the warped bamboo umbrella stand his father had bought for a quid at the Bell Street market.

He galloped down to the yard. The rain clouds had blown away and patches of blue were peeping through the skudding shreds that remained. He flicked back his bike cover and concentrated hard as he reassembled his twin carburettors. He tugged the visored helmet on, secured it, mounted the bike and reached for the electric starter. He engine throbbed smoothly into life. He pulled on his gauntlets, adjusted his visor and slid the machine gently forward from its stand. It pulsated slowly out through the yard and then he was swinging into Bell Street and accelerating throatily away towards Lissom Grove. In two minutes he had made Park Road and a right-hander took him into the circle road that bordered Regent's Park.

Cars were parked in an endless line, bonnet to tail, round the hedge side of the road. He purred on past the great Nash Regency terraces on his circuit that took in the Queen Mary Rose Gardens and restaurant, tennis courts, Bedford College, and then off on another circuit. A woman with a jacketed poodle on a lead scampered across in front of him as he approached the golden dome of the mosque, gleaming wet through the baring trees. Padded brake callipers engaged stainless steel discs front and back with immediate and total response on the slippery surface. Assymetric perforations on the discs meant no noisy squeal of brakes as he halted. He glared at the woman as she disappeared into the park with the poodle. He rode on slowly round the park again. The Scorpion was in perfect health.

Eventually he slid it into the kerb near the Albany Street entrance to the park just off Camden Town Parkway, climbed down and secured the steering lock. He tucked his helmet into the back box, stepped back to give the bike a final appraising study and wandered down ino the park.

On the other side of the railings tourists were thronging dense through the Zoo. He ignored them. They didn't bother him today, he noticed absently. Got them out of me system, like, he thought. All the same, there were plenty more wandering about the wide open spaces of the park as he cut through to the football pitches that spanned the green sward from the Zoo down to the boating lake half a mile distant. There were about ten pitches and earnest North West London Sunday League sides were locked in battle on each in a wide range of brightly coloured kits.

He stood on the touchline of the first pitch he came to and watched for a few minutes, warm in his bike leathers despite the keen wind that swept across the park. Usually he felt too self-conscious to stand for long in the park on a Sunday afternoon. There were too many people paired off together, like at Agger's parties on Saturday nights. Too many girl-friends tugging on right arms. But today he felt inconspicuous. Too inconspicuous really—none of them knew, the grunting, puffing players, the few supporters shouting them on in two and threes, the wandering lovers, the strolling tourists, that a killer was among them. A man who struck with one sure thrust. No blood, no mess, no clues. He could do it again now if he wanted. But he

58

didn't want. He could choose to wipe one out any time. But he might not feel that hate again, he thought regretfully. It was the Scotch that had done it. He had drunk that last lot too fast. He had felt superior but strangled. Then the exhilaration came afterwards and finally the peace. He would like to feel that again. There was still a bit, but not like last night. He had slept well, too! He laughed and a young couple turned to stare at him. He gazed fixedly out across the pitch.

"Right, Chuck! Through ball!"

"Man on! Man on!"

"Mine!"

"Lay it off!"

"Come on, ref! Took the man, nowhere near the ball."

"Less of the mouth, number five!"

Suddenly bored, he moved on to the next game, but as usual it was no better than the first. He could go down the boating lake. Might be open. Go for a row. Not much fun on your own.

He decided to get back to his beloved Scorpion. See if he could break his record on the run home. It did not need speeding. It was all a question of flicking through the traffic and taking the bends neat and fast, economic line and no brake. The Scorpion was easier to flick through bends than any other 250 four-stroke. That was a known fact. He approached his bike and looked at it tenderly, chrome shining in the pale sunlight. Back on board, he glanced down at his watch. No, take the time from the far end of the outer circle by the boating lake entrance. That still counted as the park.

He purred gently round the perimeter of the park again, reached the Park Road entrance by the Mosque and then was away with another throaty roar, the light machine flicking into Rossmore Road and on down Lissom Grove. Left, Bell Street, twenty seconds, left again, a fraction too fast as the back wheel started to slide, and on through the heavy iron gates into the yard of the flats again. He pulled back the flap of his left gauntlet and looked at his watch. Two minutes dead! That was seven seconds inside his record. Next time he would break two minutes. Easy. He gave the bike a final careful wipe, locked and covered it and looked up as he heard a shout from the top balcony. Wayne and Kenny were looking down at him.

"Your dad said you just took the bike round the block for a test run. We been waiting ages," yelled Wayne.

"Come on down then," he shouted. Their boots scraped and thundered down the concrete steps.

A window shot open and his mother's head came thrusting out. "Tell your friends to make less din on a Sunday afternoon," she said. "You going out again?"

"Are we?" he said as they reappeared, slithering down the final flight of steps.

"Thought we might go to the pictures over the road. First house in half an hour," said Kenny.

He brightened. "There's a mucky sex bill." He raised his voice again. "Yes, Mum. See you!"

She tutted and closed the window.

"What was the party like then?" he said as they wandered out through the yard.

"It weren't nothing," said Wayne. "Three scrubbers between ten and they spent the evening dancing with each other. Then his folks come home early and nearly went spare. Here, you have the law round this morning?"

He nodded. "About the stabbing. And you?"

"Yeah. I wonder if it was a Shed boy done it," said Kenny. "Might even be someone we saw yesterday. Someone standing there a few feet away. Didn't it look rubbish on the telly?"

"At least Agger had an alibi," said Sid with a laugh. "He'd have been first suspect on my list."

"It's funny that," said Wayne. "At first we heard it was a fight, between fans, like. It was on the *Heavy Metal Show*—in the news bit at half-way. We went round Charlie's for a burger and he had the radio on. And Agger—he come with us to get out of his old lady's hair because she was doing her nut—he said when he got rid of that blade at the game, he dumped it on you."

"Lying git," said Sid, as they reached the subway.

"Said he slipped it in your pocket when he saw he was going to get frisked," said Kenny. "And last night, when we heard about it, we was saying suppose old Sid got in a rumble on the way home. Then old Agger said you'd be tucked up in bed by that time."

"With your teddy," said Wayne, cackling. "Gerroff. That hurts."

"Well, he never slipped nothing in my pockets," said Sid, releasing him from an armlock. "He just dropped it, or slung it away. He probably never had a blade. I mean, he was bragging and then when he sees he's going to be searched and he's got nothing, well, he's got to say something, hasn't he?"

"They ask you who you went to the game with?" said Wayne.

"Yeah, and what I done after. Mum and Dad was there so they tell him I was in all evening and that's it. I had to say I went with you, though. I mean they was standing right next to me."

"Mine, too," said Kenny. "Nosy bastard Old Bill asks where the party was, what time we go to Charlie's afterwards, which way we walk home, what time we get in. Well, I'd told the old lady I was in by midnight so when I tell the rozzer it was after two she goes spare, doesn't she? Give me a right clip when he'd gone."

"They'll never bloody get him though, will they?" said Wayne. "I mean, some mad bastard goes and puts a blade in and all they got to go on is a blue and white scarf."

"They asked to see mine," said Kenny.

"Mine too," said Sid. "Funny when you think, though, I mean just suppose I'd been for a walk or come back from Agger's. On my own, like. I wouldn't have no alibi, would I? I might be over the road rotting in some cell right now. Or getting the third degree. A punch in the kidneys where it don't show."

They emerged from the subway on the far side of the flyover and gazed across at the police station.

"Come on," said Wayne suddenly. "We can pick our seats if we get there first. Last one there buys the peanuts!"

They raced away towards the cinema, swerving to avoid an elderly woman out for a lonely Sunday afternoon walk.

"Hullo, Mrs Roberts!" yelled Sid as they passed. "Turned out nice again."

The old lady turned and watched them disappear into the cinema. She smiled indulgently. It was nice to see Sidney so full of high spirits with his friends.

Harry King didn't mind the middle shift on Sundays. The small handful of reporters and subs made it intimate and chatty and there was little of the mad scramble of a normal day on the *Globe*. By middle evening things were humming almost as busily as a weekday with the early Monday editions rapidly taking shape. But that was hours away. He even liked the journey up to town, a lazy, shambling affair with the train frequently making unexpected detours to circumnavigate track repairs and the few passengers travelling up at three in the afternoon idly turning the pages of bulky and already crumpled Sunday papers, or doing crosswords, flicking through colour magazines, or simply gazing moodily out at the last hour or so of fading afternoon daylight.

61

Charing Cross, too, was deserted, in marked contrast to the Strand outside where tourists headed down towards Nelson's Column from the Savoy, the Strand Palace, the Waldorf, on their way through Admiralty Arch and up the Mall to Buckingham Palace or left into St James's Park. Harry King walked against the tide, whistling cheerfully through perfect teeth and smiling happily at any pretty girls who passed. He liked long-striding, untidy girls hurrying into the bitter wind, hair awry and cheeks glowing. And generally they liked him, although his bachelor days were ten years behind him. No, nearer twelve, he thought ruefully. But enough smiled back, all the same.

Monday's paper was always a thin one, sport and weekend political speeches seizing more space than news stories. There were few enough diary jobs on a Sunday and off-diary stories were curiously few and far between.

His walk took him past the rambling mock Gothic eccentricities of the Law Courts, always much appreciated by the more camera-conscious tourists who swayed and backstepped before him on the pavement, trying in vain to get the highest pinnacles into their viewfinders, and on over Temple Bar and into Fleet Street.

The street itself was relatively quiet at this hour, although the camera and light macintosh brigade were still much in evidence, now moving with him on their way to St Paul's which looked down from the top of Ludgate Hill ahead beyond the Blackfriars railway arches. He turned off right towards the river and then sharp left into his own paper's building. Fred, the on-duty commissionaire, looking even more bored than usual with the inactivity of a Sunday afternoon, nodded sleepily from behind his counter down the left side of the entrance hall.

He ignored the lift and took the three flights of steps at a steady trot, two at a time. The newsroom was practically tidy after the idleness of Saturday night. Three early-duty sub-editors were sorting through agency copy on the home news desk at the far side of the room. Two of the younger reporters were typing diligently in the opposite corner of the reporters' half of the area, heads down, reaching automatically for cigarettes in ashtrays every third line. Harry looked away hastily. It was three years since he had given up smoking but during the first hour at work he still felt the need for one. Once he was absorbed in what he was doing, the craving passed, but this first hour of transition from a morning in the garden and Sunday roast lunch with Maeve and the kids to the potential urgency of the newsroom was the hardest.

The deputy day news editor Jack Snellgrove waved a hand from his desk at the centre of the room. Harry drifted over and sat on the corner of the desk. He winced at a sudden twinge in his back and reached round to rub it vigorously. Snellgrove smiled with sympathy.

"Me too. Not used to bloody gardening at this time of the year. Clearing up leaves all morning. Maeve better?"

"Fine. Just a flu bug, I think. Anything doing?"

"Not really. I've got those two on follow-ups and odds and sods. New kid starting on day shifts, too. I'll save the other scraps from the Sundays for him and see how he goes. Comes highly recommended. There is one thing you might take a look at meanwhile." He shoved the front page of the *News of the World* across the desk. "This tourist murder. You seen it?"

"No, Maeve won't have the thing in the house. Irish Catholic upbringing. She and the kids were back from Mass before I woke up this morning." He scanned the ringed paragraph briefly. "So?"

"Bit more on it now. Soccer supporter apparently. The guy who did it. Or some oaf in a supporters' scarf anyway. It's not that angle as much as the victim, though. Tourist. Only arrived yesterday. Might be an angle there. How many muggings of tourists this year. That sort of thing. British going to New York always being warned about muggings and canker in the Big Apple. What about dear old London Town? Are we making it unsafe for their lot to walk the streets at night?"

"Well, are we?"

"I'm asking you," said Snellgrove patiently.

"Yes, but you generally know the answers in advance," said King with a grin. "It wouldn't be surprising if there was a trend, though. I mean, the cost of a meal and God knows what else in London these days—these rubbernecks must carry heavy wads of cash around with then even in the age of American Express. Often stray off the beaten track and get hopelessly lost, too."

"Right. Take a shufti through the cuttings. Yard press bureau might come up with some figures. Don't let Harvey nick it for a feature if you can cobble anything together, though. I need some home page leads for tonight. Sod all happening anywhere. And take your time, so long as you're free for anything that comes out of first conference at four."

63

"Yup. Anyone in the library yet?"

"Janet, I think. You hear Mike Parker's going, by the way?"

"No. Where?"

"*Express*. Been on the cards for weeks. Haggling over price, I think. Greedy bastard. *Express* pay a good three grand over our miserable rates."

"You'll be moving up one then?"

"Not necessarily. Might help my chances if you came up with something today."

They laughed.

"How about you, though, Harry? God knows, we could ill afford to lose you off the reporting strength but would you put in for this desk on which your bum is resting if I did go up one?"

He sniffed doubtfully. "Oh, I don't know, Jack. Deskbound?"

"Well, you'd have got it by rights last time if you'd put in when I did. But don't you get pissed off with rushing around in the great wide world out there, knee-deep in bloody tourists and trippers?"

Harry laughed. "Your interest in this murder a personal one?"

"One or two of my British brethren I'd rather take care of first, starting with our idle bloody copy boys. Boy! Boy! Oh, sod it, I'll make the tea myself. You want some?"

"When I get back from the library. Mug's on my desk."

He wandered down the corridor to the library. Perhaps he should put in for the deputy desk job. He was thirty-seven. He'd been on reporters for twelve years now after three in Manchester on a similar routine. And certainly the eternal battles for taxis and tubes and buses, the parking tickets, the ten-minute drives that turned into fuming hours in traffic-choked streets were all pains in the arse. The hours would be longer but at least he would be home every night, which would please Maeve and the kids. Yes, he would put in for it. The money would be handy, too.

Janet Luke, the senior assistant librarian, was busily cutting her way through the Sunday papers with a large pair of scissors. She looked up. "Hullo, Harry. You're looking very thoughtful."

"And you are the thinking man's dream in this building, as you well know," he said. "Muggings in the metropolis, streets, parks, tube trains and stations, preferably involving tourists. Anything?"

She crossed to a block of filing cabinets and pulled out a drawer. "These two might help," she said, returning half a minute later. "And I've got the latest tube statistics over here with a cross-ref to football fans, but not tourists, I'm afraid."

"Football fans are half the story, but not the important half," he said, looking down dolefully at the bulging buff envelopes she had put before him. "Thanks, Jan. You had a cup of tea this afternoon?"

"No one in until five. I'm stuck here on my own."

"I'll fetch you one. Made by Jack, I'm afraid, so watch out for stray tea-bags and biscuit crumbs."

"Beggars can't be . . ." she said. "Bless you, Harry."

Ten minutes later he was deep in his cuttings. The rising rate of muggings on the Underground seemed to have little to do with tourists who might have been ripped off by every retail and service trade in the capital, but were apparently going home intact at the end of it.

"Anything likely?" said Snellgrove, passing on the way to his desk.

"No. Mind you last night's wasn't a mugging, was it? Robbery not thought to have been motive, this PA add says. Hooligan with knife."

"Try the Yard bureau anyway. Hell, I wish something would turn up before first conference. Boy! Don't leave that there. Give it to me!"

King yawned and reached for the telephone.

"Harry, leave that!" shouted Snellgrove suddenly, hurrying back over clutching an agency news flash. "Pass it on to young Kevin. PA flash here. Private plane down on Epsom Downs. Paddy Shafto, the jockey, killed, two others seriously injured. Have a word with our stringer out there first—Campbell, I think—and get out there with a photographer. I think Shafto lived near the downs somewhere. The racing desk can dig out some bumf. Give us a ring from the course when you get there."

"If not before," he said, pulling the cuttings envelopes together into a pile and carrying them across to Kevin Toomey's desk. He dropped them next to the reporter's typewriter. "Tourist murder—facts and figures behind same," he said. "None of them exactly salient, however. See Janet gets them back today or she'll flog you to ribbons—an interesting prospect some might say."

The young reporter watched him enviously as he walked unhurriedly from the room. Everything he did had style. He was always smart, however casually he dressed. His hair generally looked as if it had not seen a comb in days and yet it was only tousled, never a mess. He had seen his wife once when she had popped in just before last Christmas after taking their kids to some Christmas matinée.

Strikingly beautiful with long black hair and wonderful skin. Smashing-looking kids too. Pair of twins—identical little girls. He wondered why Harry was still a general news reporter. Enjoyed it presumably. He certainly kept busy. He was one of the élite five or six who never sat sprawled at their desks toying with a mug of tepid tea or flipping idly through the evening papers.

"Epsom," said Harry to Terry Barber in Photographic. "Plane crash on the downs. Paddy Shafto, the jockey!"

"He's lost me a few bob in his time," said Barber. "Get me gear. See you round the back in two minutes. Oh, it's a blue Cortina with a buggered offside wing."

"Where's the Volvo?" said Harry, already on his way.

"Had to leave it for Tina."

"You haven't split up again?"

"Yip. Would have taken the car with me, but I was very pissed at the time. I'm staying with Noddy Moss."

"Silly sod," said Harry. On the way down the corridor he flicked through his memory for details about Shafto. Wonder boy jockey, had weight problems in his late twenties, married lovely leggy dancer from popular television music show, starved himself down to real racing weight again and champion jockey twice in the last five years. He had seen the home outside Epsom in Maeve's *House and Garden* a couple of months ago. Didn't they have twins, too? Yes. That brought it home all right.

"Didn't they have twins?" said Barber as they drove out of the car park. "Like you."

"Yes. Hell of a jock, too."

"In his day," said Barber. "Come on, madam, move your arse. I want to get out of here. Be a good yarn. All I'll get is some crumpled wreckage in the floodlights, I dare say. Think they'll want the house, too? Must have plenty of him and the wife on file. Saucy piece, as I recall. Went to a Taverners ball once. Legs up to her armpits. Very tasty."

Good yarn, yes, thought Harry as they accelerated away through the traffic at last. Lovely wife and twins. Married about the same time as he and Maeve got hitched, too. No denying the strength of the story on a bleak Sunday. It certainly had more mileage than a street stabbing of an unknown American tourist.

A damp Sunday evening passed into night. Harry King phoned back five hundred words from a box on the nearby racecourse. The intro would need no rewrite. The twisted wreckage, lying barely a hundred yards from Tattenham Corner where Paddy Shafto had enjoyed his greatest triumph, thundering to the front in the Derby to go away and win by six lengths not six months earlier, saw to that.

He found two eye-witnesses with the help of the local stringer, Campbell, and added their own accounts to his an hour later. Two other Fleet Street lads were waiting outside the white paddock gate of the Shaftos' luxury home nearby. The wife, of course, was unavailable. Her brother spoke to them briefly by the front gate and then, satisfied that they were all in the same boat, they drifted down to the local pub to collect some colour from the locals. There was a picture of Paddy and Mountain King, taken on the day of their Derby triumph, over the bar behind the expansive landlord. They tossed for order at the telephone, made their last calls and settled down to swap stories and racing reminiscences over best bitter and large Scotches. Harry would have liked an exclusive line but, short of nipping back and climbing in the bedroom window, there was no chance of that.

He arrived back at the office at 9.30. Snellgrove was just leaving. The night news editor was shouting across the now bustling room to the chief sub. A score of typewriters rattled and jangled and aged copy boys hurried tremulously to and fro. Snellgrove, in his overcoat, was no longer part of the scene. He was hanging on for something—or someone. He looked up from his first edition and hurried over to King.

"Ah, Harry," he said eagerly. "Others get anything we didn't?"

King grinned. "No. They've all got the eye-witnesses, though. Campbell probably made a nice fat profit on the evening's work. Still, what can you do?"

"Follow-ups all done," said Snellgrove. "Racing desk dug up all sorts of stuff. We're doing a centre spread of pix for the next run—wedding-day, twins' first appearance, Derby Day and all that. You'll have the front by-line splash though. We just used agency for the first edition."

"You need me, Phil?" Harry bellowed across to the deputy editor at the desk. He looked up, harassed. "What? No thanks, Harry. Sorry to have dragged you back in. Didn't know how we'd be fixed. Goodnight to you, too, Jack," he added pointedly.

Snellgrove grinned. "I can take a gentle hint," he said. "Come on, I'll give you a lift to the station."

Kevin Toomey looked up from his desk. He might as well go home too. He had been off for an hour and more, but hung on in case something blew up while King and the other seniors were out of the office. But it had been a dull day at the telephone and typewriter. He stubbed out his cigarette into the overflowing ashtray. He really must give them up. If Harry King did not need them, then neither did he. He had heard that bit about the front page by-line. Jammy bastard. Just routine air crash coverage really. Well, Shafto made it more than that, but there was nothing exclusive about the treatment. He would have given anything for a front page by-line.

FOUR

It was the same by-line that Tom Baxter read at his breakfast table the next morning. He remembered Harry King from his days at the Yard. They'd met two or three times. He had found him amiable and reliable enough on the whole. He didn't mind the Press. Publicity could be handy when it came at the right time. He might not have got his promotion and come across to the division when he did without a Harry King splash on that LSD racket and his own patient, not to say laborious, part in it. And it was Harry King who got him tickets for the title fight at Wembley when his brother-in-law came over from Canada. Must be over three years since they met. He scanned the story briefly over his cornflakes. The quartet had been returning from an unsuccessful but cheerful off-season week of gambling in Monte Carlo. It was all right for some. He remembered hearing one or two dodgy tales about the unfortunate Shafto during his Yard days. About a third of the gossip was generally true. And jockeys were natural targets in the heart of the gambling industry. He flicked through the pages of the newspaper. Yes, there were a couple of pars. inside. Page seven. Police questioning and searching homes in West London after blue-scarved youth stabbed American tourist to death in Edgware Road. Name and home town of victim. Widow now under sedation at nearby hotel. Poor Dave Dilley did not merit any more. He was just a straight punter.

"More coffee, darling?"

"No, better get going. I'll ring you this afternoon. You want the paper?"

"If you don't. I'll probably do the crossword at lunch-time. Anything about the case?"

"Nothing in it for them. One-off senseless stabbing with no sex interest. And if it really is an isolated drunken impulse job our only real chance is if he brags to one of his mates. They can't resist that

69

sometimes. Someone gets pulled in for something quite different—they fish around for some scrap to please you. Might happen. Doubt it, though. We'll be going through the motions today, tomorrow and the day after. Jesus, is that the time?"

She followed him into the hall. "That shirt collar's going to start fraying soon," she said as she helped him into his overcoat. "I'll get you two more today. What colours?"

"Oh, whatever you think," he said. "No, make one plain white. Then something with a stripe. Thin ones, you know. Not like pyjamas. Something green. Anything but blue!"

She turned him round and kissed him on the nose. "I hope something comes up."

"You never know," he said heavily, as he opened the door. "The terrible thing is, Di, the best possible lead we could get would be the killer doing it again."

"Clever Daddy's on the front page again," said Maeve.

"Yes," said Sally, engrossed in her comic as she reached out for another piece of toast.

"Not impressed and quite right, too," said Harry. "It just happened to be the only strong story last night. Not much satisfaction when all the others have led on it."

"Terrible, though," said Maeve. "I mean, they had twins, too. They had some film on the news last night—the whole family on horseback together. The girls are much the same age as ours. Supposing it had been you."

"Yes, I know," he said vaguely. "Sounds as if that Chelsea game was a stinker."

"What a long time since you and I used to go," said his wife. "Oh, come on, Sally, you're getting marmalade all over that comic."

" 'Morning, Daddy," carolled Sarah as she bounced in carrying a bowl heaped high with cornflakes and Shredded Wheat. She wobbled as she reached the table and milk dribbled over into the sugar bowl.

"Honestly!" said Maeve, cross. "How many times do you have to be told? Bring the packets and the milk in first and help yourself at the table."

"You're coming to our open evening tonight, aren't you, Daddy?" said Sarah through a crunching mouthful of cereal and milk.

"But don't wink at me when I'm doing my piece like last time when

70

I giggled and lost my place," said Sally, folding her comic and shoving it across the table to her sister.

"I promise you all I'll be home in plenty of time anyway," he said.

"Heard that before," said Sarah indistinctly as she studied the comic.

"So've I," said Maeve.

"No, really," he said solemnly. "Word of honour. I'm only on early today because I swapped with young Kevin. I suspect he's going for a job interview this morning."

"Not getting on?"

"Oh, I don't know. He's only been with us since Danny Hart got that telly spot. But it's difficult at his age. You never seem to get anything. He had a long story spiked last night. Jack Snellgrove showed me. It wasn't the lad's fault. Just no story there, however hard he tried. Jack wanted an alarming-trend shock horror piece, but it was never on. Just a tourist stabbed in the street."

"There was something, though. I saw it just now," said Maeve.

"Just a stick of agency stuff," he said. "I must be off. Come on, girls."

"You're always telling me not to bolt my breakfast and now you're hurrying me," Sarah complained. "And she's got marmalade all over my comic."

"It's my comic," said Sally. "Yours is *Sherry*. So there, Mouldy Face."

"All right, Cheesy Chops."

"I'm glad we didn't give them saints' names like the rest of your side of the family," said Harry mildly. "I thought you said that Catholic school went for old-fashioned virtues."

"No father figure to chastise them," said Maeve. "Will you go for that promotion you mentioned last night?"

"If you really want me to. I'd enjoy it, I know. But there won't be many early turns. Tonight, for example—I'd have missed the school thing."

"No trips away, though. You'd be home every night. I'd enjoy that."

"Yes, so would I. We might run to a second home by next year, too. Cottage somewhere. Dorset, maybe."

"Or Ireland," said Maeve wistfully.

He sighed. "Yes, or Ireland. More expensive to get there, though. Can't just throw some things into the car on a fine Friday evening and

71

drive down in a few hours."

"No, that's true. Dorset would be lovely. Summer weekends. Riding for the kids."

The twins squealed with joy. "Riding! In real countryside!"

"I'll need the car this afternoon," said Maeve. "I'll run you down to the station when we've dropped the monsters off. Pick you up tonight at six?"

"Yes, I'll get the half past, all being well. Put that comic away, Sarah! Good grief, how I ever get to Fleet Street by ten with you two to hold me back in the mornings is a miracle I'll never understand."

Sidney Dunn was in Fleet Street by half-past eight, rolling gently to a halt outside the scruffy back alley that was the AAA Ace Delivery Agency headquarters. He flicked the bike back on its stand and strolled into the dusty office where Julie Simmonds was bending to plug the electric kettle cable into the skirting-board socket. He eyed the round contours of her tight-stretched bottom hungrily but hopelessly. She turned in her crouching position and glanced over her right shoulder.

"Don't stare at me like that, you spotty creep," she said viciously.

"I wasn't staring," he said, flushing and remembering how he had walked in silently one morning and found Ronnie Swain, the manager, slowly stroke the curves of that same bottom as she was studying a paper on her desk, seen her shiver sensuously, then rise with a little scream of delighted outrage as he swiftly passed his hand under the skirt and gently up between her legs. Sid had hastily backed out of the room, sick with envy.

"You might as well take that packet round," she said now, rising from the kettle and smoothing the tight skirt over her thighs. "Carl Glover's sick. It was to have been his first run."

"What is it?" He crossed to the table and picked up a square brown parcel.

"How should I know? Does it matter? It's from one of the magazines upstairs. Something to go back to a fashion shop in High Street Ken. The address is on the label. And don't forget your radio this time. We don't want you coming back on any excuse and skiving around half the morning."

"We?" he said flatly.

She flushed.

"All right." He did not care anyway. He hated the scruffy little office. And Ronald Swain, jumped-up little shite hawk in his mid-twenties with an endless succession of natty three-piece suits and a drooping ginger moustache which he trimmed in front of the cracked mirror in the smelly bog every morning. When he was not feeling up Julie or ringing up head office, as he importantly called it, he was chucking his weight about with the bike boys who all hated him equally.

The head office spiel did not fool Sidney either. He had often run the accounts over late on a Friday. It was a similar scruffy set of offices, or partitioned rooms, in Peckham High Road with a battery of plastic name-plates beside the warped and peeling painted front door. All the titles were aimed at prime positions in the yellow pages directory. AAA Allweather Plumbing Services. AAA All Appliances Electrical Repairs, AAA Alpha Accommodation Bureau. All were run by the same fat, middle-aged cockney Eric Flushing, known to the bike boys as Bogroll. Dickie Lansing, who coined the name, said Bogroll had done time. Known for a fact round the boozers of Peckham. Dickie crawled round him, though, thought Sidney darkly. He yearned to get in on the plumbing side of the business.

"Four hundred quid for a boiler job up some smart West End gaff. Imagine that, Siddo!" he'd said.

Sidney was not impressed. "And how much of that you reckon you'd see?" he had said contemptuously.

"A third," Dickie assured him. "You have to pay for the materials off Bogroll's yard, but there's no other overheads apart from your van. A third's not bad for a few hours' work. You take off a bit of the boiler, see, and cart it off to the yard. Needs repairs on it, like. Then you ring and say you got a four-hundred-quid job here. When the party cuts up rough about it, you say in that case you'll come back and restore the part you took, only time's money so that'll cost 'em and all. By then it's in for a penny, in for a pound. Money's nothing to them flash punters in posh apartments."

"It still leaves two-thirds for Bogroll for doing sod all," said Sidney sourly. "Bleeding racketeer, that's all he is. Carl's mate Dennis, he used to work for him on the plumbing side and he got pissed off with handing over most of his bread so he went solo. Three weeks and his van gets nicked and turns up in a lay-by the other side of the Watford Gap, burned out. He buys another one with the insurance after starving for two months and the wheels go missing inside a fortnight. Bogroll's boys, even if he can't prove it. Emigrated to Canada in the end, Carl said."

"Come on, Dunn, don't stand there day-dreaming. Get your bleeding radio and get your arse on the saddle," said Swain, bursting into the room and tossing his smart black executive brief-case on to his desk. Sidney scowled and shuffled through to the store-room. He lugged a radio set down from the wall shelf, tucked it under his arm and went back to collect the parcel.

"I thought he could do Carl Glover's run. He's sick. Flu. His mum rung," said Julie, unwrapping a piece of gum. "You want a coffee, Ronnie?"

"Please, darling," said Swain. "On your bike, Sidney."

Sid sniffed and went out to the yard. As he bent to slide the radio into position between his handlebars he could hear the voices through the open office window.

"I wish they could take their radios home with them," said Julie's plaintive whine. "I hate it when they hang around the office first thing. Specially him. He gives me the creeps. Every time I turn round he's there, staring at me."

Swain laughed. "I stare at you too, don't I, sweetheart?" he said.

There was the sound of a slap and a giggle.

"No can do, Julie, doll. They'd flog their radios off the next day, then come in and swear blind they was nicked off their bikes while they was tucked up in bed with their teddy bears."

Sidney's radio crackled. "Testing, testing," said Swain's voice, thin and metallic through the small speaker at the same time as it drifted live through the office window.

"Yep, all right, said Sid laconically into the mike in his hand.

Swain stuck his head through the window. "What's your call sign for the thousandth time?" he said coldly.

"Charlie Four," said Sidney sullenly.

"Then use it," said Swain. "On your way." His head jerked convulsively in the window frame. Julie's voice giggled behind him.

"I owed you that one," Sid heard her say. Swain disappeared.

He pushed his bike through the alley and out into Fleet Street. Jesus, she had actually goosed him. Imagine being goosed by a chick like that. She was a bitch, though. She wouldn't be so bloody snooty and vicious if she knew he was a killer. They didn't know he was someone to reckon with now. They didn't know, but they would.

He roared away down the Strand. It was raining again and the

74

surface was greasy. Sodding Monday mornings. He was pissed off, with the weather, with Ronnie Swain and with the London traffic. The week was going to pass so poxy slow.

The morning certainly did. He had no time for a smoke or a break. He had two other runs immediately after the first, the first from a Knightsbridge shoe shop to a flat in Wimbledon, the next from Putney High Street to Cheapside in the City—a thick envelope of documents. He called in from the kerbside afterwards and asked permission for his lunch break. He always kept his receiver turned up full blast at times like this. He felt important again in his heavy visored helmet and leathers, microphone in hand as he bent urgently over the bike to impress the passing tourists on their way from St Paul's to the Monument or Tower Hill, and the young secretaries flocking out of the offices on their way to the wine bars and sandwich shops. Not that Julie helped his image.

Her amplified voice rang out from the bike. "Dunn says can he go for his lunch." There was a pause. "Yeah, all right, you can go, only don't go skiving off away from your radio and call back by half one or you'll be docked your next hour's pay."

He waved a derisive V-sign at the radio as he switched it off and then slung one leg over the bike, setling into the saddle as he pulled his visor down and edged slowly out into the heavy traffic again.

It had been a slow morning for Tom Baxter, too. The inquest on Dave Dilley had been opened for evidence of identification and just as swiftly adjourned. The widow had been tearfully grateful for the speed with which her husband's body was being released to her for the long journey home. A young diplomat from the American Embassy ushered her out of the West London Coroner's Court in Horseferry Road.

"I'll call you a cab, ma'am," he said. "We'll be round in the morning to take care of the rest of the details."

"Mrs Dilley can use my car," said Baxter, joining them in the doorway.

"Thank you, Mr Baxter. You've been very kind," she said. "But I have to meet my brother at the airport so a cab will be just fine. He's going to help me with the arrangements, together with Mr O'Neil here, of course."

"Well, if we can help in any other way, you tell your brother where he can find me," said Baxter.

75

"As a matter of fact, no, there's a cab there right now. Thank you, Mr O'Neil."

The young American sprinted out to the kerb and hailed the cruising taxi. She smiled again at Baxter and hurried away. He watched the other man help her into the back of the vehicle and wandered out to join him again on the pavement.

"We'll see her on to the plane tomorrow morning," said O'Neil. "Terrible thing. I was in Washington three years ago when one of your young girls at the British Embassy was raped. You kind of want to keep apologizing for your country."

"Yes," said Baxter. "She was starting to say something when that taxi turned up."

"Yes, her brother. He's in your line. Los Angeles Police Department, I believe. He'd probably appreciate a word. Don't worry, I still think London's the most civilized city in the world."

"I sometimes wonder," said Baxter.

"Anyway, I must get this paper work tied up. You know where I can find the coroner's officer?"

"Same room we met in this morning."

"OK then. Have a good day. I mean, I hope you find this guy."

"So do I," said Baxter.

"What are the chances? I'm sorry. Foolish question. My card. Give me a ring if I can help in any way."

Baxter thanked him and was tucking the card in his wallet when Frank Armstrong joined him.

"Come on, Frank," he said. "They do home-made steak and kidney pies at the Flat Ship round the corner. And I need a pint of best bitter."

It was *moules marinières* for Harry King in the Mikado Suite at the Savoy. "Find me a freeloader, Jack," he had said as he arrived that morning. "I haven't had a junket in weeks."

Snellgrove had frowned down at his list. "There's a beano at the Savoy. Launch of some revolutionary piece of office equipment from the States. Does everything for you, right down to screwing your secretary, and all for a mere ten grand. Actually, I've got young Kevin Toomey down for it."

"Much too young to appreciate all that rich nosh," said Harry. "And much too keen to want to waste three hours on something like that. Anyway, he doesn't come on till lunch-time. He'll probably have

76

grabbed a brunch on the way in."

Jack pursed his lips, still studying the list. "Tell you what," he sid finally, "you can take the lunch if you do me the bus and tube traffic survey this morning and nip up to Whitehall after the nosh-up for a press conference at the War Office."

"What about Harrop? He's defence."

"He's also on holiday. I was thinking of letting young Kevin fill for him, but if he does, then he gets the lunch, too."

"No, no, it's a deal," said Harry. "That should see me through till knocking off anyway. I want to get away early. Kids' open evening at school."

"Rather you than me. I've sat through a few of those in my time," said Snellgrove. "Meanwhile here are the shortcomings of London Transport neatly encapsulated in a mere six hundred close-typed pages. Five hundred words before you go. You'll earn your lunch."

And so he did, but the depressing statistics were soon forgotten in the first glass of Chassagne Montrachet '71 which complemented the mussels superbly. And the girl opposite, a busty redhead from *Business Equipment News*, as she breathlessly informed him as they took their seats, could prove a useful contact for the future. He was all in favour of plenty of close contact. "Sorry, Lou, you were saying?" he said to the man from the *Express* beside him.

Sidney dined less satisfactorily in the bombed-out churchyard of St Mary's in the Fields between Poultry and St Michael's. His mother had put Branston Pickle in his cheese sandwich when she knew he preferred tomato chutney and, not for the first time, his can of Coke had got so shaken up in the box on the back of his bike that it erupted in a great column of sticky brown foam all over his leathers, much to the ill disguised amusement of two girls on a nearby seat in the little courtyard. His apple had a maggot in it and she had not added his usual chocolate digestives. He slung the can in a flower trough, outstared the disapproving gaze of a bowler-hatted herbert feeding sandwich crusts to the pigeons from the seat opposite and strode down to the bike, parked at the entrance to the clearing. He switched on the radio and reported himself back.

"Are you still in the city? Confirm," said the horrible Swain.

"Roger," he said gruffly.

"Then proceed to Waring and Gillard in Threadneedle Street and collect a package from a Mr Golding, left at front reception. Package

77

to go to Greatorex and Barker of Chancery Lane. Legal documents," said Swain. "And pull your bloody finger out. We're running late everywhere today."

He repeated the message back dutifully, switched on the engine and headed west again. 1.30. Four hours left.

The checks and double checks were getting nowhere. Cook was threatening to call in the Yard, establish a pattern. But there was no pattern. He was sure of that. He had been over it a thousand times—it was an isolated lunatic or drunken stabbing. They all knew it.

His sergeant tapped apologetically at the open door. He looked up irritably from his forest of papers.

"Sorry, guv, but you got a visitor downstairs. Brother of the widow?"

"All right, Frank. Show him up." The last thing he wanted was the American Embassy stirring things for him.

"Steve Franklin," said a short, fair, stocky man in his early forties a minute or two later. He hesitated in the doorway.

"Come right in," said Baxter, rising to greet him and wincing under the tight grip proffered. "Sorry to have to meet you in these circumstances, Mr Franklin. Appalling thing for your sister."

Franklin took the battered leather armchair in the corner of the cramped room. "It happens every hour of every day somewhere," he said simply. "I hope you don't mind my coming straight here. I had a few words with Sis on the drive in from the airport and she said it was all right by you. I have to see O'Neil at the Embassy later on, but I figured as you were just across the street from the hotel . . ."

"I wish I had something concrete to tell you," said Baxter. "But you must know what these cases are like from the inside. At least, O'Neil said . . ."

The other man nodded. "That's right. Somerset Division, Los Angeles Police Department."

"Crime?"

"Every damn thing."

"You'll know the pattern then. As your sister will have told you, it was a drunken kid in a shop doorway. Very little physical description to go on, although a taxi-driver got a look at him later on as he was running. We're pretty sure it was the same chap. He was wearing a blue and white striped scarf and the main significance of that is

78

they're worn mainly by football supporters. Football, soccer, of course, is still pretty big over here with teenagers and it was a Saturday night which suggests he'd been to one of the big games. We reckon he was a Londoner and the local side are Chelsea who were at home on Saturday. We've done door to doors right across the area and we're collating all that stuff and following it up where possible. We're sure there was no clear motive. If it was a robbery bid he would have chosen a tourist on his own, not one with a wife who might scream and bring help . . . I'm sorry."

"No, no, that's OK. The fact it was my sister's husband and he was one hell of a nice guy makes me pretty damned anxious to hear this bastard's been taken, but it doesn't mean I don't appreciate the problems you face. My wife's going back with Myra tomorrow morning. The Embassy's helping with the arrangements for Dave. I figured it'd be simpler to have him cremated over here and have the ashes buried over there, but she's strong on a proper funeral back home and I guess you can understand that. But when he's safely on his way home I'm coming back into town to see how things go for a few days. Don't get me wrong. I'm not going to get in your hair."

"You couldn't if you wanted to," said Baxter, smiling. "But I'll keep you in touch as much as I can. We're only too happy to help as much as we can. That's why we had the inquest opened so quickly. The coroner has already authorized the transfer of the body out to the air base."

"Yeah, we really appreciate that, too," said Franklin. "Dave was in the Army Air Force for seven years, right through Korea too."

The tea-trolley arrived at the door. The American smiled. "This is the famous British tea-break, I guess," he said.

"It's tea," said Baxter crisply. "We don't break for it, I assure you. You have somewhere to stay? It's never easy in the heart of London. The tourist season is pretty well all the year round now."

"No problem. They had a ten-day booking so I'll take their room for the duration. They were going on to Paris and Rome. Dave had planned it for years but never gotten around to it."

Baxter watched him sip the tea and wince. "Too strong and too much milk," he said. "I'm afraid our tea-ladies all make it that way. You could try some sugar with it?"

"Hell, no, I'll take it as it comes. That's my motto in life," said the other. "Tell me, how do you operate on cases like this? Is Scotland Yard running the inquiry?"

"No, it happened on my patch so it's a divisional inquiry," said Baxter. "We're all in the Met together and everything from criminal records to fingerprints and, well, you name it, is at the Yard for our everyday use. But we wouldn't call in the murder squad unless the inquiry became a general London one which needs central liaison. That's a gross over-simplification, but it means we basically have the same resources at our disposal whether it's our case or the Yard's. On the other hand, a murder in Cheshire, say, might cover a wider field of inquiry than a provincial force can handle on their own so they call in the murder squad if they feel they need them. There may be one area where you could help. I'd like you to take a look at your sister's statement. Here's a copy. If you think she's up to talking about it, you might like to chat quietly with her this evening and see if she can come up with anything at all that she overlooked when she talked with us. She was still in a state of shock then, of course."

"I'd say she still is," said Franklin, "but I'll try." He studied the statement in silence for a few seconds. Eventually he sighed and tossed it back on Baxter's desk. "I've read a few like that in sixteen years in the department," he said huskily, "but when you get a personal stake in it, it's different. That is one grim document."

Sidney was having a grim afternoon, too. He had been late delivering the legal documents to Chancery Lane through no fault of his own. The doorman at Waring and Gillard in Threadneedle Street, near the Bank of England, had denied all knowledge of the package he was to collect. As he had failed to make a note of the sender's name during the radio call and had no intention of calling up Swain to tell him so, he had to pace the reception area for twenty minutes while the bored doorman laboriously rang number after number on the internal phone until he finally located a testy Mr Goldman who sent his receptionist down from the third floor to inform Sidney coldly that clear instructions had been left for the messenger to ask for Mr Goldman the moment he arrived as last-minute work was being completed on the documents at the time and now twenty priceless minutes had been lost.

"I was told to pick 'em up here," said Sidney equally coldly. "No one said nothing about asking for anyone."

"Mr Goldman has telephoned your agency to complain in the strongest terms," said the girl who was fat, plain and bespectacled.

"Good luck to him," said Sidney, taking the envelope and ignoring a friendly wink from the doorman.

When he returned to his bike and called in on the radio Swain was screaming with rage. Sidney listened impassively and polished his offside mirror with his sleeve as the abuse crackled through.

He did not fare a great deal better at his next port of call, the parcels office at Euston Station where a bored West Indian could find no trace of the photographs he was assured had arrived on the Glasgow train an hour earlier for a magazine publishing house on the south bank of the Thames near Waterloo Bridge. After half an hour another stationman located the package on a trolley with a basket of pigeons on platform thirteen and arrived whistling with it as Sidney sprawled across the counter uninterestedly reading the late city edition of the evening newspaper. There was a load of old mumbo-jumbo about a financial crisis on the buses and tubes but nothing he could see on the Edgware Road killing. When he did spot the likely headline the paper was snatched away from him by the West Indian who told him to sign for the photos and bugger off.

At least Swain couldn't blame him for that cock-up, he thought as he reached his bike outside the station concourse. Swain was in an even more evil mood, however, and told Sidney in a fresh flood of abuse to get back to the office pretty bloody smart the moment he had made his drop-off at the south bank.

When he slouched in Julie, painting her nails with elbows resting on her typewriter, surveyed him with some satisfaction. "Cripes, you're really going to catch it and all," she said. "We had to turn down two jobs this afternoon."

Swain strode in, furious. "How many bleeding times have I told you to write down all the details the moment you get instructions for a pick-up?" he demanded. "Those legal documents had to be in court by half three. That's two good regular customers who won't use our service again."

"Well, if the geezer had left the documents with the door bloke like what you said on the radio there wouldn't have been no problem," said Sidney. "I mean, I arrive to pick the stuff up like you said and it's not there. That's not my fault. If you ask me, the stupid berk forgot all about them and he's trying to blame us. I was waiting there twenty minutes all told."

Swain grunted. "I wasn't asking you anyway," he said. "And think yourself lucky you're not out on your ear. Now leave your radio on the shelf and piss off. And for Christ's sake pull your finger out

81

tomorrow. We got a full diary already."

He signed off in the book on the table near the door. It was exactly five. He was sick of Swain and the smirking Julie who had sat there painting her nails and singing softly to herself all through Swain's tirade. They didn't know who they were dealing with, that was the trouble. And then the useless evening paper had hardly a fresh word on the murder as far as he could see before that coon snatched it back. It was his murder and no one wanted to know about it. All the thrill had gone out of it now. He was really choked. And as he headed through the dense traffic of Fleet Street for the last time that day, making towards Trafalgar Square and then up Piccadilly towards home, he suddenly saw the answer. He gave a great shout over the roar of the Scorpion's engine.

He was home by half-past five, whistling a Buddy Holly number cheerfully as he slammed the front door.

"Nice and early, dear," said his mother as she bustled between kitchen and table. "Beefburgers and chips all right?"

"Yes, ta," he said. "You put the wrong pickle on my sandwich and there was no chocolate biscuits."

"That's right," she said. "You scoffed the last of the biscuits when you got back from the pictures and you finished the chutney on Friday. Did you have a good day?"

"Oh well, you know, Monday," he said, washing the oil from his hands at the kitchen sink. "Traffic was bad."

"You still getting them headaches?" she said, coming back into the kitchen and looking at him anxiously as he dried his hands on the towel beside the sink. "Here, your spots really are going."

"Yes, I think they are," he said. "And I haven't had a headache for days now. I feel great, honest."

"Your dad's doing overtime," she said. "You can eat at six. That ironing-board folded up on me again this afternoon. Wretched thing."

"It only needs a new pin through the joint," he said. "I'll fix it for you."

"Ah, there's a good boy," she said. "It's in our bedroom. I'd almost finished when it happened. If you do that before tea I can get the last of the sheets out of the way before your dad comes home tonight."

Whistling again, he went through to his own room for his tool-kit. "Evening, Buddy," he said to the wall poster. He lugged the tool-box out of his wardrobe. He certainly did feel great again. Funny how he

82

hadn't realized what had to be done. He went to find the ironing-board. The sound of sizzling fat from the kitchen was another reminder of just how hungry he was. As his mum always said when she worried about his feeling out of sorts, he certainly had a healthy appetite.

Baxter was coming downstairs after seeing the old man when Frank Armstrong raced in with the news. "We've got another one, guv. In the Regent's Park boating lake bogs. American tourist. Stabbed in the back."

FIVE

"Give it the klaxon and shift!" he said to the driver as Armstrong piled into the back of the moving vehicle. They squealed out across the heavy traffic and raced up the centre of the road towards the park.

"What have we got, Frank?"

"Bloke went in for a slash and found this guy sprawled on the floor," said Armstrong. "Small but clear wound between the shoulders of his mac. Pan Am shoulder-bag on the floor apparently unopened. Bloke ran for a park keeper who called us in ten seconds so we're quick on to it again. I was in the radio room when the call came in."

"We were bloody quick to lose him last time," growled Baxter. "The old man's just off to a Home Office dinner. He won't want this one cocked up."

"Do we park by the mosque, guv?" said the driver as they arrived with a screech of brakes.

"Christ, no, drive straight through," he said. "We haven't called to see the fornicating rose garden." He nodded curtly to the uniform boys on the gates as the big black car slid past them and on down the tarmac track. Knots of curious tourists stood by the exit, police among them, questioning, studying, searching. They drove on to the boating lake and then he was out of the car and running, Armstrong close behind him. They crossed the footbridge as a family of black swans swam slowly past and then they were pushing through a thicker cluster of onlookers to a small group of police and park keepers who stood guarding the entrance to the lavatories.

" 'Evening, sir." It was Sergeant Billington again. "Not much question it's the same bugger done it, sir."

He hurried on past the trim privet hedges that lined the entrance to the toilets. He recognized several of the faces about him, at least three of them from Saturday night in Edgware Road. Something to

85

write home about in letters to Glasgow, Nantymoel and Ipswich. Two murders in a week. It's an exciting life in the Met.

The body lay face down in front of the urinal. He crouched carefully, well to one side of it. "Who found it?" he said over his left shoulder. There was a shuffling behind him. An anxious-looking man in a trim brown suit clutching a leather portfolio and a collapsible umbrella was ushered forward into the doorway.

"Tell me," said Baxter.

The man stuttered nervously in a West country burr.

"Gordon Davey, Hi-Con Electronics. We're having a sales convention at the Phoenix for three days. I was taking a stroll through the park between seminars. I just came in to relieve myself and he was lying there. I thought he'd just collapsed, heart attack or something. Then I saw the dark hole in the light mac, between his shoulders there."

"Time?"

"Twenty minutes past five." He was clearly proud to be so exact. "I'd looked at my watch as I came in, you see, not wanting to miss the next talk at six. I was making for the exit on the other side of the lake to grab a cab and as I came in I just checked I wasn't cutting it too fine. He has been murdered, hasn't he?"

"We don't know what's happened to him yet, sir," said Baxter. "Which direction were you coming from?"

"From the zoo side of the park," said the salesman eagerly. "I looked at the elephants over the fences and then at some kiddies playing baseball in the middle of the park. Then I made for the lake straight across the football pitches."

"Did you see anyone coming towards you as you approached the toilets? It was only a quarter of an hour ago so you'll never be able to remember as clearly again as you might now."

"Two women," said the man suddenly. "Walking towards me and eating ice-creams. Girls really, early twenties. Attractive, wearing raincoats and eating ice-creams. I thought it was pretty chilly to be eating ice-creams."

"Anyone else?"

"No," he said sadly. "There were plenty of people strolling around in the rose gardens earlier on and again by the lake and the zoo, but round this side, well, there's only football pitches, isn't there? It struck me how quiet it was."

"Did you look in the cubicles when you spotted the body?"

86

"Oh, they were empty," said the man definitely. "My first impulse was to call out for help but I could see they were empty. The doors were open."

"I want you to go with one of these officers and sit in a car outside for a few minutes and think of anything else that you can remember about the walk over towards the toilets."

"The women—that won't help you, will it?" said the man miserably.

"Oh yes, it will," said Baxter. "If nobody passed you as you approached the toilets, then someone may have passed them, going back towards the lake. And we'll find them if your description jogs a memory at the nearest ice-cream selling shop."

The man's face cleared. "Yes, I understand." He was ushered out.

"Forensic outside, guv," said Armstrong.

"Right. Everyone out of here while they take a look." He turned to the nearest park keeper. "Your guv'nor around, is he?"

"Making the nearest lodge ready for you, sir," said the man.

"Show me the way. Frank, bring forensic over after—ah, Colin, give me something as soon as you can. We can't keep the park surrounded for too long and I've got a good hundred citizens rounded up out there."

"Will do," said the sergeant laconically, pushing past with his little square case. "Keep the ambulance boys out for ten minutes Frank, will you?"

Armstrong grunted. The toilets were empty as the forensic sergeant crouched beside the body, legs wide apart. Baxter lingered for a few seconds.

"Tiny point of entry, but plenty of force," said the sergeant. "Other was frontal, of course, but they look bloody similar." He shuffled backwards a few inches. "Might be a good footprint in all this wet stuff. Heavy boot there, I'd say. I'll be over in ten minutes with a first outline, guv." He sounded reproachful.

Baxter sighed. "Yes, carry on. I'll leave you in peace."

He joined the group at the end of the privet-lined path.

"We must have a witness this time, Frank," he said. "This is a park, for God's sake, not a deserted street. See how the questioning's going before you come over to the lodge. We must get him this time."

"OK, Harry, that's fine," said the night news editor. "See you tomorrow."

"Cheers," said King. "Good-night, young Kevin. Keep taking the statistics."

The young reporter looked up from the Government Green Paper. "Three hundred words from 50,000!" he said dolefully. "Half of which I don't understand. I'll never get a front page by-line this way."

He watched Harry King make his cheery way out across the newsroom, pausing for a chat here, a laughing insult there. He sighed and hunched over the report again. The figures danced before his eyes.

There was a loud shout from the news desk. "Harry!"

"He's gone," he called. "Shall I get after him?"

The night news editor, Mike Bostock, shook his head. "No, he's got something on, anyway. Here, young Kevin, you did a piece on that tourist killing yesterday, didn't you?"

"Three pars.," he said sadly. "At least, that's all they used. I couldn't get any sort of pattern from the Yard press bureau or the files and they killed the quotes I did dig out."

"Well you could be on to something now," said Bostock. "Another one just came through. Stabbing in Regent's Park—in the loo by the lake. Another American tourist, they think. Bugger those figures. I'll get someone else on that. One of the Westminster boys can have a shifty when they get back. Get up to the park and ring back in half an hour. I must know the strength of it before second conference. All right?"

"Great! Yes, terrific!" He jumped from his desk, grabbed his coat from the peg and was out in the corridor in five seconds flat.

The news editor watched him go with an indulgent smile.

Harry King was still waiting for the lift as Kevin reached the end of the corridor. "Hullo," he said in surprise. "You haven't told that nice Mr Bostock to stuff his statistics up his posterior, I hope?"

"No, I've got a story," he said. He stopped suddenly and the lift arrived just in time to cover his confusion. They stepped in and King chatted easily with two advertising men from the third floor on the way down. Kevin was glad. He had wondered for a moment whether he should tell King about the story. He had handed it over yesterday when the air crash story broke and might still feel he had a stake in it. But now they were all moving out through the foyer and King had forgotten him as he walked off into the street in deep conversation with the other two. A taxi crawled slowly past in the

88

heavy rush-hour traffic. He jumped into the gutter and bellowed. The cab drew in.

"Regent's Park," he said. "Gloucester Gate."

The journey seemed to take an age. The driver was distractingly chatty and anxious to discuss—or rather deliver a monologue on—the Battle of Britain of all things, in which he appeared to have taken an improbably active part. As the taxi finally approached the entrance to the park a policeman stepped into the road and urged them past.

The driver promptly stopped. "What's up, Doc?" he said with interest, pushing down his window.

"Murder inquiry," said the young policeman importantly, as Kevin started to open the rear offside door. "You'll have to drop your passenger somewhere else."

"Hell, no," said Kevin, climbing out. "Press. *Daily Globe*." He fished for his press card.

"I can't help that, sir," said the young officer officiously. "You can't come in here."

Kevin thrust a couple of pound notes through the driver's window. The driver stuck them in his wallet and showed no sign of moving off as he continued to listen to the conversation with interest.

"I'm following press inquiries," said Kevin.

"I can't help that," said the constable again. "No one's going in that park. Not tonight."

Kevin sighed. He never had this trouble in Melton Mowbray. Everyone co-operated with the *Courier* there.

He had to climb over the railings and squeeze through the shrubbery twenty minutes later. There was no other way. He could imagine the night news editor, a man who lived on a very short fuse indeed, not taking kindly to being told lamely on the telephone that he had not managed to get into the park yet, let alone find the strength of the story.

"Hullo, hullo," said a vaguely familiar figure in a dirty crumpled macintosh, half smoking, half chewing on a thin cheroot as he loped steadily along the path by the lake. "It's young Scoop of the *Globe*. I would have thought they'd have sent Harry King on this one."

"Why?" said Kevin, offended. Mulvaney from the *Express*. They said he had four wives. He had pinched his pen and then his winegums on a doorstepping job in Devonshire Place.

"It's Tom Baxter's patch, isn't it?" said the other. "Harry knows him, doesn't he? Old mates, he always claims."

"How did you get in, anyway?" said Kevin, struggling to keep up with the surprisingly fast pace the long-legged Mulvaney was setting in his down-at-heel Hush Puppies.

"I knew a man on the gate," said Mulvaney, tapping the side of his nose significantly. "Cousin of the second wife. Yes, Harry knows Tom Baxter as well as anyone—which isn't saying much. Stand-offish sort of bastard. Hullo, stroke of luck, here's the great detective now."

Baxter surveyed the two pressmen without enthusiasm as they hurried down the path towards his car. The driver reached across and opened the door for him to get in.

"Hullo, chief. Mulvaney, *Express*, we met . . ."

"I remember," said Baxter curtly.

"I'm from the *Globe*," said Kevin eagerly.

"Give my regards to Harry King," said Baxter. "Try the press bureau at the Yard."

"Give us a break," Kevin pleaded.

"You shouldn't be in here," said Baxter severely. He started to climb into the car, looked at Kevin's crestfallen face and hesitated.

"I can't tell you any more than the bureau will later," he said. "But we've found the body of a middle-aged American whose identity we cannot reveal at this time. He was lying face downwards in the urinal by the lake and the doc estimates his death at about five or shortly afterwards. He is aged about fifty, white, and has a single stab wound in the back. A number of people have been helping us with our inquiries, but we are most anxious that anyone who was in the park between four and five this afternoon, particularly in the vicinity of the boating lake, should contact us or their local nick as we are attempting to piece together a picture and description of the person or persons concerned."

"Nothing to go on at all then?" said Mulvaney sympathetically.

Baxter frowned. "Our inquiries are at a very early stage," he said. "A description may be released later. Now if you will excuse me, gents."

He slammed the car door.

"Pompous bugger," said Mulvaney out of the side of his mouth. "You got a pen?"

Kevin darted forward as the car started to move. He placed one hand on the window as the policeman started to close it. "Could there be a link between this and the Edgware Road killing on Saturday night?" he said softly. He started to trot as the car accelerated gently.

"Too early to say," said Baxter. "Good-evening."

"They were both American tourists," said Kevin, starting to run.

"Possibly," said Baxter calmly. "There are about two million tourists in the West End and a fair proportion are American. And two Scottish shorthand typists may be attacked between here and Marble Arch in the next fortnight but that won't mean there is any connection. And if you don't want your hand crushed to a pulp I suggest you withdraw it."

He stood aside as the car roared off. Mulvaney panted up beside him. "Hey, what was that all about?" he wheezed. "Play the game. No whispering in the back row."

"I have to find a phone," said Kevin hurrying off towards a distant park keeper. "I can't stand here gossiping to you."

"Well, five's not bad out of that little lot, guv," said Armstrong, an hour later over their third cup of tea in the smoke-filled office.

"Yes, but look at the descriptions," said Baxter. "Your actual pin-striped city gent with brolly and brief-case, two painters in dungarees, one motor-cyclist in crash hat and leathers, face invisible, and one wild-eyed scruff of advanced years, talking to himself."

"Any favourites?"

"Not out of that lot. They were all hurrying, but who isn't—in the park near closing time? They were in the right place at the right time, but so were thirty others we've interviewed out there. I don't fancy the painters. The bloke's wallet hadn't been touched so this was a satisfaction job and they're single-handers."

"Unless they were disturbed as they started to rob him."

"Yes, well, they weren't, were they? No, forensic says the wounds are almost certainly made with the same blade as Saturday night and that seems to let out the city gent. I doubt he'd have been lurking in a shop doorway pissed out of his mind and wearing a football scarf."

"The nutter then?"

"We're looking for a nutter of sorts, not much doubt about that. But this is the wrong sort. Too old for the Saturday job."

"You said yourself they might not be linked, guv. One blade's much like another and he might have read about the first one. Trigger impulse."

"No, I'm not going to buy that, Frank. We'll pick this old bugger up easy enough. He'll be living rough in the area. One of the young PCs reckons he knows him by sight. Dosses out in a derry round the back of Praed Street. He's gone for him now. It's a possibility still, I suppose. He could have picked the scarf up anywhere on a Saturday night and the woman could have been wrong about the age—it's the hardest thing to judge in circumstances like that. But we'll know soon enough. That leaves the motor-cyclist. He sounds likely. Probably a youngster—which tallies with Saturday night, but no one noticed the bloody bike anywhere. Still, why should they? And wearing a crash hat with a visor he could have been the invisible man. I hope that young reporter's not going to go over the top with some yarn of a blood-lusting tourist-killer at large in the West End, that's all."

"Certainly pile up the pressure on us," said the sergeant gloomily.

"It's the last thing I need," said Baxter.

But it was what they all got the next morning at breakfast and it gave Harry King no more pleasure than it gave Baxter. The 132-point heading fairly screamed at him from beside the milk jug.

YANK-HATING
RIPPER IN
WEST END
Report by Kevin Toomey

So the youngster had got his front page by-line. He felt a pang of annoyance. Not jealousy—the story amounted to little more than a few bare facts about two possibly linked murders with some highly emotive padding. No, it was the thought that he had been given the story first, had taken out the background notes from Janet, made a couple of calls and then dumped it without success when the air crash story broke.

He thought back to the previous evening in the lift. The lad had looked excited, awkward. He must have been going out on the story then. Ah well, bugger it. Good luck to him. He started to read.

TERROR stalked the tourist-filled hotels of London's West End last night after the second American visitor to the capital in 48 hours was found murdered.

A 54-year-old oil company executive from New York, Earl Henry Masterton, was found stabbed in the back in a public lavatory in Regent's Park just after 5 p.m.

On Saturday night a school teacher from East Lansing, Michigan,

David Delane Dilley, aged 58, was stabbed to death in a shop doorway while on an evening stroll with his wife.

Both men were killed with single wounds inflicted by a narrow bladed instrument, possibly a stiletto or long scalpel blade, said police last night.

Detective Chief Inspector Tom Baxter, in charge of the inquiries at Paddington Common police station, said the two murders were "not necessarily connected", but news of the second killing spread like wildfire through hotels and restaurants in the West End during the evening.

One American tourist, Mrs Edna Schucklefeld, from White Oaks, New York, said: "We always thought London was the capital of the civilised world. We don't intend to stay here after hearing this terrible news."

Another, a visitor at the Mall Hotel, who preferred to remain anonymous as he will be staying in London until the end of the week, said: "We knew and liked the dead man, Mr Masterton. We spoke at breakfast only this morning. It is an outrage when tourists cannot walk in safety in the open heart of a foreign city. We intended to stay for two weeks but will leave for Paris on Saturday morning . . ."

Maeve brought in his scrambled eggs.

"You can't have the front page to yourself every day," she said mildly.

"Sorry, what?" he said.

"Your face. Like thunder. Is it the story?"

"No, no. Not really. Only I started it on Sunday, made a few half-hearted pokes at it and then dumped it on the kid when the air crash broke. Normally I'd have followed it up yesterday if I'd been at a loose end on day shift. And if I'd been on the evening shift I'd have gone out there, Tom Baxter's patch. As it was, I buggered about on diary jobs all day and then left just as it broke. Swapping with young Toomy worked out very nicely for him."

"Well, and quite right, too," said Maeve, sitting opposite him and pouring herself a cup of coffee. "He needed the story more than you and if you hadn't swapped shifts you'd have missed the kids' open evening and broken your promise to them."

"You're right, of course," he said, cutting his bacon with difficulty. "I'll sharpen these knives for you at the weekend. Where are the monsters anyway? It's uncannily quiet for this time of day."

"Sally's hamster has just had quads in the garage. They're administering post-natal care and quarrelling over names. You will have a word about that promotion today?"

93

"If I get the chance. No, no, I promise. I'll stake a claim before the day is out. Go and round up that bunch of midwives will you? If I get in early I can have a word with Jack Snellgrove about the job. I think he'd like me on the desk, assuming he gets Parker's number, which is virtually certain."

"Good," she said, rising and kissing him on the back of his left ear. "So long as it's what you want. Don't let me nag you into it."

"You haven't succeeded in doing that in the last ten years, have you?" he said with a grin. He ducked as she cuffed him. He grabbed her round the hips and nuzzled her belly. "I'm glad I swapped shifts with young Toomey anyway. Last night was fun."

She stroked the back of his neck. "It was," she said. She giggled suddenly. "That joint portrait of you on the art room wall. It dominated the whole room. The art teacher said she thought it looked like a cross between Jack the Ripper and God. I said that was remarkably accurate."

"Very witty," he said, pinching her bottom hard. "I offered her a fiver for it, for school funds. 'We could use the fiver,' she said. 'I promise you shall have it for your living-room wall the moment open week is over.' I said I was thinking more of giving it Lady Churchill's treatment of the Sutherland portrait."

"Oh you didn't," said Maeve.

"Well, honestly," he said. "I saw at least three of the darts team from the Old Plough grinning up at it. I'll never be able to show my face in there again. I mean, I didn't know kids of that age were allowed to paint nudes."

"It's all part of the open approach to education," she said. "That's why you wanted them to go there, I thought. Old-fashioned discipline, but forward-thinking and adventurous, that's what you said Donald Wickson told you."

"Yes, he was one of the darts team," he said. "And now kindly allow me to finish my breakfast while you round up the delinquents. Oh, and expect me when you see me tonight. We're a bit short-handed. Some flu bug. Bloody nuisance. I could have done with a lie-in this morning."

Sid had risen early, too. His dad was still eating his porridge, paper spread out on the table before him. He looked up from it. "You slept well again," he said. "I hear you were in bed by eight."

Sid yawned. "Yes, had a hard day yesterday. Anything in the

paper?"

"I should say so," said his mother, returning from the roof with an empty washing basket. "There's only been another murder down the road—in the park."

"Honest?" he said, wandering through to the kitchen sink. "That's two in a couple of days."

"Stabbing again," said his mother. "They do say the two might be connected."

"Nasty," he said. "Very nasty."

"Ought to bring back hanging, if you ask me," said his father. "That'd cut it out. Stands to reason. I mean, life sentence for murder and they're out in eight years or so, aren't they? Ready to do another one. You want to see this paper, son, you'd better take a quick shufti right now because I'm off in five minutes."

"No, ta," he called, starting to shave. "No football last night, anyway." He'd buy one on the way to work, go the back way and have a proper read of it. "No breakfast either, Mum. I got to get some petrol and things. I'll grab a bacon roll somewhere on the way in."

"All right," said his mother, waiting patiently for the sink with another pile of washing. "See you do, though. You're not starting the day on an empty stomach. Here, I wonder if we'll have the police coming round the buildings again."

"Waste of time, innit?" he said easily. "I mean, any nutter doing murders like what these are wouldn't do them on his own doorstep would he? He very likely lives miles away. In and out in the car. Home in the hour and no one any the wiser."

"Football fan, the Saturday night one, though, wasn't he?" said his father. "Local one, too, they reckon. And it says here there could definitely be a link. Done with the same weapon, see. Long thin blade, they say. So you're wrong there, my son. It's someone from round here, right enough. There's no fathoming a killer's mind." He nodded over the phrase approvingly.

Stupid old berk, Sid thought, wiping the last traces of shaving-soap from his chin. His mother pushed him away from the sink and started to clean it out after him as he wandered back into the living-room.

"Someone who hates Americans, they say," said his father, getting up from the table and folding the paper neatly. He stuffed it into his uniform jacket pocket.

Sid, on the way through to the bedroom to collect his clothes, hesitated. "Is that what they say?" he said. "Still, who are they to know? I mean there's no 'they', is there? It's just some newspaper geezer having a guess, isn't it?"

He kicked the bedroom door shut behind him. He was annoyed. The geezer had got it all wrong, too. It was not just Americans. There were some good Americans. Plenty. Buddy Holly was an American. And Elvis. All the really great rock stars from the golden days. Of course, most of them were dead. But the ones that were left were better than all this punk crap that Agger and his mates went a bundle on. English punk, skinheads, cheap rubbish, through and through. He had no time for any of it. But that was nothing to do with the way the tourists were buggering up his beloved London, his own patch. If only he could explain it to the geezer.

And the story hardly appeased him when he read it twenty minutes later in a back-street café off Lissom Grove. It was a load of old cobblers. Man with a vendetta against Americans! Balls. The last two paragraphs gave him a shiver, though.

Police are anxious to interview four people who, they believe, may have been near the lavatories at the time of the killing.

Descriptions: Two young men in blue boiler suits streaked with white paint; one young motor-cyclist in brown leathers, wearing a dark brown crash helmet with Perspex visor . . .

Christ! Still, it wasn't a lot to go on, was it? He laughed. Bloody master-stroke, wearing the helmet like that. Bloody odd, he would have sworn there was no one around at the time. Not a soul in sight. Must have been mistaken. No room for mistakes. Have to make doubly sure next time. And he'd enjoyed it, all right. No Scotch necessary to boost him up this time, either. That was interesting. One minute he'd had that sick, screwed-up feeling and a thumping head, pissed off with Swain and Julie in particular and the whole world in general and then afterwards everything was fitting together real neat. Just right. And the guy couldn't have known what hit him. He hadn't even looked round. It was all so easy again. One thrust between the shoulder-blades—a powerful one, mind. He had felt the strength of ten men—and down he went with a sigh.

He was annoyed they had not mentioned the—what would you say? The clinical efficiency of the operation. That was it. He had hoped for something on the lines of its clearly being the work of a trained killer, possibly a former member of the armed forces, an élite

96

group with the ability to kill swiftly and surely with one stroke. He'd have to watch it with the bike, though. Like the blue and white scarves. Two murders and they already had two pieces to fit together. Three really if you counted the fact that they were both so near home. He wondered if the young copper who called round had linked him with the tarpaulin-covered bike in the yard below. And he had been stripping down the carb on the landing when he came. No, altogether, he would have to be much more careful next time. A little farther from home, maybe.

Still, what could they prove so far? He had a scarf. So did thousands. He had a bike and brown leathers and hat. So did thousands. And he had left Fleet Street at five and been home by half-past. Not many juries would swallow a killing between those two times, specially if they had sweated and groaned through the London traffic to get to the Bailey by ten that morning!

"Do you seriously believe, members of the jury, that my client, having left his office at five that evening to do battle with the rush-hour traffic in the heart of this great capital, popped off in Regent's Park for a quick killing before arriving home at half-past to sit down to beefburgers and chips at his mother's table?"

He realized regretfully that there would be no Old Bailey trial. That would really have been the big time. Front-page reports. Yards of them. The days in the dock. Then—innocent! Down the stairs, outside, the television lights glaring. On *News at Ten* that night. Maybe even a studio interview afterwards. "I bear no grudges. The police have a difficult job to do. Yes, I shall be back at work on Monday morning as per usual." And see how Julie looked at him then!

Still this lad Kevin Toomey had not done a bad job. He had put him in the big time. Maybe he would put Toomey in the big time. Good for each other. He might have a word.

He swallowed the last third of his bacon roll in a gulp and left a 10p tip in a puddle of cold tea. Big time! He laughed again and hurried out of the café. It wouldn't do to be late after yesterday's cock-ups.

This time Harry King had beaten him to Fleet Street.

"Sorry I couldn't make that tourist-killing story fit on Sunday, Jack," he said as they sifted through the rest of the dailies over a tea at the news desk.

Snellgrove shrugged. "Second killing made the story," he said.

"Bostock gave it to the boy because you'd just gone. He didn't make a bad job of it, though. Still, I think we might pass it back to you today. Tom Baxter's an old buddy, isn't he? Have a word during the day, will you, Harry?"

"I'm putting in for your job when you get Parker's, by the way. You were right. I can't go on as a legman forever."

"I've already got it," said Snellgrove, grinning widely. "The old man rang me last night."

"Great. I'm pleased," said Harry sincerely. "Did you, um . . ."

Snellgrove continued to grin, dragging out the awkward pause.

"Yes, I did put in a word for you," he said, eventually relenting. "He asked who'd I like to have and I told him you were thinking of going out to grass." He enjoyed another pause.

"All right, you bastard, what did he say?"

"He said the saving on expenses could put the paper in profit for the first time in three years," said Snellgrove.

"Do I ring him?"

"I think not. He's not putting it up for grabs outside and he'll let you know in his own good time. Meanwhile let's have a good week with these killings, just to seal it for the pair of us."

"It needs sealing, does it?"

"Oh for Christ's sake, Harry. Don't worry about it. It's yours. All wrapped up. No one else has a tenth of your experience and if I'm to be day news editor I want someone I can work with easily. I want you. Now, these killings—hey up, here's Kevin. Nice one, son."

Kevin beamed as he joined them at the news desk. "Thanks, Jack," he said. " 'Morning, Harry."

Harry nodded.

"I'm bunging it back to Harry today because he's got the police contacts on division," said Snellgrove easily. "Old mate of Tom Baxter and as you no doubt found last night Baxter doesn't take to strangers readily."

Kevin stared at him and then at King. "But you can't do that!" he said." The night news editor said I'd made a good job of it. And you know how hard it is to please Bostock."

"Yes, leave it to the lad," said Harry awkwardly. "He made a good job of it. I've plenty to do. There's a follow-up to . . ."

Snellgrove cut in angrily, waving Kevin away to his desk: "Good job it's not your first day on the desk, Harry. Never do that when I'm the number one day man."

"OK, I'm sorry," said King. "Point taken. But that doesn't mean I agree with it, or that I'll be your yes-man for the next few years. The story needs two on it. Why don't Toomey and I do it together?"

Snellgrove hesitated and then nodded. "Fair enough," he said. "Go and tell him."

Kevin looked across the news-room and sniffed resentfully as Harry King drifted over. He was not about to be mollified by some Dutch uncle act. His telephone jangled shrilly. He picked it up.

"Kevin Toomey?" said a gruff voice.

"Speaking," he said.

"You got it all wrong," said the voice urgently. "It's not Yanks. They're all right. It's bleeding tourists. It don't matter where they come from."

He sighed. All he needed now was a nutter.

"You listening to me?" the voice demanded.

"Yes. You're the Regent's Park killer, I suppose?"

"And the other one. You better believe it," said the voice.

Harry King raised his eyebrows questioningly.

Kevin rolled his eyes and tapped the side of his head significantly. "And why should I?" he said. "Unless you care to prove it to me".

"All right then," said the voice. "Next time I'll do a Jap. Fair enough? Only don't make out I'm against Nips then because they're all right too. Make the best bikes in the world."

"Hang on," said Kevin. "Let's meet and have a quiet chat about this. Just you and me."

"Naff off," said the voice, jeering. "You'll be hearing from me—in a manner of speaking."

The line went dead.

He looked up at King, puzzled, and then dialled for the switchboard. "Could you find out who put that call through to me?" he said.

"Ninety-two? I did," said the girl.

"Was it a coin-box?"

"Yes, that's right. Asked for you after the coin went in."

"OK, thanks," he said. He replaced the receiver slowly.

"Well?" said King.

"I thought it was a nutter," he said. "Claimed he did both stabbings."

"So I gathered," said King. "We're on this together now, by the way. What else did he say?"

"Just that it wasn't Americans he was against. Tourists in general."

99

"Nutter," said King decisively. "You ask any of the LBC crowd in the Red Lion of a lunchtime. They get enough of them on those phone-in shows. There's a million nutters manning the phones in London day and night."

"He said next time he'd do a Jap, just to prove it," said Kevin.

King stared at him. "Did he now?" he said. "That's a bit different. Not a lot, but enough."

"Do we use it?"

"Oh sure, but how and when is the question. Come on, let's grab Snellgrove before first conference."

They caught him at the door. He chewed thoughtfully on the stem of his pipe. "Difficult," he said. "Almost certainly a nutter in which case we'd look bloody silly splashing it if some other bugger is arrested on the other side of London two days later. On the other hand, if he does do what he threatens . . . Take it to Baxter, Harry. You know him. He can hardly ignore it. Did this charmer say he'd be in touch?"

"In a manner of speaking, he said," said Kevin, recalling the voice with a shudder.

"Actions speak louder than words, mm?" said Snellgrove. "Let my murders do the talking." He jabbed his pipe back in his mouth decisively. "I must get to conference. We'll have words later. Oh, go and see Baxter personally, Harry. If you tell him on the phone he'll thank you kindly and then ring off."

"Golly, gosh, yes, I never thought of that, sir," said Harry.

Snellgrove looked at him and sniffed. "All right," he said.

They watched him hurry away.

"Can I come?" said Kevin hopefully.

"Kevin, you shall go to the policeman's ball," said King.

"Thanks, Harry," he said. "And thanks for putting a word in back at the desk."

"I just pointed out that it was a two-man job," said King. "And as for coming with me—you don't think Baxter would be satisfied with a second-hand account, do you? Besides, you can pay for the taxi. My expenses are running rather high this month."

They found a cab cruising round the corner of Chancery Lane.

"How many times have nut-cases rung you over the years?" asked Kevin as they settled into the back. "I mean, pretending to have done a serious crime."

"Oh, I dunno," said Harry, pushing the window down and blowing

100

a loud raspberry at the sports editor scurrying across Temple Bar, late for the morning conference. He sidestepped their taxi at the last second, to the rage of the driver, and leaped for the safety of the pavement.

"Call yourself a sports editor!" Harry bellowed. "My old grandpa could run faster than that."

The other shook his fist. "British high-speed bleeding Rail," he said. "Signal failure at Purley Oaks."

Harry laughed and slammed the window shut. "Bernie and I started the same day," he said. "Sorry. You were saying?"

"Nutters. Crimes. Confessions. How often?"

"Oh yes. Well, can't say I've had any personally. But they pop up over the years. Old Luke Bingley—before your time—he had a series of phone calls from some silly old sod who claimed to have done the Shepherd's Bush prostitute murders back in the early sixties. Claimed he cut 'em up with a carving knife. Police didn't go a bundle on it, but the old berk—Luke, that is—fixed up a meet somewhere ridiculously remote on the waterfront, out Limehouse way, I believe."

"Did the bloke turn up?"

"Oh, he turned up all right. Brought the murder weapon with him—or what he claimed to be the murder weapon. Luke expressed some doubt until the loony dug it into his ribs."

"Blimey," said Kevin.

"No great harm done. Blade broke off in his waistcoat and the nutter burst into tears and ran off. They picked him up later in the day and took him back to the madhouse."

"He hadn't done the murders?"

"Good Lord no. And the knife was plastic and wouldn't have cut butter. Then there was Dick Brandon's mysterious blonde bomb-shell. Heavy breathing down the phone and a sexy catch in the voice. Claimed to have shot Harvey Crown, the financier. Said it was jealousy. Wanted the world to know what a bastard he was. Kept it up for six days. Police couldn't find any trace of another woman on his background file. Apart from his wife, secretary and two part-time mistresses, that is. Then they finally got a phone trace on her and she turned out to be a 58-year-old spinster clerk in one of his offices."

"Another nutter."

"Christ, no. Well, an honest one, anyway. She really had shot him. Harboured this passion for him for years. She killed herself on remand. Hanged in her cell. So you see young Kevin, it's fifty-fifty. You never can tell. Ah, here we are."

Kevin paid the driver off hastily and followed King up the stairs of the police station.

"Just going through to CID," said King airily. "I know my way."

"I dare say you do, squire," said the stolid desk sergeant drily. "Your face looks familiar enough, so you may well know your way through to the cells too. Got your initials on the wall, have we? Barge in here like that and you may be retracing them soon enough. What's your name?"

"Harry King, *Daily Globe*. Now can we go up?"

"Oh yes," said the sergeant sardonically. "Send the Press up any time, Fisher. That's what the CID guv'nors say to me all the time. No, you can't bloody well go up."

"Then would you mind picking up the telephone and telling Mr Baxter I would like to see him and I am not seeking information from him. On the contrary, my colleague here has some for him. Can you remember that?"

Muttering, the sergeant picked up the telephone and dialled.

"Yes, yes. I told them that," he said loudly. "Right." He put the phone down with some satisfaction. "Mr Baxter's too busy to see you right now. Someone may be along to see you later if you care to wait. I expect they'll send one of his young aides." Smiling happily, he opened a ledger on the desk before him and started to turn the pages slowly, whistling through his front teeth.

"Tell whoever does come down that when Mr Baxter has time for me I have vital information concerning the Edgware Road and Regent's Park murders," said Harry, making swiftly for the door. "He can reach me at the *Globe*."

Kevin scrambled after him into the street. "Was that wise?" he said. "Won't we have to get something this morning?"

"We'll wait here for a taxi," said Harry. "That should do the trick."

"Harry King?" said a voice behind them. "I understand you have some information for Mr Baxter."

"For Mr Baxter. Correct," said Harry. "We did have."

"Oh Christ, don't go all moody on me," said the young man. "I'm DS Armstrong. You were told someone would attend to you and here I am. Do you think Mr Baxter's got nothing better to do than come skidding down the stairs on his arse to get his name in the bleeding newspaper? What's the information?"

102

"I'll tell him next time I see him," said King, waving to a taxi which, Kevin noticed, was clearly already hired.

"Blast!" said King unconvincingly as it drove past.

Armstrong sighed. "I'll see if I can get you five minutes," he said.

"Lead on, sergeant."

They followed him back into the police station and up the stairs. "He does know me," said King as they reached the first landing.

"If he didn't you wouldn't be coming with me now," said Armstrong, opening the first door on the right.

"Harry! Long time! Hullo, son. We met yesterday in the park, didn't we?"

King sensed the young reporter's surprise at the geniality of the big man's welcome. "Don't be put off by that," he said. "It's all part of his be nice to the bastards and they'll bugger off in five minutes and leave me in peace approach."

"Just get to the point, there's a good chap," said Baxter. "Take a seat. And you, son. I'd offer you a cuppa but you wouldn't thank me if you tasted it."

Kevin pulled a notebook from his jacket pocket. "I had this phone call at the office this morning," he said.

Baxter groaned. "Don't tell me. I've had six in the past twenty-four hours, including one from a woman who said her husband's been at it for years, ever since he caught her having a knee-trembler with a US Marine round the back of their garage in late forty four. Says he's committed to wiping out the entire American nation, or as many as he can squeeze in before we catch him. What did yours say then?"

"I typed it out," said Kevin, unfolding a sheet of paper from between the leaves of his notebook.

"That was smart," said King.

"It was when you were chatting up that new girl on the way to get your coat," said Kevin.

Baxter reached out for the sheet of paper and scanned it in silence for half a minute. He rubbed his nose slowly. "Next time I'll do a Jap," he read out thoughtfully.

"It is different, you must agree," said King. "I mean, if he's another attention-seeker and wants us hanging on his every word when he rings again, then why would he set himself up like that? I mean, another American gets knifed and Kevin here isn't going to have a lot of faith in him, is he?"

Baxter sniffed noisily. "Since when did one of these merchants

103

have a logical mind?" he said. "They're rarely intellectual giants, you know. Their powers of reasoning often extend just about as far as being able to look up and dial a phone number after a great deal of calculation. You intend to use this?"

"Of course."

"Tomorrow?"

"Yes."

He tapped his teeth with a ball-point pen. Kevin wished he wouldn't.

"This motor-cycle reference is interesting," said Baxter. "As you know, one of the people we're anxious to interview was a biker. The voice was young, Keith?"

"Kevin. Yes, I'd say so. A teenager, I should say."

Baxter's heavy eyebrows shot up. "That young?"

"It was gruff, but yes, I think so."

"Londoner?"

"Certainly. No question."

"Well," said Baxter, "we get plenty of hoax calls from kids. Trouble-makers. And plenty of kids like Japanese bikes. Maybe it's just some yobbo who wants to put the wind up tourists."

"Like the killer, for example," said King. "You can see we have to use it?"

"Oh, I want you to use it, all right," said Baxter. "If this call is genuine, then nothing would upset the lad more than to be ignored. He'd probably go out and do the first Japanese gentleman he saw clicking his camera in the street. And it's a nice little story for you as it stands. Gives you a scoop for tomorrow, even if it is a hoax and a one-day wonder. And if it is the killer, you are really sitting pretty. But it doesn't do much for me at present, does it?"

"I wouldn't say that," said King. "You said yourself that the motor-bike thing could be a lead. And the tourist angle."

"We do already have several hundred policemen in London keeping a sharp look-out for a motor-cyclist showing a marked distaste for tourists," said Baxter pleasantly. "We had actually got that far. And if this friend of yours does go out and help himself to a Nip, all it does from my point of view is make me look a very silly bugger indeed."

"We've brought it straight round to you," said King. "We could have led with it tonight and then come and seen you for a follow-up once the first edition was out. Hell, the call only came through forty minutes ago."

"Very grateful I'm sure," said Baxter sourly. "What you want—a Queen's commendation?"

"Just a few answers you haven't processed through the press bureau," said King.

"As you must know, we have to keep back forensic facts only the killer could know. Print the details and we'd get every nut-case in London turning up with a confession. Do you think your chief would let my boys tap your line—just the one to your young friend here?"

"Oh, come on," said King.

"Just his extension."

"That really would go down a treat if it leaked out," said King. "Can you imagine anyone ever ringing the *Globe* again with a tasty titbit if they thought the Old Bill was listening on a wire tap?"

"Just one extension with one of your people listening too," said Baxter.

"In return for what?"

"Well, there is one line—might make you a feature piece. The widow of the first victim—her brother came over to help her. He's in the Los Angeles Police Department."

"In the business, is he?" said King. "Thinks our policemen are wonderful?"

"He's staying on for a week or so. Nice chap. I'd have to check with him first, but if he thought it might help to find the killer, he'd probably be glad to chat to you."

"Might turn into a why don't the Limey police find the killer of my brother-in-law," said Harry.

"He's a copper. He knows the problems—which is more than I can say for some people. You're the journalist, but I would have thought a comparison of those difficulties might make a good piece, coming from someone directly involved. He thought a lot of his brother-in-law."

"I'll have a word with the news editor when I get back and then we'll have a word with the old man," said Harry. "Heaven knows what he'll say to the line-tapping idea, though. Of course, the more co-operative you are with us, the more kindly disposed he'd be."

Baxter frowned. "I can't spare you any more time now, Harry. You might like to know we've accounted for most of the people we asked for overnight. The tramp was dossing in a derry in Paddington. We've seen him and eliminated him from the inquiry. And the pin-stripe job came forward first thing this morning. Phoned in from Esher when

105

he read his *Times*. He's been checked out, too. The decorators were a couple of Irish lads on their way through to Baker Street to catch a train home to Kilburn. They'd been repairing an air duct on the tube, the other side of the park. They're cleared."

"And the motor-cyclist?"

"Not yet."

"Oh really? That makes out friend on the telephone particularly interesting to you, doesn't it? OK, Tom, I know how busy you must be. Say goodbye to the gentlemen, Kenneth."

"Kevin," said Baxter. "I remember his name, don't I? I want that wire tap done within the hour, Harry. My guv'nor'll ring yours in forty minutes. You'll be wanting to see him first."

"On our way," said King, rising. "Just what precautions are you taking to protect the tourists?"

"What can we do?" said Baxter, seeing them to the door. "We get over two million of them a year in London. On the record, we are keeping a close watch on the situation. Off the record, he's killed in the middle of Edgware Road and in a Regent's Park bog. They're not exactly renowned tourist traps, are they?"

"No, I can see you've got a problem there," said Kevin.

"That, son, is the understatement of the week. Now bugger off, the pair of you. We'll be in touch directly."

"So it's motor-cyclists all the way now, guv?" said Armstrong as the door closed behind them.

"I want a list of every motor-cycle delivery agency in London— West End, City, suburbs. They're mushrooming all over the place, that's the trouble. Some of them aren't much more than a boy and a bike. We'll probably not have them tabulated. Try everything. First yellow pages, classifieds in the *Standard*, *Time Out*. I want every one visited today. I want the names, addresses and ages of every delivery boy at every agency. I want the logged movements of every rider yesterday between four and six in the evening. We can't handle this from within division any more. The old man will see that. But take the more central ones yourself. The likeliest will be West End, or this side of the City, anyway. The bastard's out there, riding the streets somewhere."

Sidney's sturdy frame was hunched over the handlebars as he turned the bike left and right through the heavy City traffic. Gilchrist and Bourne were at the far end of Leadenhall Street. The doorman had actually been waiting for him with the packet, which made a change, and while he was running on schedule he figured he might take a brief break before the long run west to Fulham.

He roared across Tower Hill, slung the machine to the right and aimed for the coach park opposite the Tower. He left the bike in a quiet corner and strode confidently through the parked coaches, past the queues of tourists on the other side of the road, and on down to the waterfront.

The sun was shimmering on the river, dark gold through his glasses. *HMS Belfast* rode at anchor out on the ebb tide. He wandered along the embankment past the heavy cannons, past tourists feeding pigeons and licking ice-creams, munching toffee apples and hamburgers. Beyond the farthest cannon sat a lone figure with a map of London unfurled on his knees. It fluttered in the stiff breeze blowing in from the river, then took off in a sudden gust. Sid caught it deftly with his gloved hand and offered it back to the tourist.

"You can't be lost here, mate!" he said. "This is the Tower of London!"

The man bobbed and flashed an uncomprehending smile rich in gold fillings.

Sid realized his helmet was muffling his voice. He pushed the visor up. "Hullo," he said with interest. "You from Japan?"

SIX

It was Armstrong's seventh call. He was getting increasingly tired of seeing the same dusty little offices down the same drab alleys with the same bored girls manning the same radio transmitters. Mind you, this one was not a bad looker.

"The manager Mr Swain is out—over at head office," she said in a South London nasal whine. "I can't let you see no books and that when he's not here."

"I don't want to see your books," he said, "just a list of your bike boys. We're checking out every one of these outfits in London. I've done six myself and they've all co-operated."

She nodded doubtfully. "They all fill in forms when they join us," she said. "For insurance and that." She crossed the room to a green metal filing cabinet and bent to pull out the middle drawer. Nice little bum, he noticed absently.

"These are all the lads we've had here in the last year and a bit," she said, coming back with a thick cardboard file. "There's ever so many of them, though. Some only last a few weeks. They're always moving on. Some can't keep to time. Some get better offers. And lots of them smash their bikes up. They have to supply their own, you see, so when the bike goes, so does the job. Sometimes they smash themselves up something terrible." She laughed.

He smiled. Charming. "Could you sort out your present lads from that lot, miss?" he said.

She smiled back. "Julie," she said.

"Julie. I might be interested in going through the lot later, but the current ones first would be ideal."

She bent over the file, tongue between her teeth as she concentrated, taking forms out of the file and tossing them on to the floor. She pushed the drawer closed with one elbow and bent to pick the papers up as he seated himself at the table.

109

He grunted as she shuffled through the forms and placed them before him. She leaned over his right shoulder, pressing slightly against it as he studied the first form. The cheap scent was over-powering in his nostrils. He did not mind. He always found it more of a turn-on than more subtle fragrances. It seemed to promise more. But it was distracting.

"How about a coffee?" he suggested. "I really appreciate your help. You wouldn't believe how some of these offices are run. I've had a hell of a day. Tell you what, I got tickets for the Sinatra concert at the Festival Hall on Saturday. Big charity do. I couldn't afford them, of course. Gift from a grateful punter. Fancy it?"

"Frank Sinatra? Would I!" she said, eyes shining. She stretched as she stood. Figure was fantastic, he noticed with surprise. Pity about the voice. Still, you couldn't have everything. "He's my favourite, after Barry Manilow, of course. I hate these filthy pop groups. I like entertainers with a bit of class. Sorry, I didn't catch your name?"

"Frank," he told her. "Frank Armstrong. Least I can do. Some of the girls I've seen today—no files, no records at all to speak off. Faces like hatchets."

She giggled. "I'll put the kettle on."

"Ta. This one, Fred Waring. Lives in Paddington. Been with you long, has he?"

She considered, kettle in hand. "Haven't I put the date on?"

"I don't think so."

"Left-hand side. Top corner?"

"So you have. Efficient isn't the word. And lovely with it. Yes, he's been with you a year. Where would he be today?"

"St Mary's Hospital," she said promptly. "He bust a hip. Hit a truck ground round Trafalgar Square one lunch-time about a week ago. He's in traction."

He put the sheet back in the file. "And William Dent?"

She giggled. "Little Willie I call him. He'll be back soon. He does the airport runs mostly. He's a good boy, Willie. He was here before I come. We don't see much of him. He lives over Harmondsworth way, not far from Heathrow, so he does trips from there out to Slough and places out west. Only comes in the office for his pay."

"He never does central London runs?"

"Oh yes, between here and the airport. But he's on holiday right now. He's got a mate works on aircraft maintenance. They've gone off on holiday to Bermuda! Only nineteen, the pair of them. But his mate

110

gets cheap tickets, working on the airlines. Willie's joining British Airways next year, he says. Going to night classes."

"And Sidney Dunn? Lives—where's this?"

She peered over his shoulder at the spidery, backward-sloping scrawl. The scent wafted over him again. "Dunno. I can't read that neither. Typical. He lives just off Edgware Road, though. I do know that."

"Does he now?" said Armstrong with sudden interest.

She pouted. "Can't you tell me what all this is about?"

"Not just yet, love," he said. "Wouldn't be fair to the lads until we know who we're after, now would it? What do you know about this Sidney Dunn?"

She screwed her face up. "Not much. He's horrid. All spotty and sort of funny. Bit of a loner, I think. I mean, the other boys talk to him and that, but I don't think they ever see him outside work. The rest of them are always going off to gigs and bike meetings at weekends, but he never goes with them. He stares at me."

"I bet he does. I bet they all do," said Armstrong. She started to giggle, but then stopped and frowned suddenly.

"No, in a nasty sort of way. I really hate him. He's slimy. Gives me the creeps."

He was startled by her vehemence. "How carefully do you log their movements? You keep a full record?"

She poured the water on the coffee powder and stirred slowly. "Well, most of the time," she said. "Only sometimes calls get missed off because of the rush and I have to do everything here because Ronnie—Mr Swain, the manager, he has to go off to head office from time to time. Like now. I mean, it happens to be very quiet now, but if the phone starts ringing while I'm talking to you and then one of the boys calls in on the radio to say he's got a breakdown—well, I can't do everything, can I?"

She placed the coffee in front of him, drew up a chair on his left and reached across the table to a large red ledger. "What days was you interested in?"

"Well, how about yesterday for starters?" he said.

She turned back a page. He passed her a cigarette and lit it for her. "Ta. Let me see, Sidney Dunn," she murmured. "Here we are. Oh yes, he come in early and hung about getting in my way and staring at me, all creepy. Then he done a run to a fashion shop in High Street Ken, some design sketches I think. Then he had a trip from Knightsbridge to Wimbledon, then Putney to Cheapside in the City. He took his lunch there and went from Threadneedle Street to Chancery Lane with some legal documents, only he made a mess of that and they was late. He took some press pictures from Euston to the South Bank and finally checked in here just before five."

"What time did he leave?"

"Dead on five. That's the only time you know he won't be late—when he's going home!" she said. "Ronnie—Mr Swain gave him a right rollicking and he left."

"So he'd have ridden home from here in Fleet Street at five, heading through the West End for the Edgware Road, assuming he was going straight home," said Armstrong. He rose and peered at the large street map on the wall over the radio console. "Yes, I see." He returned to the table. "And today?"

She turned the page over. "He was late in this morning. He'll get docked a quid for that. Then he went to Bowling Green Lane, off the Farringdon Road. It's up the Angel end. Took some photographic stuff from an advertising studio to a printer's well out east, Hainault way. It's on a trading estate. They use us a lot. From there he went to Whitechapel and fetched some rag trade samples to Margaret Street off Tottenham Court Road. Then a private address in Blackheath— he took his lunch break out there—to pick up some share certificates to go to a City address off Poultry. He called back at two thirty and had a short run in the City, just down Leadenhall Street. From London Wall, it was. You'd think they'd have taken it round themselves, wouldn't you? Made of money, some of these City firms. His last call was from Fulham to Shepherd's Bush. I gave him that well in advance at lunch-time because I knew we wouldn't have anyone else this afternoon and he'd need to get right across town for it after his City job. He'll call in on the radio from Shepherd's Bush—the BBC at White City—and I'll probably send him home from there. No point in him coming all this way east again. I certainly don't want him hanging round here till five."

He finished scribbling, stubbed out his cigarette and drained his coffee cup. "Delicious," he said. "Our canteen makes it with Bisto, I swear it."

"That's Gold Label," she said proudly. "Ronnie—Mr Swain won't drink any other instant. He likes his coffee tasty."

"Like his secretary," said Armstrong putting the top back on his pen and rising. "I'll ring you on Thursday about the concert, all right?

Better still, why don't I pick you up and we can make arrangements over a drink and a spot of dinner on Thursday evening?"

"Ooh no, don't pick me up here," she said in sudden alarm. "Mr Swain might not like it. I mean I keep my private life well away from him, from the office, that is." She looked as confused as she sounded.

"OK, tell you what. You ring me at the nick. There's the number."

"Ta." She took the card and popped it into her handbag on the desk beside the table. "If I do give you a ring and we do have a drink—and I don't know whether I'm going to be able to make it, I got one or two things on this week—are you going to tell me what all this was about?"

"I promise," he said. "You may know before then, as a matter of fact." He flipped through the forms one last time as she took the cups to the sink in the far corner and rinsed them rapidly under the running tap. "This Sidney Dunn," he said. "Bit of a football fan, is he?"

She dried her hands on a torn tea-towel and walked back across the room towards him. He hadn't seen knockers bounce like that in years.

"Football? Yes, I think he supports Chelsea," she said. "I've heard them arguing about it out by the bikes in the alley first thing. I don't know about that drink on Thursday night. Still, I should be safe with a policeman." She giggled.

Christ, he thought. A possible lead and a probable score.

He put in a call to the Criminal Records Office from the car on the way back to the nick. There was nothing on Sidney Dunn. He was not surprised. It was not a professional villain they were chasing. The surprise was waiting back at the nick. It was nearly five as he plodded wearily up the back stairs. He had had enough bloody stairs for one day after all those grotty offices. Baxter came out of the murder room and motioned him curtly into his own office across the corridor.

"Sorry, guv, just got back."

"So have we," said Baxter. "We've had another one."

"Another one?"

"At the Tower. On the river bank. A Jap."

"A Jap," said Armstrong. "Bloody hell!"

"Mr Hutchinson's at the Tower now with the Assistant Commissioner," said Baxter. "And the City boys are in it, of course. Their patch."

"And I was tramping round sodding offices. But I think I found something. What happened and when, guv?"

"Jap was slumped on a seat by one of those old cannons they've got down on the embankment by the Tower. Old boy cleaning up litter found him just before three. Doc was there in ten minutes and reckons it happened not earlier than half-past two."

Armstrong pulled out his notebook and flipped through the pages. He gazed at his notes for a full half-minute. "Jesus, it could still fit," he said. "The last of these bike delivery outfits I checked out has a lad living just off Edgware Road here. That makes him about half a mile from the Saturday night job. On Monday he left his office off Fleet Street at five. He could have made Regent's Park some time after quarter past on a nippy bike and then made it home by, say, half-past. And this afternoon he was on a run in the City between London Wall and Leadenhall Street around two thirty. So he was certainly within a mile of each killing at the times in question."

"Don't get too excited," Baxter warned him. "So were you."

"I don't have a motor bike and I'm not a Chelsea fan, not by any means," said Armstrong.

"No. I am, though. And the lad is?"

"Apparently."

"Where is he now?"

"Just finishing his last run out West somewhere," said Armstrong. "I've got an address. Horrible handwriting he had. Giles Buildings, it looked like."

"That's two minutes from here," said Baxter, rising. "Let's have a look at those doorstep lists. I was going through them when the Tower call came through." He reached for the top file from the pile on his desk. "Bell Street, Penfold Place, yes, here it is, Giles Buildings. What was his name?"

"Dunn. Sidney Dunn. Nothing known. I checked on the way back."

"Got it. Seen by PC 495 Ernest Welch at noon, Sunday. Aged 19. Well built. Chelsea supporter. Produced blue and white scarf when asked. Parents Elsie and Jim vouched that he had gone to bed at eleven on Saturday night. Eliminated but he's cross-referenced it for the red file."

"Worth a possible second look, he reckoned? Red file in the murder room?"

"Yes. I think we'll have Welch up instead, though." He picked up the phone and dialled. "Ken? Tom Baxter. One of your chaps, Ernest Welch. Is he about? No, no, nothing like that. Done a job well. What's he like? Fine. Well, give the canteen a buzz and tell him I want him here pronto, will you? Thanks."

"He could have done all three, you know," said Armstrong, looking up from the file.

"I told you, don't get too excited," said Baxter. "So could almost anyone with a floating job like that. Mini-cab driver, for instance. Come on Welch, where are you?"

"Give him a chance, guv," said Armstrong. "What's the form on the inquiry now? The chief giving you your head?"

"I'm going to the Yard with him at six. So I'd better have something by then or else."

There was a sharp rap at the door and a young policeman poked his head nervously round the door. There was custard on the side of his mouth. He wiped it away, hastily swallowed what must have been a particularly troublesome lump of pastry and gulped. Baxter waved him in.

"Welch, this report of yours from Sunday. Sidney Dunn."

"Yes, I remember him," said the constable promptly. "Top-floor flat in the buildings opposite. I recognized the father. Seen him coming home from Paddington in uniform at night. Stationman."

"The boy?"

"Seemed, well, sure of himself," said Welch. "That's all I could put in the form for the red file. Nothing dodgy. But I'd seen a lot of lads that morning and he wasn't nervous or anything. And the other thing was—he was nineteen and he looks it all right but he acts like sixteen. I couldn't put my finger on anything, but, well, sir, I'm nineteen and he seemed much younger than me. I saw his mates later on to check him out and they were all about sixteen. He—well, he semed a bit of an odd bod, sir."

"He showed you his scarf."

"Oh yes. No bother. Never misses a home match at the Bridge. Not a skinhead Shed lad with the boots and that."

"Different from the other lads you saw that day?"

"That's it, sir. Different."

"What about the parents?"

"Respectable folk, I'd say, sir. Straight. I'd seen some scruffy beggars that morning. Truculent, too, some of them. But they were keen to help. Both certain the boy was in bed by eleven. He'd watched

115

the football on telly with his dad. The mother had gone to bed earlier. Other two turned in after the programme. The father locked up. Said good-night to the boy in his bedroom."

"Had he been out drinking earlier?"

"No. Been in all evening. Eliminated him clear enough. But I wasn't entirely happy about him."

"You've seen this afternoon's briefing sheets? Have you checked back on any of your Sunday calls for anyone with a motor-bike?"

"No sir. I'm not on for another hour. I only came down to get some grub first. Of course, we weren't looking for bikes on Sunday, but there could have been one down in the yard under a cover. Mind you, he was cleaning something on the outside landing when I got there. Oily rags and one or two tools." He looked excited. "In fact, I'd say he could easily have been stripping a carb down, sir. Are we on to something then?"

"It might be nothing," said Baxter. "I think we'll borrow you for an hour, Welch. We'll get round there now, Frank. Does this lad finish at five, Frank?"

"Could be earlier today, the girl said."

"Blast. I'd have liked a word with the parents first. I'll tell you the form on the walk over."

The young constable swallowed the last vestige of his apple pie as he hastened down the corridor after the two detectives. His helmet. He had not got his helmet. He hesitated.

"Come on, Welch," said Baxter. "Time's short."

Outside, they threaded their way through the rush-hour traffic with difficulty. "If there's no bike down in the yard, then he's not home yet," said Baxter. "So we'll leave you down there, Welch. Stop him when he comes in. He'll remember you, of course. Say you're continuing with the same inquiries. You just want a check on the bike insurance and stuff while you're at it. Give us at least five minutes with the mother. I doubt the father will be in yet."

"He might be, sir. They work funny shifts."

They went down a wide passage from the busy main road and on through the back of the buildings, watched curiously by a knot of women with shopping bags on the corner of the street. There was no sign of the bike in the yard. Welch wished he had his helmet. He felt undressed without it.

Baxter grinned. "Improperly dressed, constable?" he said. "Makes you feel a foot shorter, doesn't it?"

They left him in the yard below and puffed their way up the concrete stairs. By the top floor they were both breathing heavily. "Wouldn't fancy this too many times a day," said Baxter. "Now, we'll keep it very low key. Don't want to alarm anyone."

He knocked at the last door on the top landing. They could hear the sizzling of a frying-pan inside and the smell of liver and onions was overpowering as the door opened.

"Yes?" Grey-haired, fiftyish, flushed from the kitchen, wearing a large plastic apron over a tidy blouse and skirt.

"Mrs Dunn? I'm sorry to bother you. What a splendid smell!"

"Are you selling something?" she said suspiciously.

"No, no."

"Not Jehovah's Witnesses or Mormons?"

"We're police officers," he said, producing his warrant card. "We're just continuing inquiries we made at the weekend. One of our younger colleagues called to see you."

"Yes, I was cooking when he called, too," she grumbled.

"And very co-operative you were, too," he said.

"I don't know about that," she said. "There wasn't anything we could tell him. Only that Sidney was in bed by eleven on Sunday."

"Yes, we know that," said Baxter. "But he still might be able to help us. You see, we now know we're looking for a motor-cyclist. And your lad having a bike himself, he might have noticed something or someone that could help."

"Motor-cyclist?" she said sharply. "Yes, my Sidney's got a motor-bike. But he doesn't go around with other bike boys. Look, my liver will burn."

"May we just come in for a few minutes then?" said Baxter. "He's not back yet, I take it?"

She opened the door to let them in grudgingly. Armstrong shut it behind him as she hurried off to the kitchen. "He'll be in any minute," she called through the doorway, busy at the cooker. "He's later some nights than others. Depends where his last call is. Half five last night despite the traffic."

The two policemen exchanged glances. "Rotten old job in that traffic, I should think," said Armstrong. "Do you worry about him?"

She emerged in the doorway again. "Oh, he grumbles about it sometimes. Take last night. He said it had been terrible. Choked up everywhere. But he was bright as a button. When you can see he enjoys his bike so much, well it'd be mean to suggest he did some-

117

thing else. Of course, it takes it out of him. But he's a good boy. He hadn't been home five minutes last night before he was mending my ironing-board for me. Then in all evening, good as gold. It's not all mothers could say that of a teenage lad."

"No, indeed," said Baxter.

She seemed more relaxed now. "Sit down, the pair of you," she said. "I'd get you a cup of tea only I've his tea to fix and his dad to get off to work."

The throaty roar of a motor-cycle engine drifted in through the living-room window as the blue smoke from the kitchen drifted out. "That'll be Sidney now," she said. "You're not going to fire questions off at him the moment he gets in, are you? He deserves a rest. Never any trouble. Just his bike, his football and his Buddy Holly records."

The bedroom door beside the kitchen opened and a short, thickset man appeared, slipping a British Rail uniform jacket on over his broad shoulders. "Hullo," he said. "I thought it must be the insurance man. I'm just off then, love. You got my sandwiches?"

"In your overcoat pocket," she said.

"Mmm, I'm beginning to wish I had that liver after all," he said, sniffing appreciatively. "I had poached eggs. At four. You eat at funny times in my game. You showing the new chap the ropes," he added to Armstrong.

"It's not the insurance," said Elsie Dunn. "It's the police. Again."

"You're the dead ringer for our insurance man, that's all," said Dunn, unworried. "You still looking for that football hooligan? Sidney's told your chap all he knows. Which isn't much."

"They're looking for a motor-cyclist now," said his wife.

He looked alarmed.

"We just wondered whether your son, having a bike, might know one or two other bikers in the neighbourhood," said Baxter reassuringly. "I think we just heard him arriving. I promise we won't keep him from his dinner. It smells too good to spoil."

Dunn grunted as he did his jacket up. "You must have plenty of manpower, three of you calling in a couple of days," he said. "I thought we were the ones who were supposed to be overstaffed on the railways. Police always claim to be under strength, seems to me. I mean I told that young copper on Sunday, I saw Sid off to bed myself on Saturday night. He was sitting up in bed drinking a Coke. He was having the bathroom after me on account of the sugar rots the teeth.

118

He knows that. As I went out fishing first thing Sunday I could hear him snoring away like a good 'un in there."

"Don't you worry yourself about that, Mr Dunn," said Baxter. "Our constable reported that you could account for Sidney's movements on Saturday night. We're just here to ask one or two other questions."

"Well, it was just in case you imagined that him having a bike had anything to do with these killings. I mean, the other one across the park. You blokes reckon it was the same chap done it. 'Course you do. Stands to reason."

The front door opened and Sidney strode in, whistling. "Goodo, liver and onions," he said, rubbing his big hands. "What a great smell!" He stopped and stared at the two policemen sitting on the sofa.

"These two gentlemen are from the police station, dear," said his mother.

"Stroll on!" said Sidney. "I've just had me licence and insurance checked over in the yard by that one who came on Sunday and now there's two more waiting in the living-room!"

"Well, as the constable probably told you, we're looking for a particular young motor-cyclist who might live in the locality," said Armstrong.

"He never said you'd be up here and all," said the youth slowly.

"He probably hadn't realized we come as far as this on our inquiries," said Baxter soothingly. "We started the other side of Lissom Grove."

"Many of your mates round here own bikes, do they?" said Armstrong.

"No. None," said Sidney promptly, unzipping his leathers. They were brown. "As a matter of fact I don't know any bikers up this end of Bell Street. There's one or two on the estate the other side of Lissom Grove, but you'll have spoken to them already, of course."

"That's right," said Baxter. "Everyone's been most helpful. I tell you what, son. You have your liver and bacon. We don't want to spoil your dinner. Then why don't you come over the station after dinner and look at some photos. You might be able to pick some familiar faces out for us. Up to you, of course. We're asking as a favour. I'd understand it if you didn't fancy a trip to the nick!" He laughed genially.

"He'll help, of course, won't you. Sidney?" said his mother

119

sharply.

"Yes, all right. Glad to," he said. "Be interesting to see inside, like."

"And, of course, you're very welcome to come along with him, Mrs Dunn," said Baxter. "I assume you'll be busy at work, Mr Dunn."

"That's right," said the man. "And I'll be late if I don't get away now. You do what you can to help, Sidney."

"Righto," said Sidney, stepping out of his riding suit. "Is that it then? I want to change me things."

"We'll see you in an hour or so then," said Baxter, getting up from the sofa. "And you, too, Mrs Dunn, if you like?"

"Well, if it's all the same to you, I'll not come," she said nervously.

"Yes, that's right," said Sidney. "You don't want to come, Mum. I'm not a kid. I'll be all right."

"Fine. And now we'll leave you in peace," said Baxter as he followed Armstrong to the front door. "My name's Baxter, Sidney. Just ask for me at the desk and they'll show you up."

They smiled pleasantly and walked away across the outside landing. They heard the door close behind them.

"It really could be him," said Armstrong softly as they reached the next landing down.

"I know. There's only the Saturday evening to put it out of joint."

"He could have nipped out later, guv. Unless they're covering for him."

"Oh no. They're straight. No question. Nipping out? It's possible, of course. But it's a small flat. They haven't even got a bathroom. He's a big lad to unlock that heavy mortice and let himself in and out in total silence. Their bedroom door's barely eight feet away from the hall. And when did he get so pissed? The wife was sure on that point. And the cabby."

"Glue-sniffer, maybe," suggested Armstrong as they continued on down the final flights. "Doesn't take long to act, does it. He might have it stashed away in his bedroom."

"No sores round his nose or anything. Doesn't go with the biking either. He'd have hit trouble by now. I'd like to see round his bedroom, though." He looked about them as they reached the yard. "There's about eight exits from these places. We'll have to have people in the two outer blocks if we tail him. All right if he uses the bike but then we've got the problem of keeping up with him. Car's no competition in London traffic. All right, Welch? I want you to hang on

120

in the hall opposite for ten minutes. I'll have a couple of CID over and you can get back to your helmet and your beat."

The young constable looked disappointed.

"You'll get your chance, son. We haven't finished with this young man. Not by a long chalk."

SEVEN

"All circumstantial, of course," said Baxter back in the office. "There's several hundred lads round here who could have nipped out on a Saturday night, most of them a bloody sight more easily than young Sidney Dunn. And most of them are out of work so they could have been in the park any time they pleased early on a Monday evening."

"You reckon he'll come over the nick tonight?"

"He'll come all right. That's our best hope. He's cool, or thinks he is. I mean, routine inquiries with a bobby at the door is one thing, but a couple of middle-aged detectives come round two days later and invite him round the nick for a chat . . . Well, I'd be jumpy, wouldn't you?"

"I'm not middle-aged," said Armstrong. "I'll make sure we get him taped tonight, anyway. Maybe we could ring him later, too. Get a tape of his telephone voice."

"I want a long talk with him. Find out what makes him tick. But we have to keep it light-hearted. Yes, we'll get young Kevin Toomey to listen to a tape later. We really need something positive."

"Great dinner, said Steve Franklin, leaning back and sighing. "Now then, how can I help you?"

"Help me?" said Harry King innocently.

"Baxter rings me to say I'll appreciate your newspaper is the only link with the killer and he'd be grateful if I meet you. He also tells me the link is a pretty goddam direct one as some freak on the phone has told one of your guys that he's the man. And now you tell me that, having threatened to do a Jap tourist, he appears to have done exactly that! Now you'll appreciate my concern in staying over here is that I don't want to go back to LA without knowing who killed my brother-in-law and why. What I can't figure is your concern with me. You've

123

had two more killings since I came here. A guy rings up and claims he did the first two and tips you off about the next one. Seems to me, I'm pretty much yesterday's news in all this and yet here you sit wining and dining me. You must have a pretty hot front page coming off those presses up the road. So how can I help you?"

"How well do you know Baxter?" asked King suddenly.

Franklin shrugged. "Not at all. We had a couple of chats. I understand his problems."

"You're happy with the way he's handling them?"

He shrugged again. "I figure he's doing all he can. We had the Boston Strangler, Son of Sam in New York, the Atlanta, Georgia, killings and I've even worked on one or two vicious chain murders at home. Your Jack the Ripper may have started the trend, but the English don't have a monopoly of them."

"No, and Baxter's a good copper, all right. Plays things close to his chest, though. He's not exactly PR conscious. We're useful to him at the present so he's playing ball. And, yes, we've got a pretty good front page for the morning. One or two Fleet Street news editors are going to be green when they see it. But unless this kid rings us again tomorrow we'll be back in the pack tomorrow. How long do you propose staying over here?"

"Depends. As long as I can. I want to see the killer caught. It's important to me."

"Where are you staying?"

"I'm keeping on Dave and Myra's booking. It's too damned expensive, though. I can sleep anywhere—and Myra's going to need every cent she can get now. They saved for that holiday for years."

"I'd like to do a feature piece on the tragedy of innocent tourists who have saved for the holiday of a lifetime being senselessly slaughtered in the most civilized city in the world," said King. "I'd like to write it from your viewpoint, specially as you're a police officer, too. And in return, we'll pay your hotel and living expenses—somewhere cheaper if that's what you'd prefer—and see there's a nice lump sum for you to take back to your sister in the States. We'd want exclusive quotes from you if they catch the killer, of course. How does that sound?"

"Too good," said Franklin. "Like you said, I'm a cop. I don't have enough to offer. Keep talking."

King sighed. "I didn't want you to misunderstand," he said. "But I'll word this carefully. You could help us with Baxter. He likes you.

He told me so this morning. You're personally involved and you're a cop. Now I don't say he's going to share his innermost thoughts with you, but he'll drop the odd word about his progress."

"Which you would like to print? No thanks. He's going to like me then, all right."

"No, not for publication. Guidance, shall we say?"

"I'm not going to be kept in style on newspaper money," said Franklin. "And I'm surely not going to be your Deep Throat! But I'll tell you what I'll do—I'll find a cheap hotel in Paddington. I noticed plenty of cheap bed and breakfast places when I was out for a walk. I'll take the cheapest I can find. You can look after that bill and the sixty pounds a day Myra had paid in advance for the other place. She'll need that back. You want to throw in another couple of thousand bucks when it's all over—well, she'll be glad of that, too. But you get no promises. If there's anything I can tell you in confidence that I know won't louse up Baxter's inquiries, you'll have it. And I'll tell you why I'm going this far. It was Baxter who steered me in your direction. He set this dinner up for us. Did you ask yourself why?"

"He owed me," said King unconvincingly.

"Garbage," scoffed Franklin. "For one thing, he figured I could use the cash which you would almost certainly offer me. And for another, he promised he'd keep me in touch with developments. We're meeting for a drink tomorrow and he'll tell me exacly what he wants you to know."

"That," said Harry, "is all Tom Baxter tells anyone, including, I suspect, his wife. But any link is better than a morning press conference with the rest of the Fleet Street crime squad sitting beside me. Let's go and find you another hotel then. Tell you what, we'll buy a bottle of Jack Daniels on the way and I can get some stuff for this feature over a few drinks in your new room. Dear Lord in Heaven, look at that bill!"

Baxter pushed his empty plate across the desk and wiped his mouth with a paper napkin. "I should have had the tongue sandwiches at the Yard meeting," he said. "Get that clutter out of the way, Frank. Dunn will be here in a minute. Have you dug out some mug shots?"

"Old ones. No danger. Lads we nicked for minor naughties back in the early seventies. Probably got two wives and six kids and living out in Milton Keynes by now."

There was a tap at the door. A young constable looked in with a curious Sidney peeping over his shoulder.

"Ah, come in, son," said Baxter genially. "Take these plates and things downstairs, Arnold. Good of you to come over so quickly, Sidney."

"No bother," said Sidney settling comfortably into the chair pulled up in front of Baxter's desk. "I never seen round a nick before. Very interesting." He spotted the Chelsea calendar on the wall. "Here, you a Blues supporter?"

"That's right," said Baxter. "And I go back well before your Clive Walker."

"So do I," said Sid. "Peter Osgood was my first idol. Ossie the Wizard. Some of them goals . . ." He shook his head.

"He scored some good ones," Baxter agreed. "They've had some scorers in their time. Before Osgood it was Bobby Tambling and Barry Bridges. Three years of Jimmy Greaves before that. And even earlier it was Roy Bentley. Won them the Championship in their golden jubilee year."

"You still go?" Sid inquired.

"When I can," said Baxter sadly. "Not often."

"No, I suppose you can't make it much, keeping busy in your line of business," Sid agreed. "Me, I'm in the Shed every match. Never miss. Be there tomorrow night and all. Leicester City. I suppose you'll miss that one and all. You must be having a busy week."

"Busy week?"

"Well, I mean, three killings in four days. Hey, it makes you think, don't it?"

"Think what?" said Baxter gently.

Sidney stared at him. "Well, I don't know. Figure of speech."

"But what do you think about it, Sidney? You know the Shed boys. You know the bike boys in the area. Any real animals among them? Because it's a sick animal we're looking for here."

Sidney considered for a few seconds and then shook his head slowly. "No one I know could do things like that," he said. "But then I wouldn't know, would I? Like my old lady says, he's someone's son. He's not going to go around shouting he done them, is he?"

"Well now, these pictures we've put together," said Baxter, pushing the heavy album across the desk. "Let's see if any of these faces mean anything to you."

Sidney pulled his chair closer to the desk and surveyed the eight photographs before him. He picked his nose as he studied them.

126

"No," he said eventually. "No, sorry, chief. I never seen any of them before. Who are these geezers anyway—suspects?"

"Not exactly," said Baxter. "Boys living in the neighbourhood. Shed boys with bikes. They've all been in trouble for violence over the years. Not your sort, I dare say. You've never been in any trouble, have you?"

"Never," said Sidney promptly. "Not even down the Bridge. I keep out of the aggro. I don't see no point in it. That's why I never go to the away games. I mean, it's childish, that seat-slashing and frightening old girls on the train home. Or twenty of you doing over some poor sod who happens to be wearing the wrong-coloured scarf. Where's the fun in that?"

"I'm glad to hear you say that, son," said Baxter solemnly. "Still, it may not be a Shed lad we're after. Could be Rangers or Spurs. He nips round London on a bike, but then so do several thousand of you. More."

"Anyway, I don't know these faces," said Sid.

Baxter's phone rang suddenly. "Yes," he said angrily.

"Sorry to bother you, guv," said the desk sergeant below. "But it's that American chap. He's in the waiting-room. Just passing, he said and wondered if there was anything new. I know you didn't want to be disturbed and normally I'd have sent him on his way, but he is one of us, so to speak, sir."

"No, that's all right," he said. "Send him up. He knows the way." He replaced the phone thoughtfully.

"Just take a final look at each photo before you go, son," he said. "You'd be surprised how suddenly the penny can drop sometimes."

Sid sniffed doubtfully, wiped his nose on his sleeve and bent reluctantly over the album again. "No," he said definitely. "I'd help if I could, Mr Baxter, but I don't know them. That's for sure."

There was a tap at the door. "Come!" shouted Baxter. Steve Franklin walked in. He looked with surprise at the youth sitting in a careless sprawl before the desk. "I'm sorry, I didn't realize," he said. "When they said to come on up I figured you were free."

"I am now," said Baxter. "This is Sidney Dunn. He's been giving us a hand on the case, as a matter of fact. Looking over a few photos. He lives in the locality, you see. Sidney, this is Mr Franklin. It was his sister's husband who was killed in the Edgware Road on Saturday night."

The boy rose awkwardly, knocking his chair over. Armstrong came forward from his slumped position against the far wall and set it upright.

"How do," said Sidney. "Nasty business. I wish I could have helped in some way."

"Yeah," said Franklin. "I wish I could, too. I just had dinner with Harry King. He told me about the third one. Terrible thing."

"Yes, but a break for us," said Baxter. "Our killer blundered badly. How did you hear about the third one, Sidney?"

"What? Oh, it was on the telly headlines," said Sid. "At half seven. Turned my mum up something dreadful, it did. She said she was surprised you hadn't mentioned it."

"I must get on. King's waiting in the car outside," said Franklin. "That was the other thing I came about—I'm moving somewhere a little cheaper—the Maxwell in Sussex Gardens."

"I'll keep in touch," said Baxter, scribbling on his desk pad. "How did the dinner go?"

"Oh, you can guess," said Franklin. "You know Harry King."

"Fairly well," said Baxter, deadpan. "What are your plans?"

"I'll just hang on for a few days anbd see how it goes," said Franklin. "I'd like to go back knowing you've caught this guy. Anyway, King's helping me move. I wanted you to know I'd had my chat with him."

"I understand," said Baxter.

Franklin looked curiously at Sid, lolling between Armstrong and the desk. "Right, we'll meet again soon then?" he said.

"Promise," said Baxter. "I tell you what, if we get this thing sewn up swiftly—and I'm pretty sure we will after this bungled job at the Tower—you must come round and have dinner with my wife and me before you go back. We could swap yarns."

"I'd like that," said Franklin. "I'll say good-night then."

He went out.

"Is he a cop, too?" said Sidney. "Hey, I never met a real American cop before."

"Must have met a few Americans, though," said Baxter. "All these tourists in London."

"Tourists!" said Sid. "Don't talk to me about tourists!"

"Don't you like them then, son?" asked Armstrong pleasantly.

Sid winked at Baxter as he jerked his head towards Armstrong. "Naughty!" he said. "Tourist-hater with a knife. I read that in the *Globe* this morning."

128

Baxter laughed genially and patted him on the shoulder. "You wouldn't be walking out of here if I thought you were mixed up with that little lot, Sidney lad," he said. "And you're going out right now because I've got some paperwork to catch up on. It's nothing like American cop series on the telly, you know. Even a murder hunt is routine paperwork most of the time. Watch those programmes much, do you?"

"Some of them," said Sid. "Not *Starsky and Hutch*. That's bloody ridiculous. *Kojak, Streets of San Francisco, Delano*. But it's mostly old cobblers, isn't it? I'd rather play my records."

"What records are those?" said Baxter, seeing him to the door.

"Oh, Buddy Holly mostly," said Sidney, suddenly bashful.

"Buddy Holly?" Baxter whistled. "That's going back way beyond Peter Osgood, isn't it?"

"He's been dead a long time. Yeah," said Sidney. "I got pretty well all his albums. That's what I like best really. Just playing them in my room. Better than the telly."

"Oh you must get out sometimes, though?" said Baxter. "No girl-friend?"

Sidney scowled. "Not my style. Not at the moment. I don't have the time, not with the bike and that."

"What is the bike?" said Baxter as they walked down the corridor.

"Kawasaki Panther. Two-fifty four-stroke. I done ten thou on it already. Course, I use it all day for work."

"You like the work?"

Sid sniffed. "I like the biking all right. But not the office. They hate me there. Swain, the manager and his chick, Julie. They're really shitty to me. Well, nothing else I can do for you, chief?"

"No, that's it, Sidney. Thanks for your trouble."

"It weren't nothing. I enjoyed it. Really. I'll say tara then."

"Cheerio. Take care on that bike tomorrow."

He watched the boy jog down the stairs, round the corner and out of sight. He went back to his office, sucking his empty pipe thoughtfully.

Sid swaggered back through the buildings. This was the big time. No one could deny that. The top brass. And they thought they had him fooled. It was the other way round. Mind, they were no slouches—had to give them that. It had not taken them long to get on to him. The phone call had been a saucy stroke, of course, and he shouldn't have

129

made that remark about the motor bike. That was careless, specially after some berk had seen a biker walking across the park. But they had been dead lucky there. Because the more he thought about it, the more sure he was that it had not been him. He had been through the shrubs and over the railings in thirty seconds. Down the ring road on the bike in forty-five. No, they had a big stroke of luck there, specially as it was the bike link that put them on to him. How did they do that though? Christ, probably went round the bike agencies checking out. Yes and Miss Snooty Julie Simmonds would have been quick enough to tell them all she could about his movements.

Well, so what. Made it better. More of a challenge, giving them a fair chance. If they had checked him out, they knew he might have done them, but they could prove nothing. He laughed as he climbed the stairs. Old Baxter trying the Chelsea bit. Probably put the calendar on the wall half an hour earlier just for his benefit! Boring old bugger. Sounded just like his old man with all that Roy Bentley and Jimmy Greaves bit. Chelsea wouldn't have the same excitement tomorrow night. Not now. Kids' stuff with Wayne and Kenny and that pathetic Agger. Still, he would go. Have to. They would expect it of him. Fatal to change his normal pattern. The old Bill would be watching for something like that. He glanced down from the second open landing. The yard was still and silent as ever, the landings in the block opposite black and deserted. They would be watching somewhere, though. Oh yes, they would not be letting Sidney Dunn out of their sights now. Twenty-four-hour watch very likely. Right round the clock. He laughed again. They would have their bloody work cut out trying to keep up with him in that London traffic. He would have to make the next one a real teaser.

He stopped suddenly on the third landing. What had Baxter said about the Tower job? Bungled? A blunder? That was bluff, man! Nice try, Baxter. Six out of ten for effort. He carried on up to the top floor, whistling cheerfully.

His mother looked up, worried, as he came in. "Everything all right, son?"

"Yes, yes, fine, Ma," he said soothingly. He patted her on the shoulder as she looked up from the settee, knitting-needles still flying. "I'll make you a cuppa, shall I?"

"Yes, all right, love. Thank you," she said. "What happened?"

"Oh, they showed me a few mug shots, snapshots," he said, filling the kettle at the sink. "Mr Baxter talked about Chelsea after that. He saw all the same players as Dad."

"Oh, he was friendly then?"

"Oh yes, he's a really nice bloke. I hope they catch this kid. Giving Baxter a really hard time, I reckon."

"Well, when they do, perhaps they can stop bothering respectable families," said his mother. "I wonder how many other boys they're hauling round the police station like that."

"Dozens, I expect," said Sid cheerfully. "And they didn't exactly drag me round, did they? They reckon it's probably a local bike boy so naturally anyone who might know him . . ."

"Have you got to go again?"

"No. He was very grateful. You want a biscuit with this?"

"No thank you, dear. There's some chocolate ones in the blue tin if you want any. Don't take more than three, though. You don't want those spots coming back. It's marvellous how they've cleared up in the last few days, I must say."

"Yes, good, isn't it?" he said. "Here, Mum, can I borrow a couple of quid for tomorrow night? Chelsea got a midweek game."

"All right. See you give it back Saturday morning, though."

"Sure," he said, bringing the tea through from the kitchen. The phone rang as he set her cup down on the coffee-table. "I'll get it. Hullo? Oh, hullo, Mr Baxter? What? No, not mine. No, they're in my pocket here. No, that's all right. No bother. It was very interesting. Yes. Right. Cheers."

"Not that man again!" said his mother, laying down her knitting in alarm.

"Don't take on again," he said. "He found a bunch of keys in his room and thought they must be mine. He said they must belong to one of the other lads they had in to help them earlier. See, I told you they were seeing plenty, didn't I? And he apologized again for spoiling my evening. So have your cup of tea and stop worrying. It's no hassle."

"Well, I don't like it and neither does your father," she said.

"I'll take my tea to my room," he said. "I'm going to play my records. I'll be back for *News at Ten*."

"They'll have some more on those murders, I expect," she said with a shudder. "What sort of person does things like that?"

He wondered if they were talking aout him over at the police station.

131

"There was more than a flicker when I told him who Franklin was. No question," said Baxter.

"One stroke of luck there anyway," said Armstrong. "And his job is another. Tailing him on a bike through London traffic would have been murder, if you'll pardon the phrase, guv. As it is, if I get back to that office in the morning we can keep a track on him by radio all day long. You're sure you don't want to pull him in tonight? Catch him off his guard. Sixteen hours of hard questioning's a bit different from a friendly half-hour chat."

"I've lost surer things than this in court," said Baxter grimly. "You've seen what a cocky young bugger he is. If we didn't break him down we'd give some ambitious defence counsel the dream of a lifetime."

"We could turn his bedroom over."

"And find the blade? He's not that daft. No, we'll build what we can, but our best bet is to keep watching until he tries again."

"The *Globe* reporter, Toomey, might make a positive ID on the voice."

"Yes, how positive in court? And what would it prove anyway? That he was the caller, not necessarily the killer. We'll have a couple of young guys with him in the Shed tomorrow night. It's vital they stick close to him after the game. I think that was what triggered it off the first time. The togetherness of the game and the Shed, the excitement and then the anticlimax afterwards. His mates all going off to a party while he went home on his own. He's still on a high. He's enjoying it and he thinks he's cleverer than we are. He might want to prove that—to himself and us. If he does go home after the game we can keep close tabs on the flat all right. He slipped out last time without his parents knowing. He could do it again."

"Shall I get young Toomey over to hear the tape?"

"Not tonight. Probably lives out in the suburbs. We've got Master Dunn under close watch for the night and we might as well allow Toomey a decent night's sleep. I could certainly do with one myself."

Young Kevin was, in fact, many miles from his bed in the locked back bar of a hostelry behind Fleet Street, nursing a large gin and tonic and scanning an early edition of the *Globe*.

"Admiring our by-line, are we?" said Harry King who had finally left the group at the bar to take the seat next to him.

"Our is the word," said Kevin. "And your name first, I see."

"Alphabetical order, old lad," said Harry. "Not a bad splash."

Tourist-killer strikes again
MANIAC CARRIES
OUT THREAT
TO GLOBE

Kevin looked up reluctantly from the headlines and his own photo set into the second and third decks of the main headline. "When are we using your Franklin piece?" he said.

"Next edition," said King. "It made a good yarn actually. We're flogging it to the agencies for the States."

Kevin looked down again at his own self-conscious picture on the front page, telephone to ear, cigarette drooping from lower lip.

King grinned. "Cross between Bogart and Clark Kent," he said.

"I wonder if it really was him, though," said Kevin. "I mean, it bloody well makes you think, doesn't it? Just over twelve hours ago I was actually talking to him on the phone and before the day's much older he's out there at the Tower sticking a blade into some poor sod's heart, just because I didn't sound as if I believed him."

"Not some poor sod. Mr Yokomo Akimoto," said Harry. "I wonder if we can work up something exclusive for the Japanese papers. I met some guy from Tokyo at the video freebie the other day. Had an office off Fetter Lane somewhere. Got his card in my other suit."

"Where did you get this quote from Baxter then?" said Kevin. " 'We are pursuing definite lines of inquiry and are confident that with the co-operation of both the London public and the capital's tourists we shall catch this merciless killer before he can strike again.' "

"Oh, I just worked that up from a word with Armstrong this afternoon," said King. "He can hardly take exception to it, can he? I mean, mercy isn't the bloke's strong suit and they would presumably rather like to catch him in the not too distant future."

"What about the definite line of inquiry?"

"Oh, them. They're always pursuing them, aren't they? Same again? What was it—gin?"

"I can't shift all that beer any more. Not when you're slinging down Scotches at such a rate. Besides there seem to be less public bogs in London than we had at home. I've had enough, though. Really, Harry. I'll go and see if I can bum a lift home from one of the late

133

subs. Not that I'll sleep much."

"Over-excited?"

"That phone call—I keep hearing that voice. Shouldn't you be at home?"

"Oh, Maeve will sleep through till seven come what may," said King. "Never knows what time I get in when I'm on late. So I make the most of it when I am. Anyway, I'm on late tomorrow so I can lie in."

"I wish I was," said Kevin.

"It's best we overlap on a story like this. I'll see you in here at lunch-time and then we can sort ourselves out before the afternoon conference. Snellgrove will want to know the position for that."

"Is it right you're going for his job?" asked Kevin as he slipped his anorak on.

"Well, yes. I should have gone for a desk job years ago really. Couldn't bear the thought of finally reckoning up my expenses. I always seem to need three advances to clear my bills. No, actually it's more for Maeve than anything else. I'm away four, five nights at a time. Not much fun for a wife and kids, year after year. And she's always fancied a litle holiday place somewhere for weekends and odd breaks, so perhaps we might run to it now. So you see, young Kevin, be very nice to me on our assignment together for I may be controlling your fortunes in a fortnight's time."

"I can't wait," said Kevin cryptically. "Are you seeing Franklin again tomorrow?"

"I'll keep in touch with him. Might have a jar in the evening. He's going to see a few sights while he's over here. Might just as well—there's nothing to gain sitting in his hotel room waiting to hear from Baxter."

"I don't see any point in him staying on at all."

"No, well, he's very close to his sister. Got on well with his brother-in-law, too. You know, fishing holidays together and things. I suppose you don't want to go home and leave it all unresolved. Specially if you're a copper yourself."

"It could be weeks though."

"I don't think so. Nor does Baxter, according to Armstrong. I mean, Christ, three murders in four days is going some. This nutter of yours is coming on strong. But we'll want something new tomorrow to stay ahead of the pack, specially now we've used up the Franklin piece as well tonight. Perhaps your chum will ring you

134

again."

Kevin shivered, despite his zipped-up anorak. "Yes," he said slowly, "that would keep us ahead all right. I don't know that I could handle it again, though. Bloody hell!"

"Oh, you'd handle it," said King. "Yes, coming, Ken! We're off for a poker session. See you midday then. Sweet dreams."

EIGHT

Sidney woke late from his untroubled slumbers. It was nearly eight when he finally heard his impatient mother's call. "You never used to need more than one shout," she said as he shaved at the kitchen sink. "You've been sleeping so deep lately."

"I need it, don't I?" he said. "No breakfast, ta. I'll grab a bite."

"Oh, there's a letter for you," she said. He tossed the towel down, grabbed the envelope and hurried back to the bedroom to dress. He recognized the office letterhead as he opened it. It was from Swain.

"Following police inquiries we have decided to dispense with your services," he read in that bitch Julie's shaky typing. "I enclose two weeks' pay plus holiday money as I do not want to hear any crap about industrial tribunal appeals against wrongful dismissal. Your inefficiency and poor punctuality is recorded on the staff log with warnings administered and is sufficient cause for your dismissal. Your tax form is also enclosed."

The bastard had fired him! That cow must have put him up to it. She hated him. She didn't know who she was working with. None of them did. He was famous and they thought he was nothing. They would find out different. He would see to that all right.

"What was it, Sidney?" called his mother.

"Just an insurance form about the bike from the office," he said. "I'll fill it in at the weekend. Right, I'm off, Mum. I'll see you tonight."

"Will you be late?"

He tucked the letter and cheque firmly into his pocket and zipped it up, thinking rapidly. "No, usual time. Perhaps a bit earlier."

"I'll be at bingo this afternoon if I feel up to it."

"Yes, all right. I'll grab a quick tea because I'll be off down the match with the lads." He was proud of that—taking it in his stride. Never let on. Not a quiver in the voice. He kissed his mother on the

137

cheek as she emerged from the kitchen again, drying her hands on a tea-towel. "Don't forget your lunch," she said. "It's on the hall table. And I haven't forgotten the chocolate biscuits this time!"

"OK. Ta, ma." He slammed the door and set off down the stone stairs, boots clattering. Down in the yard, the bike started as easily as ever. He looked casually about him. No sign of the Old Bill. Lurking on the landing opposite, very likely. He grinned to himself as he suddenly roared out of the yard and accelerated away down Bell Street to Lissom Grove. Keep up with that, coppers! He raced left, right and left again through a maze of side streets and screeched to a halt beside a newsagent's. Inside, as he waited for the old duck to emerge from the murky back room behind the shop he scanned the front pages on the counter before him. Front page lead in the *Globe*—Christ, the whole bleeding front page! That was more like it. Yes, he was glad he made that phone call, all right. That was what got them going. He glanced at the *Sun* and *Mirror*. Down page in both. No sex interest, that was the trouble. The Yorkshire Ripper, the Cambridge Rapist, the old Shepherd's Bush killings they still went on about in the pubs down the Broadway, they were all meaty sex cases. Still, there was always Julie! That was a thought. Not too quick, neither. Tell her who he was before he done it. That would give them all something for their front pages.

He bought a *Globe* when the old lady emerged at last and scanned it briefly again on the way back to his bike. Young Toomey had done him proud again. What was all this guff inside from the American geezer, though? Bleeding hell, that must have been the guy in the nick last night. By Harry King, too, the one who shared the front page credit with Toomey. That wasn't right, either. Getting his name in first, too. And the piece inside: "crazy animal . . . society must be protected . . . sub-human . . ." He didn't like that one bit. King and Franklin needed taking down a peg or two and all. He glanced up and down the street. Not shadowing him then? He was disappointed. Had he shaken them off that easy? Of course, they were probably expecting him to go straight to work. He had left at the usual time. He coasted off down the street, turned back on to his usual route and headed east for Fleet Street.

No way they could have kept up with him at that hour of the morning. And Fleet Street was already busy. He threaded his way through the rush-hour traffic heading towards Ludgate Hill and the City, swinging back into the main stream as an equally heavy convoy

made its way back down the Strand towards the West End. He negoti-
ated a line of tourist coaches, parked outside the post office and slipped
into the entrance hall. The telephone-boxes were empty at this hour of
the morning. He took the middle one and dialled the number on the
masthead of his paper.

"*Daily Globe,* can I help you?" said a sexy young voice.

"I want to speak to Kevin Toomey," he said gruffly.

There was a brief pause. He felt uneasy.

"Trying to connect you, caller," said the girl.

He fidgeted with the pile of directories in the pigeon-hole.

"Toomey," said a voice, breaking into a cough.

"I rang you yesterday," said Sid. "I just wanted to say, like, thanks for
the coverage. You done all right."

There was another pause. He wondered whether they were bugging
the phone—and getting a trace on the call. You read about it. No time
to hang around.

"What coverage?" said the voice, sounding wide awake now.

He grinned at his reflection in the little mirror over the instrument.

"You know," he said. "Keep it up. I'll be in touch."

"Hang on," said the voice urgently. "We get all sorts of calls from
cranks. You read this morning's paper. You could be . . ."

"Nice try," Sid cut in. "You know it's me. You recognize the voice,
right? Cheers, Kevin."

He hung up, wiped the receiver carefully with a tissue, then the
handle of the revolving door. He was on his bike in seconds and
accelerating away down the Strand.

Kevin stared at the receiver as the dialling tone buzzed back at him.

"He's gone, Mr Toomey," said the operator downstairs. "The
gentleman from the police says would you come down please."

He slammed the phone down. Snellgrove hurried over. "Well?"

"Same guy, no doubt about it," he said. Snellgrove stared at him.

"I was holding a call for you from the Paddington nick," he said.

Kevin hurried over to the news desk. "Yes?"

"Morning. DS Armstrong. We'd like you to come over and hear a
tape. See if you recognize the voice."

"I was on my way downstairs to see your bloke here," he said. "I've
just had a call from my friend again."

"Stay there," said Armstrong crisply. "I've got one quick call to
make on my way but I'll be right with you."

Armstrong used the klaxon on the unmarked car and the traffic slid reluctantly to one side for him as he took the great crescent curve of the Aldwych and headed on towards Fleet Street. He turned left into Chancery Lane against a long line of taxis and slid the car into the back yard of the agency. He ran up the alley.

The girl in the office looked up, startled, as he burst in.

"No bikes outside—your Sidney Dunn not arrived yet?" he panted.

She stared at him. "He's been fired," she said. "Mr Swain dictated a letter when he came in last night. I had to tell him you called, of course."

He swore. "Yes, sorry, love. Not your fault. He'd have got the letter this morning?"

"Oh yes, I posted it first-class in Fleet Street on my way home."

"Sod it," he said. He apologized again. "I should have dragged you off for a drink last night," he said. "Then your boss wouldn't have heard about it till this morning. Is he coming in to collect his cards?"

She shook her head. "We posted them and his money and all. We don't want him back here."

"My inquiries, they were confidential," he said. "Not grounds for dismissal."

She shook her head more firmly than ever. "Mr Swain said special in his letter—he was sacked for inefficiency and lack of punctuality. He won't be back."

"I will, though," he said. "Well, I'll be in touch, anyway. We've got a date, remember."

She pouted. "You'd be welcome to a coffee, only Mr Swain'll be in any minute."

"No time anyway, love. Got to dash." He hurried back to the car, locked it and strode up Chancery Lane to Fleet Street.

They were playing the tape through for the third time when he arrived in the switchboard room. He listened carefully, controlling the twitch of excitement he felt.

"Is that the same voice, Kevin?"

Toomey nodded. "And yours?"

"Mine?" said Armstrong.

"You said you had a tape for me to hear."

"Oh," said Armstrong. "That. False alarm, I'm afraid. No, this is much more interesting. I'll be in touch. You can give me a bell this afternoon if you like. Might have something for you. I must dash."

He made his way out of the building and into Fleet Street. The post office was barely fifty yards from the *Globe* office. The young CID man dusting for dabs in the middle phone booth was not encouraging. "Probably this one," he said. "Greasy dabs all over the others but the door handle and this receiver has been wiped clean. I'll go over everything, of course, but you'll get bugger all out of it."

"OK," he said resignedly. "Pop in and see me when you've finished, anyway."

He collected his car and headed back to the nick. Baxter had just arrived from the Yard. "I heard," he said. "Toomey quite sure?"

"Oh yes. Same caller."

"And?"

"I'll play it for you," said Armstrong, fishing the cassette out of his macintosh pocket. "It's Dunn all right."

They listened together.

"Not much doubt about that," said Baxter. "You didn't play Toomey our tape?"

"No point," said Armstrong. "Was there?"

"Quite right. None at all. Master Sidney really is a saucy boy, isn't he? Must have known we'd have him taped. Figures it's not enough to go on, maybe. Where is he?"

"That's the bad news," said Armstrong. "They sacked him."

"They what?"

"Last night. Girl in the office said they caught the last post. First-class. Told him not to bother to come in again."

"Bugger," said Baxter. "Where was the call made from?"

"Box in Fleet Street outside the post office probably. They found one wiped down. You want a call out for his bike?"

"Not yet. I've a fair idea where he'll be."

"I'll buy it."

"At home, having a quiet cup of tea, playing his records and reading his press reviews. He's enjoying every second of this, Frank. Fairly swaggered across the road when he left the nick last night. He knows we're on to him and it just makes it better as far as he's concerned. That's why he rang young Toomey again this morning. Just underlining the fact that he's number one suspect. I bet he was disappointed when he left home this morning and didn't spot a tail on him. And what did he say to Toomey—thanks for the coverage. Loving it all."

He checked a number in his pocket-book and started to dial it. "I'll

141

prove it," he said.

"Isn't that pushing our luck?" said Armstrong. "Supposing he takes fright and simply stops. We'd never get him then."

"He can't stop. Now now," said Baxter.

Sid was immersed in Harry King's feature on Steve Franklin when the phone rang. And it did not improve one bit on the second reading. Crazy animal . . . subhuman . . . The more he read it, the more it upset him. He was not sure who he was madder at, King or Franklin. They both deserved the treatment.

The phone jangled on. He scowled at it. His mother was visiting his Auntie Eileen in Esher before going to bingo. It couldn't be for him, though. Still it rang. He pushed the paper aside and reached for the phone on the sideboard.

"What?" he said irritably.

He grinned at his reflection in the mirror on the wall as Baxter's voice drifted down the line. They had heard about the phone call then. Well, they would need a bloody sight more than that.

"We've been checking out the bike agencies this morning again," said Baxter, "and I was most disturbed to hear you'd been dismissed."

Sidney's reflection frowned back at him. "I was leaving anyway. No loss."

"All the same such precipitous action was most unwarranted," said Baxter.

Sidney's face grinned back again. Pompous sod. "It's all right, honest," he said. "I don't mind."

"Well, I do," said Baxter. "If firms dismissed every employee we made a routine inquiry about, we'd have an even higher rate of unemployment. Would you like me to put in a word with the man at the top?"

"No, don't bother, ta," mumbled Sid.

"What will you do now?"

Sidney smirked again. Give-us-a-clue time. "I'll sit around here till it's time to go to football," he said.

"I meant about a job," said Baxter.

"I'll find something," he said. "One thing though, Mr Baxter. Don't tell the old lady. She'd worry. And my dad. I'll tell them I got a few days off. All right?"

"Of course. But I don't suppose I'll have cause to bother any of you

142

again," said Baxter. "Good luck in your job hunt, anyway."

Sidney put the receiver back and jabbed two derisive fingers at it. Lying bastard. He wasn't worried about his losing his job. Just checking him out. Had a man watching the flat at this very moment, very like. He crossed to the window and looked across at the dark landings opposite. That phone call would have made them jumpy. But what could they do? He dug into his jeans' rear pocket and pulled out the giro cheque. Plenty there for a week or two anyway. He would play some records for the rest of the day, make the match tonight and then maybe spend a few quid tomorrow. Have some fun.

"Well?" said Baxter.

"It's dead dodgy, guv," said Armstrong. "I mean, we lose him for half an hour and we could have another dead body. More. The bigwigs happy about it?"

"No," said Baxter. "They're not. And nor am I, but they agree we can't pull him in without a shred of evidence and if we turn his place over and find nothing—which we would—we'd have to pull him in and go for the circumstantial line—which we would lose."

"All the same," said Armstrong slowly. "Suppose he did another one and it got out that we'd pulled him in for questioning not a day or so earlier . . ."

"Suppose nothing," Baxter cut in. "We'll never let him out of our sight. The game itself'll be easy enough. He'll be there with his usual mates, we can depend on that. But it's what he gets up to afterwards that could be the clincher, bearing last Saturday night in mind. I want two guys with them, close up, mind, from Edgware Road tube all the way to the ground. His little mates could be very useful to us. Our Sidney's led quite an exciting life since last Saturday afternoon. He meets them tonight and they'll be talking about the latest signing, what Buggins at work got up to last dinner hour, Kojak on the telly, the Nosepickers' new release—all pretty small beer to the ruthless Sidney. He's going to find it hard to adjust back to that. If he resists the temptation to brag, or drop a heavy hint, he might still let something slip. I must have another word with the old man. We'll pick the tails this afternoon. Think about that meanwhile. We'll want the best. I'll get another dozen from the Yard."

"And you and me?"

"We'll go to the match, too," said Baxter. "Oh, don't be nervous. I won't drag you into the Shed. We can watch from the news stand.

You're an Arsenal man, aren't you?"

"Come on you Gunners," said Armstrong.

"Yes, I'll never forgive you for those two Cup semi-finals in the early fifties," said Baxter sourly. "Two up in the first, we were. You got one back and the wind blew Denis Compton's corner in in the last minute."

"Before my time," said Armstrong.

Baxter looked at him hard and sniffed.

"You're very quiet, Sid," said Wayne as they swayed from their strap handles in the rattling tube train.

"He's in love, very like," jeered Agger. "That bird at your place, the one we saw that night when we come round to pick you up for the West Ham game. What was her name? Lovely arse in a tight skirt."

"Julie," said Sid. "No, she's horrible. I really hate her. Anyway, I slung the job in."

The train had drawn into Fulham Broadway station and jolted to a halt, but Kenny, Wayne and Agger still stood staring at Sid as the fans behind them pushed past with muttered oaths and complaints and clattered away up the platform. Sid followed them to the stairs.

"Here, hold on, when was this?" said Kenny.

"This morning. Sarcastic cow. Her and that Swain. I told them to stuff their job," said Sid. "So what's the odds? I can get a job like that any day." He lengthened his stride, shoving aside an elderly couple as they handed in their tickets at the barrier. The other three hurried after him, followed closely by the two young plain-clothes men who had followed them from Edgware Road. All six were out in the Fulham Road now as a heavy crush of fans drifted slowly down towards the ground in the cold evening air.

"Well, you never said nothin', Sid," said Wayne as they caught him up again.

"Didn't get much chance with Agger going on about his boring tart," said Sid. "Irene Croft! Christ!"

"What's wrong with her?" demanded Agger fiercely.

"What's right with her, more like," Sid scoffed. "She's got tombstone teeth and a jaw like Jimmy Hill. I know she shags like a rattlesnake. Everyone in West London knows that. And I know you don't look at the mantelpiece when you're stoking the fire, but, bloody hell, Agger, fancy having those legs wrapped round you! They're like my old lady's sideboard."

144

Agger grabbed him by the lapels. "You take that back or I do you," he hissed.

Sid pushed him away contemptuously. "Leave it out, Agger," he said. "Like a kid in the bleeding school playground, you are. She's not worth getting steamed up. Anyone could do better than that, even you." He skipped hastily to one side as Agger charged him, close-cropped bullet head down.

"Here, watch it," said a middle-aged fan walking down the centre of the road with his wife.

Agger charged in ahead. A group of youths walking beside them in the kerb stopped and cheered. "Action, action," chanted one. "Four to one on bullet bonce!"

Agger, cut off by the press of bodies from the evasive Sid, swiped out at random, catching the chanting youth on the bridge of his nose. He put one hand up to his face and then looked at it slowly as the blood trickled down his finger. "He whacked me," he said in wonder. "That ugly bastard whacked me." His nearest mate, a tall youth with trousers at half-mast above his boots, lashed out with his right foot, catching little Kenny a painful blow just below the knee.

"Right!" said Wayne. "I seen that."

"All right, leave it out," said a special constable, stepping off the pavement and moving in among the two groups. A sergeant on a horse steered his way through the throng.

"What's the trouble?"

"No trouble, they're on their way," said the foot bobby confidently.

"I want him done for assault," said the first lad indignantly. "I'm bleeding, aren't I. Look!"

"I hardly like to. I might faint," said the constable.

"I got witnesses," said the youth. "I was just walking along and he belted me."

"Well, you could press charges, of course. Come up the nick now and miss the match," said the constable. "That what you want?"

The youth muttered.

"Right, you lot. On your way. Not you three—wait. Let them get well ahead. And behave yourselves."

Agger, Wayne and Kenny waved derisive fingers at the second group and slipped away through the crowd.

"I'll still have that Sid," said Agger. "Where is he?"

"We lost him. He's miles ahead now," said Wayne. "Forget it, Agger. He's out of sorts. Just lost his job."

145

"I'm glad," said Agger. "Serves him right. Always going on about that bike of his. He can get a really bum job like mine now and see how he likes it, sitting in a bleeding office making tea and fetching doughnuts from the corner shop all day long."

"Bugger it, we've lost Dunn," said the first detective behind them. "You stay with this crowd, Fred. I'll see if I can get after him."

"You'll be lucky," said Fred. "You'll never get through this lot. They leave it so late for these midweek games, all rolling up together. Must be fifteen thousand up the road there. You stay with these and I'll nip in that gateway and call up the old man."

"Rather you than me," said the other.

"Bloody hell, a football crowd like this isn't exactly the easiest place to tail someone," said Fred. "Go on, they're shoving their way ahead."

Baxter took the call in his car in the park near the news stand. He swore. He turned to the uniformed inspector beside him. "There's still only the one entrance to the Shed?" he said.

The inspector nodded.

"Then we'll have to pick the shadowing up there. I don't want him out of sight again for the rest of the evening."

The inspector shook his head. "It's impossible," he said. "We never expected a crowd this big for a midweek League Cup game. There's no way any of your boys could stay with him. You can get carried twenty, thirty yards in one surge when they start shoving in the Shed."

Baxter hesitated. "Fair enough," he said finally. "You know your ground. I want the others picked up straight away, just in case we don't find him again. But Dunn's number one."

"I'll see to it," said the inspector. "Give you a shout in five minutes."

"Sid'll be waiting on the corner of the gate, very like," said Kenny, as they neared the entrance. "It's where we always meet up if we lose each other, right, Wayne? Like the Arsenal cup game last year."

"If he is there, leave it out till after the game at least, Agger," said Wayne. "I want to see this one. I'm not getting slung out just as they're kicking off."

"I'm not standing with that sod," said Agger.

"He's not there, anyway," said Wayne. "Hey up, they're frisking them again."

"All right, you three, stand over there out of the way," said a large

146

sergeant.

"Oh bloody hell, not again. You lot frisked me on Saturday," said Agger. "What's up with you? You fancy me or something?"

"I'll fancy flattening your right ear if you give me any lip," said the constable. "Yes, I do remember him. He was saucy last time, too."

The sergeant moved to one side to greet the inspector who had arrived hot-foot from the main entrance. Another constable moved in to help with the search. The CID men hovered on the fringe before joining the inspector.

"Mr Baxter wants this lot pulled in now," he said. "You'd better see if you can pick Dunn up. He can't be far ahead."

"He's certainly not come in here," said the sergeant. "No way we could have missed him on that description. They have to funnel right in here."

"He won't get in the main entrance either," said the inspector. "He can't be far away."

"Hullo, what's this then?" said the constable searching Wayne.

"It's a bleeding comb, isn't it?" said Wayne. "Like I run it through me hair from time to time."

"What hair?" said the constable, surveying his close-cropped head. "Scrubbing brush would do the job better. It's a metal comb."

"Oh my word, so it is," said Wayne. "I'd never noticed that."

"Do a lot of damage with that, couldn't you?" said the constable. "That could definitely be an offensive weapon. What you got, Chas?"

"This naughty boy's got a chain," said the other constable.

"Oh leave it out. It's got a padlock on one end," said Agger. "It's for our shed. I forgot to lock it last night, didn't I?"

"Offensive weapon," said the other constable.

"This one's clean," said a third, stepping back from an alarmed Kenny.

"We'll take 'em in together though, I think," said the first.

Kenny yelped. "You can't. I ain't done nothing."

"The thing is, sonny, we'd like a chat with you all and we can either have it nice and private down the nick or take you home and do it in front of your dad. Would you prefer that?"

"No," said Kenny, sulking.

The inspector joined them. "Where's the big lad you came down the road with?" he demanded.

"We had a row. He went on ahead," said Agger. "Lucky bugger. He'd fall down a sewer pipe and come out smelling of roses. Look, do

147

we have to miss the game?"

"You do," said the inspector curtly. "And you'll be the ones smelling of roses if you help us with our inquiries. On the other hand, you could be in a big bother if you don't. So what's it to be?"

Sidney sat back comfortably in the back seat upstairs on the number 11 bus as it rumbled slowly down the King's Road towards Sloane Square. He had not fancied the match anyway. Funny, that—for the first time in his life he had not looked forward to a game. But none of that mattered now. There were things to be done and time was running out with bloody Baxter hanging round his neck. He looked down on the colourful parade of King's Road on a weekday evening. Groups of punks in pink, purple and green hair, sometimes stripes of all three, wandered along the pavement as listlessly as the white macintoshed tourists among them. There were knots of mod revivalists in their oversize green parkas, astride motor scooters bedecked with six mirrors, radio aerials with pennants on top and their names emblazoned in cut-out letters on their bikes and their backs. New romantics drifted down towards World's End and live gigs at the pubs in matching hair-styles and fashions, hand in hand. The gaily coloured and brightly lit boutique windows winked and gleamed in the enfolding darkness and then were gone as the heavy bus swung round Sloane Square and headed on towards Victoria.

Outside the railway station a group of tourists clattered noisily upstairs, disturbing Sid's peaceful solitude. He scowled. They filled the three seats in front of him, chattering about stand-by fares and food prices, their conversation punctuated with cries of recognition as the bus reached Parliament Square.

"Westminster Abbey! The Houses of Parliament. My, they look so old!"

"Not more than a hundred and fifty, honey. Mid-Victorian Gothic."

"Is that right? My, but they look so antiquated."

And they were heading down Whitehall.

"Downing Street. Isn't that the home of the Prime Minister? Not exactly the White House!" More laughter.

"Hey, Warren, what say we walk back from here? It's so full of historical interest."

"I've had my bellyful of historical interest for one day," said Warren, a heavily built man sprawled across the seat in front of

Sidney. "Hampton Court, the Tower and St Paul's is about all the historical interest a man can take without a large drink inside him. I'm for a large Scotch on the rocks."

"I'm game, Della," said the woman at the front. "Come on, Maxwell, be real nice to walk back. It all looks different at night."

"Sure, you go ahead," said Warren good-naturedly. "I'll see you back at the hotel. In the bar!"

"If you're sure," said Maxwell doubtfully. The three of them rose and lurched towards the top of the stairs as the bus braked suddenly. "See you around nine then?"

"Fine, fine," said Warren. "You take good care of my wife, now, you hear?"

Cries of farewell were followed by laughter and a brief but noisy exchange of repartee with the conductor below and then they were spilling out on to the pavement outside the Whitehall Theatre. Warren looked down and back to wave farewell as they looked up. Sidney could smell his powerful aftershave. He hated aftershave. Poofter stuff.

As the bus headed on round Trafalgar Square, Warren pulled out a large cigar from an expensive-looking leather case. He stuck it between his teeth and started to pat his pockets, exclaiming to himself in dismay. He swung round. "Say, boy, you got a match?"

"Don't use them," said Sidney shortly. He looked out of the window at the fountains illuminated in the evening lights. Warren sighed and put the cigar slowly back in the case.

Sidney whistled to himself quietly. Yes, he would bloody give them two weeks' pay and no compensation all right. He happened to know the small bay window had a loose catch. And, best of all, he happened to know that Mr Smart Arse Ronald Swain had his own little private deposit account in the locked drawer of his desk, built up over months of pilfering from the petty cash box in Julie's desk. He had come in early one Wednesday morning and seen him at it. Taking out the petty cash, extracting a couple of oners and then over to his drawer, out with the old Oxo tin and counting the stack of notes in their rubber band before kissing them and locking the drawer again. Must have been a couple of hundred quid there. And who could he complain to if they vanished overnight? Yes, he could be in and out in a couple of minutes, nip back to the ground on the tube, pick up Agger and the lads outside the ground and be home with an alibi they would never break. He would pick up the drift of the match easy

149

enough from little Kenny's excited chatter. They would never know he had missed it.

They were half-way down the Strand now, past the Adelphi Theatre, as the man turned again in his seat. "Would you happen to know if we're coming to the Waldorf Hotel, son?"

"No," said Sid. "Piss off. I'm thinking."

The man turned to the front again, a slow flush spreading up the base of his fat neck. His resentment too much, he started to turn again and Sidney slipped the blue and white scarf from his neck, flicked it deftly over the large head, then rose and pulled with one great savage twist, relaxing for a brief second to loop the extra footage round his wrists as the man kicked out convulsively with an astonished gurgle. Then he pulled again, swinging the head from side to side and pulling tighter and tighter with such strength that he banged his left elbow hard on the window.

"I banged my funny-bone," he said with a giggle. The tourist gave a final gurgling sigh and was still. Sidney relaxed his grip and un-looped the scarf. The man's body slumped forward over the seat in front. Sidney pulled his shoulders back into a more restful position, stepped out into the aisle and took the steps two at a time as the bus passed Temple Bar and approached the Chancery Lane stop. There was no one waiting and as his feet hit the pavement the conductor rang the bell briskly and the bus gathered speed along Fleet Street towards Ludgate Hill. Sid watched it go with satisfaction. No one would be getting on in the City at this hour. And if they did go upstairs they would see a sleeping drunk.

He turned and walked briskly down an alley to his left. It was dark. He hesitated as he reached the courtyard at the end. There was a light on in the office. No mistake about it. The reflection shone in the puddles outside. He approached the little window with care. Voices. A girl's cry. Bugger it. The window blind was drawn and he edged slowly past and turned the handle of the front door. It opened easily and he slipped inside, shuffling into the narrow hall. The door to his right was ajar. He could hear the murmur of voices more clearly now and then the lighter, excited cry of the girl again. He peered through the crack in the door.

Julie lay back in the leather armchair in the far corner, the one Swain used for his catnaps when he came back late from the Red Lion on a Friday afternoon. Her blouse was open, her heavy breasts were bared, nipples erect, and she was smiling brilliantly up. A hairy

150

hand slid over her right breast and caressed it slowly and repeatedly, fingers widespread round the nipple. Sidney fought to control his rasping breath as he stretched on tiptoe to see more clearly through the crack. Her bare legs were spread out, one across each arm of the chair. Swain was crouched between them.

Sidney pushed the door open with one foot. "Here," he said, "I'm not having that—or perhaps I am."

NINE

"I think we'll start with you," said Baxter pleasantly to a nervous Agger who sat uneasily on the other side of the table in the tiny interviewing room. "You seem to be the biggest—after Sidney, of course."

"Sidney?" said Agger. "He's here? But we lost him."

"Tell me about him," said Baxter.

Agger stared. "He's watching the match, I suppose. Tell you something, I hate the bastard. He's not one of the lads. Never has been."

"I had him round my nick last night," said Baxter. "Did he tell you?"

Agger shook his head. "Is he putting the finger on me?" he said. "Rotten, stinking . . . That's it, isn't it? The blade. You're too big to bother with Shed lads and football aggro. This is the tourist killings, innit? The fan in the blue scarf. Here, that bastard Dunn never told you I done them!"

"Didn't you?"

"Oh, leave it out, guv! I admit the blade. At the Sunderland game last Saturday. They was frisking us on the gates and I was carrying this blade I bought off a geezer on the train coming back from Cardiff the week before. It was just like something to show off with, you know?"

"You were done for having an offensive weapon in December last year."

"Oh yeah, brass knuckles. Just for show again. I mean, you're outnumbered at an away game and you need some protection if you don't want your head kicked in. Anyway, I got off light, first offence and that, but when I seen them searching the lads on Saturday I knew I had to get rid of it pretty quick or it'd be sixteen Saturday afternoons of the old community service so I slipped it into Sid's pocket. I got

153

searched and he didn't so it all came out hunky-dory, only I forgot about it afterwards and he never mentioned it."

"Describe it."

"It was, you know—a blade. Unusual one, mind. Long and thin, like a skewer almost. Medical it was, apparently. That's what the bloke on the train said. Wicked sharp, though. I had to blunt the sides before I could carry it. But the tips was—here, that rotten bugger never really said I had anything to do with them killings? He bloody did, didn't he! He would and all."

"Did he mention them tonight on the way to the match?"

"He never hardly said anything on the train. He'd just lost his job. I slipped that blade in his pocket Saturday and I haven't seen him since—not until tonight, that is."

"The blade answers the description of the one we're looking for," said Baxter carefully.

Agger stared at him again. "Christ! Then it was him! Yeah, that's what you do think, isn't it?"

"I think you're in serious trouble either way, son. It rather looks as if you might have provided the weapon. So sit tight and think hard about that for a few minutes. I'll be back."

He slipped out through the communicating door to the room next door. Armstrong and a station inspector were confronting a terrified Kenny.

"Where's the third?"

"Gone for a slash, guv."

"Any joy?"

"We told him. We don't know nothing about what Sid gets up to," jabbered Kenny. "We saw him on Sunday and we talked about the law coming round all our places after the stabbing in the street and then we went to the flicks and we ain't seen him until tonight. He says nothing on the train till we get to Fulham Broadway and then we hear he's lost his job. Then he gets stroppy with Agger over his bird in the Fulham Road and then we get picked up."

"Close mates, are you?" said Baxter.

"I saw him more than the others, maybe. But Wayne's my real mate. Sid's older than us. And he liked his bike and his Buddy Holly records. We got no bikes and we're more into heavy metal and that. That Holly stuff, it's yonks old, isn't it?"

The door opened and Wayne appeared with a constable close behind.

"Look, what's this all about, mister?" he begged. "We never been in no trouble. Not Kenny and me at any rate!"

"I know that," said Baxter. "Nor has your mate Sid."

"What about him?" said Wayne. "He's all right. He's at the match. Jammy bugger."

"Yes, why do you all keep going on about Sid?" said Kenny, bolder with Wayne beside him.

"Put these two in with Agger and get them some supper," said Baxter to the constable. "Your mate Agger will tell you all about it. You'll all make statements about Saturday and Sunday, where you went with Dunn and what he said to you. And then you can go home."

The constable took them through.

"He's doesn't seem to have done any bragging to his mates," said Armstrong.

"He sounds in an ugly mood, too," said Baxter. "Brooding about the lost job, they reckon. He certainly didn't seem to care much about it earlier today. All day to think about it, of course. Doesn't seem to have been in much heart for the match either. I doubt very much whether he's shouting his head off in the Shed right now. Besides, the lads would have picked him up."

"You think he might have gone round to the office to do the place over?"

"He hasn't gone in and he hasn't gone home and I don't like it one little bit," said Baxter. "We'll get round there."

Harry King and Kevin Toomey were glancing idly through the early editions over a coffee in the heart of the bustling newsroom.

"Nothing from Baxter still?" said Kevin.

"I couldn't get hold of the bugger," said Harry. "He's definitely up to something. They've got their suspect somewhere. I mean, Baxter wanted Armstrong to come and play you a tape, right?"

"Right."

"Then Armstrong hears about your second call from the killer, comes round to hear your tape, and suddenly his tape's not news any more. Why?"

"I see," said Kevin slowly. "He recognized the voice on our tape was the same as the one he brought over. He didn't need my identification then."

"Exactly. And just where did his little tape come from?"

"Maybe that was a phone call from the killer too."

"I doubt that. I mean, you ring a nick in the middle of a murder inquiry, you know you're going to be taped. With us, he might not have suspected that. And even if he did, we represent the publicity he loves. No, I reckon Baxter's got someone very much in mind for this little lot. I think I'll go and have a word with our American friend."

"Steve Franklin? How could he help?"

"He was anxious to see Baxter last night when I helped him to move hotel rooms so I dropped him off at the nick for a few minutes. He said Baxter had a kid with him, showing him some photos of local lads in case he could help. Does that sound to you the sort of vital inquiry that would engage a detective chief inspector after three murders in four days?"

"Could be," said Toomey. "He seems to have precious little else to go on."

"Mmm, well, I didn't give it a thought last night," King admitted. "But I think it's worth a follow-up. Anyway, you've got your latest phone call piece for tonight. I've got Fanny Adams. Tell Arthur I'll be back for a final check before I go home."

Kevin nodded and watched him make his jaunty way across the room and out through the double doors at the end. He started to doodle idly on the newspaper on the desk in front of him.

"Kevin!" The night news editor's bellow startled him. He threaded his way through the desks to the news desk.

"Come on, you dozy bugger, get your skates on. They've just found a body on a number eleven bus at the top of Ludgate Circus. American tourist, they reckon. Ken Ashton was on his way back when he spotted the action so we'll have the first on-the-spot pictures, but it's on every bugger's doorstep so they'll be there in seconds. Ken coming back with his film but he'll hang on for five minutes to put you in the picture on the scene. We'll revamp the front for the next and splash it, so shift your bloody self!"

St Paul's was floodlit at the top of Ludgate Hill as the driver accelerated under Blackfriars railway bridge. "No Harry King again?" he said chattily. "Must be losing his touch. I seen him drive out of the car-park not two minutes before you come down. There, that'll be the one." He jabbed a finger at a bus drawn into a lay-by, rear seat slung across the back of the platform to warn traffic of an out-of-action vehicle.

Ashton waved from the pavement and climbed into the car beside Kevin. "Have to get this back in a rush," he said. "I got a beauty of the

156

body before I got slung off. Conductor spotted it not five minutes ago. Dancing up and down on the pavement with his driver when I came by in a cab so I hopped out. I'll get a credit on this one."

"How was he killed?"

"Strangled with a blue and white football scarf. It's still round his neck! Bloody fantastic picture. I could even pick up an award for this one. Ken Ashton, News Photographer of the Year. Bloody hell, I hope the Old Bill get here before the *Mirror* and *Mail*, though. Ah, here come the boys in blue now. It's all yours, Kevin, my son. Here, how come you keep beating Harry King to these tasty little jobs."

Kevin grinned and climbed out of the car. He hurried over towards the bus.

Five hundred yards down the hill Baxter and Armstrong were making their stealthy way down the alley towards a pool of light in the yard beyond as their driver backed into Chancery Lane and parked the car. The light from the small office window cast a pale shimmering gleam in the puddles among the cracked paving stones. The front door was open. Baxter pushed it gingerly with a gloved finger and they both moved quietly forward. They paused in the hall and then stepped quickly into the office.

They both took involuntary steps backwards in the two seconds that followed, stunned by the scene before them. At a desk in the window bay at the back was the sprawled figure of a man, slumped sideways and still tied to his upright chair. Blood dripped steadily from his open throat to the threadbare carpet. The naked figure of a girl lay sprawled in an old leather armchair beside the desk, her legs wide apart.

The mutilation was more than Baxter for all his experience could contemplate beyond those fleeting seconds.

The two men looked at each other in horror. "Check the room at the back," said Baxter in a low rasp. Armstrong moved forward and Baxter spun round in the same moment as running footsteps echoed through the yard outside and the driver burst in.

"On the radio, guv," he panted. "American tourist found strangled in a bus just up the road." His voice died away as he took in the terrible scene.

Armstrong returned from the back room. 'Blood in the sink. No sign of the blade," he said.

Baxter nodded. "Double that watch on Giles Buildings," he said.

157

"You take the bus. Back to your car, Jackson. You know what we'll want here."

The driver, pale, gulped and nodded, escaping thankfully into the night air. They heard hs footsteps running back up the alley.

"Go on, Frank," said Baxter.

Armstrong hesitated. "He might still be around," he said. "He's gone right over the top now."

"Just get over to that bus before the City men run all over it," he said curtly.

He gazed down at the girl's body.

"I was taking her out tomorrow night," said Armstrong dully. He turned and walked out through the front door.

Baxter looked round the room. There were few signs of a struggle. He must have been on them like a savage animal. But what else was he? God, he had been talking to him that morning, had him in the office twenty-four hours earlier. These two need not have died.

There was a stir in the alley. A uniform sergeant in a City helmet appeared in the doorway. "Sir," he said. "Christ, what a mess."

"Yes," he said.

"That's three in one night. Six in a week," said the sergeant almost chattily.

"Five days," he said. "It's six in five days."

"Bloody hell," said the sergeant. "Jack the Ripper wasn't in it."

Baxter pulled himself together. He had to finish the job. He knew it would be his last.

"So by the time I'd completed the paperwork at the embassy I didn't get round to any sightseeing," said Franklin.

"Cheers," said King, raising his glass to the light and watching it wink back, golden brown. He sat gingerly on the edge of the bed as Franklin settled in the only chair in the corner. "When you popped into Baxter's office last night, did you get a good look at this lad he was chatting to—the local lad looking at the photos?"

"Not really," said Franklin. "But it's strange you should mention that. I had just an hour to kill before I went to the embassy this afternoon and I went for a walk up Praed Street and wandered into a record bar there. I was just flipping through a few albums when I heard this kid at the counter talking to the guy behind it about a Buddy Holly revival album. It seemed an odd sort of thing for a kid to be asking about and I looked up. His face seemed kind of familiar and when I turned to go out of the place I saw him looking at me across the rows of albums. It gave me quite a scare, the malevolent expression on his face, I don't mind telling you. And in my line, I don't scare easy. I walked out and flagged a cab to go to the embassy and as I looked out of the window the last thing I saw was this same kid on the pavement—still glaring at me with that same expression. I knew I'd seen him before—at least I felt I had. Then I remembered—I bumped into him on the hotel steps as I came out this afternoon."

"And are you saying . . ."

"I'm saying it was the same kid who was in Baxter's room," said Franklin. "The moment you mentioned it just now, something started to click into place and as I was telling you about the record bar I knew it was the guy. Why did you ask me about him?"

"Well, this morning Armstrong, Baxter's sidekick, was coming round to our office to play young Kevin a tape—to see if it was the same voice he'd heard on the phone. But Kevin had another call from his sinister friend and when Armstrong heard our tape he suddenly grew rather coy about playing his to Kevin."

"He'd recognized the voice for himself?"

"Right. And I remembered you mentioning this lad in his office after you'd called in at the nick."

"Christ!" said Franklin, finishing his drink with a gulp. "I was about to say it wasn't so strange seeing this kid again as he lives in the neighbourhood, but if he's a goddam suspect and he's been following me around . . ."

"You could be lucky to be alive," said King, finishing his own drink. "I think we'd better finish this bottle."

Sidney knew where he was going. His dad had often mentioned the trouble they had with dossers and drunks on the station late at night, particularly over the suburban side where they tried to kip on trolleys, under benches and even inside the parcels office. Well, he was going to find himself a train to bunk down in. His own personal sleeper. Only it would not be going anywhere—leastways, no farther than the sidings at Old Oak Common half a mile outside Paddington. And right now he could certainly use some sleep.

He had cut swiftly down Chancery Lane into Holborn when he left the office, business completed and two hundred smackers in his pocket. His walk had taken him through the relative peace of New Oxford Street and then on to Oxford Street itself, more crowded with window gazers and evening strollers. He had had enough of buses for one night, he thought with a giggle. And the tube might be dodgy. No, walking was safest. Straight on to Bayswater Road and then cut right through to Paddington. Plenty of time to think things out in the morning. He had to get his head down first. The man on the bus had not been as satisfying as the others. But the office made up for that. The looks on their faces as he moved in on them—oh yes, that made up for everything. No contempt any more. The scream of the girl as he wiped out Swain. The pleading as he turned to her. Then the satisfaction.

"Watch where you're going!" snarled a middle-aged business type as he cannoned into him on the corner of Bond Street.

"Sorry," said Sidney meekly.

He passed Selfridges on the other side of the road, then the big Marks and Sparks where his mum always bought his underpants and then he was looking down the Edgware Road itself. Funny to think Mum and Dad were sitting there in front of the telly not a mile away. He realized, of course, that he would not be seeing them again. But that had to come. You could not go on being a kid for ever. And he had grown up in the past few days. That was why he had left the scarf on the bus, the blade in the sink. The time for playing games with Baxter was over. He had to finish the story and move on. But not till the morning. As he neared the subway at Marble Arch he took one last long look down the road. They would be in the yard, on the landings, up on the rooftops. He saw a uniformed bobby crossing the road and he hastily headed on down the subway. He had to get to Paddington. He was knackered.

Baxter was crossing the yard when the shadow loomed up out of the darkness. "All quiet, sir," the man reported. "The old man came home in his uniform not half an hour ago. Must have just finished work."

"Right, I'm going up," he said.

"Have they any idea?"

"No. I don't think so."

He took the stairs slowly and heavily.

The man opened the door cautiously. "Mr Baxter, isn't it?" He motioned him in. The woman was sipping a steaming mug of something milky. She looked alarmed.

"Is something wrong?"

"Yes," he said. "Would you sit beside your wife on the sofa, Mr Dunn. I have some bad news for you."

"Sidney?" Now the man looked frightened, too.

"He's at the football," said the woman.

Baxter sat in the armchair opposite, leaning well forward. "He's not at the football," he said. "I'm sorry to have to tell you that we are looking for Sidney. We followed him to the ground tonight, but he gave us the slip and took a number eleven bus up the King's Road. Half an hour later a man was found dead on a number eleven near Fleet Street. We found Sidney's boss and secretary dead in their office shortly afterwards. He didn't tell you he'd been sacked?"

"No. Sacked? He hadn't been sacked. These people dead? Murdered? He wouldn't. He couldn't." The man's mouth trembled, lost shape. His wife started to sob silently, swaying from side to side on the sofa.

Baxter hoped the doctor and the policewoman would arrive on time.

"We believe that last Saturday night after you went to bed Sidney slipped out of the flat. We think he had been drinking in his room. He got involved in a clash with an American tourist down the road and stabbed him with a blade which we know one of his football mates had planted on him during the afternoon."

"But . . ."

He held up his hand. "Two days later on his way home he parked his bike in the ring road outside Regent's Park and he killed a man in a public toilet with the same blade. Then he came home as usual. He telephoned the *Globe* newspaper the next day. We have a tape of a subsequent telephone conversation and there is no question it was Sidney who made the calls. He threatened to kill a Japanese tourist and he did exactly that the next day. We could prove nothing at this stage, but tonight he went right over the top and killed three more times. There was no way I could tell you this terrible news other than brutally. I'm sorry."

"Not our boy," said the man, weeping as he clasped his wife's hands fiercely in his own. "He's a loner, I know. Always has been. Just the football matches with his mates. I could never get through to him. But not these terrible things!"

"We must find him and help him," said Baxter. "You must see he's ill. He'll go to—a sort of hospital. Psychiatry, with time, can achieve amazing things."

161

The couple on the sofa continued to weep together.

"Bloody hell," said Harry King in exasperation, "it really does fall into your lap, this one. Every time I turn my back the bugger does it again. You could have rung me at the hotel."

"Didn't have time, did I?" said Toomey, lighting his twentieth cigarette of the day and slipping a new sheet of copy paper into the old Remington. "You'd only gone out of the door a minute when we got the bus call. I was on my way back ten minutes later when I saw Larry Jenner going across to the carnage in the office."

"Did you get on to Baxter?" said Bostock, the night news editor, coming over.

"Fat chance," said King, scowling. "I spoke to one of his team. There'll be a statement within the hour."

"Every bugger'll have it then," said Bostock. "How much will they spill?"

"The whole beans, I reckon," said King. "Sure to say they want him for all five. Hell, half an hour ago I was the only one who knew they had a clear suspect."

"They'll have the parents in their pockets by the time they release a name and address," said Bostock. "Pity, I'd have liked an exclusive with them. Still, at least we know Baxter had the guy at the station a clear day before tonight's three killings. That gives us a powerful enough exclusive—the one they let get away to slaughter again." He hurried away to answer the insistent jangle of his internal phone.

"If he's really following your American friend . . ." said Kevin.

"I know," said Harry King. He glanced at his watch. "I wonder if he's managed to contact Baxter yet."

"He was planning to?"

"Oh Christ, ay. Wouldn't you? We didn't know about tonight's horrors when the penny dropped, but he wasn't too happy about it then, cop or not. Said the look the kid gave him was pretty bloody scaring even before he'd put two and two together."

"That was it," said Bostock, coming back. "Sidney Dunn, aged nineteen, of Giles Buildings, NW1. Wanted in connection with inquiries into tonight's three killings and three other murders during the past week. Motor-cycle messenger who worked for the tourists as his pet hates. I'll get the others to check out what they can on his home and work. You'd better do him an open letter for the front, Kev. You know, appeal to him

162

personally to give himself up. Tell him you feel you know him. You've talked together. He only has to ring you any time day or night and you'll go to him and help him to give himself up to the police peacefully."

"Will do," said Kevin, lighting another cigarette.

"And I suppose I'll have to crucify Baxter," said Harry dismally.

"You will," said Bostock. "Well, Christ, the bugger asked for it, didn't he? They clearly had this lad lined up and then lost him again. It's not as if you're wrecking your contact with him. You'll be on the desk next week."

"Maybe."

"No maybe about it, not after this little lot. Harry Snellgrove has given you his stamp of approval and the old man'll be getting mine in the morning. The three of us'll run a bloody good desk, Harry. I'm delighted."

"I feel like Dracula," said Harry, still gloomy. "I start my new life by giving Baxter the treatment."

"It'd all come out soon enough, whatever you wrote," said Bostock, "so stop parading your conscience while the precious minutes tick away. Start typing."

Baxter closed his garage door as quietly as he could. He had always been considerate to his neighbours in Adeline Avenue. He walked with equal care along the path to his front door which opened with a sudden shaft of bright light as he reached the final rose tree.

"Darling! What a lovely surprise!" said his wife. "I was just drawing the bedroom curtains when I saw you turn in the drive. You said you wouldn't be back till Friday."

He followed her in and collapsed into his favourite chair in the corner beside the fireplace. "Did you hear the late news bulletin?" he said, kicking his shoes off as he leant back.

She frowned. "No. There was a film on the other channel. What is it?"

"There were three more tonight," he said. "A tourist in a bus and a couple making love in an office."

"God," she said faintly.

"And I had him in my office last night, Di. A kid of nineteen. We knew it was him. We had circumstantial evidence to make a case, but not one that would have got a conviction at the Bailey with a top brief on legal aid. So I let him go and we watched him. I spoke to him on the

163

telephone this morning! And tonight we watched him and he killed three more people." He crouched forward and buried his head in his hands.

His wife knelt beside him and stroked the back of his neck. "Policemen are allowed to cry, my darling," she said gently.

He shook his head, fought for words and hugged her fiercely instead. Half a minute passed. "I'm sorry, Di," he said eventually.

"You've never come home this late without ringing," she said. "Have they . . ."

"Taken me off the case?" he said with a thin smile. "No, they only do that on the telly. Oh, Tarrant's running the show from the Yard now. The old man explained that all right. It was natural. Tonight's three were all on City ground, anyway. But the lad's on my patch. Do you know he lives about two hundred yards from the nick! 'We played it your way and you blew it, Tom.' That's what the old man said. 'We backed your judgement and experience and we were wrong, too. The responsibility is mine.' Big of him!"

She continued to stroke his neck.

"I'd just come back from telling the kid's parents. Can you imagine what that's like? 'The search is fully co-ordinated. Just go home and have a good night's sleep,' he said. Sleep! 'Then, when we pick the bastard up, he's all yours. It's still your case and you'll see it through to the end,' he said."

"Is that so very bad then?" she asked.

"He saw me down to my car. On the way he said he'd been meaning to have a chat for some time, but the last two months had been hectic, which is true enough. Said Sinclair's Bank were looking for a security director and if I wanted to go three years early he'd recommend me. Wouldn't do it for anyone else. But they wanted a top man and I was ideal."

"It's the sort of thing we'd often imagined you might do eventually," she said softly.

"I wanted those three years, Di," he said angrily. "I wanted to finish back at the Yard and I wanted to go all the way."

"It's not the end of the world. It's been a very successful career," she said.

"I know," he said. "It's not just that. I might have stayed on for the final three in uniform somewhere in the suburbs, bored out of my mind. But to go like this. And to know there are three bodies in the City mortuary tonight, three lives lost that I could have saved. Christ, do you know Frank Armstrong had a date with that girl for later this week?"

"Yes, well, knowing Frank Armstrong, I don't expect that was a tender affair of the heart," she said, unexpectedly tart. "And didn't you say the couple were making love?"

He nodded. "Anyway, you'd better be prepared for some rather unpleasant newspaper stories tomorrow," he said.

"About you?"

"Indirectly, maybe. It's my inquiry and I cocked it up. The Assistant Commissioner will do a good cosmetic job on it. But they'll add two and two all right. Harry King must know we were making some sort of progress."

The phone rang in the hall. He sighed. "That's probably him now. We should have gone ex-directory years ago."

"I offered," she said quietly. "You said it would upset my Guild and Oxfam engagements. Shall I pour you a drink?"

"Please." He rose heavily and went out to the hall.

She poured him a large Scotch and then one for herself. She pulled the dressing-gown more tightly round her and shivered. The nights were getting colder.

He was gone five minutes and came back looking strangely excited.

"Who was it?"

"Steve Franklin, brother-in-law of the first victim."

"How on earth did he track you down?"

"Well, he is a copper, if you remember."

"Yes, I do. You liked him. And he said some nice things about you in that *Globe* piece by King. And some very nasty things about the killer."

"Yes, that's partly the point. He looked in last night when I was talking to the lad, Dunn. Then later on he bumped into him on the steps of his hotel and then again in a record bar in Praed Street. He had to grab a cab to go to the embassy, but said Dunn was there on the pavement, giving him a malevolent look as the cab drove off. He didn't make the connection with my office at first, but Harry King went round to see him tonight."

"Harry King again!"

"I know, I know. They didn't know about tonight's killings then, but they realized Dunn was more than a casual caller in my office. When King left he tried to get a call through to me at the nick but I'd gone. He said they seemed evasive about when I'd be back, as well

165

they might, so he found my number. Then King rang to tell him about tonight's carnage."

"Does King know he's contacting you?"

"No. But Franklin's sure the kid was following him. And it makes sense. Those killings tonight—the first was another tourist, but then ten minutes later he takes care of a couple of personal grudges, quite different from the rest. After reading Franklin's words about him in the *Globe*, he might well have him marked down as another victim. He's obviously gone right over the top now. Anyway, I've told Franklin to hop into a mini-cab and get over here right away."

"You what!"

"I know, darling, but you must see how important it could be. Make him up a bed in Shirley's old room, there's a love."

"Yes, but what on earth do you think you're going to do?"

"Talk. Then sleep. I must make some calls. The lads'll need to know about Franklin's hotel, just in case Dunn is skulking around outside somewhere tonight. Then I must get hold of Harry King."

"Oh, for God's sake, Tom. You're not taking him into your confidence?"

"Only as much as I have to. He's probably finishing off a late story right now. No time to waste. The bed, love. I'll take that drink to the phone with me."

"Harry King." The voice sounded weary.

"Tom Baxter, Harry."

"Christ!" There was an awkward pause. "This is a bit difficult, Tom."

He grinned at the banisters despite himself. "Just doing a nice hatchet job, were you? Listen, Harry, I've just had a call from Steve Franklin. If this kid's really after him it could be our best chance of picking him up swiftly before he slaughters anyone else. You can gather from tonight's events just how dangerous a state he's in now. Splash a story about him tailing Franklin and you could send him to cover for a week. And God knows what little diversions he might dream up, to keep himself from getting bored in that time."

There was another pause. "I'm writing the story now," said King.

"I knew you would be, of course. And I can imagine what else besides. He was a suspect, Harry. No more. If we'd picked him up and he hadn't broken . . . If we'd found nothing in his home—and I doubt we would have—we'd have either had to let him go or we'd

166

have seen him discharged on trial."

"But you were following him," said King. "You must have been. And you lost him."

"I'm not asking you to lay off me," said Baxter quietly. "You've got to ask the questions in tomorrow's paper. I know that. But not the Franklin angle. Don't warn the kid off."

"What would I get out of it?"

"I'm sending Franklin out sightseeing tomorrow," said Baxter. "You can go with him. I'll be following."

"Done," said King. "We'll hold the 'questions that have to be asked' piece for twenty-four hours. We've got the killings, this morning's phone call and a direct appeal to the killer from Kevin Toomey filling the front together. No need to gild the lily, specially if I'm in on the arrest."

"Isn't this an executive decision, though? Can you give me a positive guarantee?"

"I'll be an executive myself next week," said King.

"I'm glad this horror story's doing someone some good," said Baxter acidly.

"Nothing personal," said King cheerfully. "I still think you took too much of a chance. And I don't know the half of it yet, do I?"

"You'll get the rest tomorrow. Meet Franklin at Westminster Pier, nine thirty."

"I'll be there. Can I bring a photographer?"

"You can wear a camera round your neck. You'll be sightseeing," said Baxter.

"One thing, though," said King. "I tried to get hold of you on your private line at the nick half an hour ago and only got Armstrong who sounded pissed off and extremely evasive about when you'd be in."

Baxter grinned again. "I'm still on the case," he said. "Oh, it's not a divisional inquiry any more. Even you must understand that. City and Met together, co-ordinated at the Yard. I prefer it that way. Gives me more freedom."

King sighed. "All right. I'll buy that—for now. One last thing, though, Tom."

"Well?"

"I hope like hell you do pick him up tomorrow—for your sake as much as mine."

"Yes, I think you probably mean that. I'll try not to imagine what I'll be reading in the *Globe* the day after tomorrow if I don't," said

167

Baxter.

He dialled his own private office number. Armstrong answered. King was right, He did sound pissed off.

"It's me, Frank. No, no, I'm fine. Listen, Franklin thinks Dunn was following him today."

"When?" said Armstrong.

"This afternoon, when he left his hotel. And then he spotted him again in a record shop up the street. And he's a copper and that's good enough for me. You'll know what's to be done up there. Meanwhile, Franklin's coming down here."

"To your place?"

"Why not? He's a nice guy. We're in the same line. I could do with the company and he'll be safer here with me."

"That's true enough," said Armstrong. "I'll have someone watch the hotel just in case Dunn should turn up. Can't see it, though. When's Franklin going to you?"

"Right away. I told him to get a mini-cab."

"We'll keep an eye open till he's safely aboard," said Armstrong. "I'll pass it on."

"You do that, Frank."

"And guv . . ."

"Well?"

"Hurry back."

"I will. See you soon."

Steve Franklin sipped his brandy and soda cautiously and settled comfortably into the deep leather armchair on the other side of the fire. "I appreciate your hospitality," he said, "but I think you're going for a very long-odds shot."

"It's only a suggestion."

"I know. I know. And I grant you something drove him over the top today and after that interview I gave King I can't be the kid's number one favourite."

"Well, that's right. You said—or at least King said it for you in his own turgid prose—that you felt no bitterness towards Londoners because of this one sick animal, in fact you still planned to see as much of the city as you could. You particularly mentioned the river."

"I said I planned to go down river to Greenwich from Westminster because that was what Dave and Myra had planned to do before that little bastard got him. But you really want me to go down to

168

Westminster Pier tomorrow for two, maybe three hours or more, just in case he turns up? I mean, Jeez, I might as well have stayed in the hotel."

"He wouldn't have gone back there. Not now," said Baxter. "Even my sergeant observed that and he's one of life's pessimists. It's too near his home. I'll be behind you."

"Can I have a gun?"

"I'm sorry."

"Will you have one?"

"I'd have to draw it officially and I don't want my lads all over the place to frighten him off."

"So it's just you and me?"

"And Harry King."

"Harry King!"

"Oh, not for the publicity. It's just that if our psychopathic friend is intent on wiping the slate clean, he may feel as powerfully about King as he does about you."

"I see. Two tethered goats for the price of one," said Franklin dubiously. "So what do we do?"

"Let the first couple of boats go if you see nothing. Then take the third one anyway. Take in the Cutty Sark, Naval College, usual sights, Greenwich Park, Observatory, spot of lunch in the park and back again. I'll be behind you all the time."

"With the greatest respect," said Franklin, "I'm not sure that's good enough. Not if nobody's carrying a gun."

"Dunn won't have a gun," said Baxter. "But you can always say no. It's a long shot, all right. I know."

"You also know I'll come," said Franklin with a grin. "But since this is a remarkably fine brandy and it's getting kinda late to go to bed anyway, I'd like to tell you about a case we had a couple of years ago back home because it sure as hell reminds me of this one, only the ending was written different from yours."

"Shoot," said Baxter, reaching for the brandy bottle.

"Oh I had to," said Franklin grimly, "or I wouldn't be here today."

TEN

The first grey shafts of dawn woke Sidney from his deep sleep in the first-class compartment of a grimy commuter diesel unit outside Old Oak Common engine sheds. He yawned and stretched. Finding a place to kip had been easy. There had been a few old dossers like his dad had often complained about after a night shift, but the cleaners had turfed them out with the help of a couple of transport police just after two. Too fuddled with booze to keep out of the way and nip in and out of the bogs ahead of the cleaners, like he did.

He rubbed his eyes and yawned again. He would have loved to have taken care of Baxter who had been playing ducks and drakes with him all week, but the events of last night must have shaken the bugger up nicely and that would have to do. The rest of the programme would run according to timetable, folks. He laughed as he walked stiffly down the central aisle of the carriage to the end door and dropped down to the trackside.

The first diesel units of the commuter timetable were roaring into life on the other side of the sheds. He jumped over two sets of rails and moved unhurriedly to a stony path that followed a high brick wall, running back towards Paddington Station. He could cut across through the next gap and nip over to Royal Oak on the Metropolitan Line without a ticket, change up the line on to the Circle and pay at the other end with the rush-hour crowds. It was time to get out of town, like it said in the song. But he was staying cool, like Buddy.

"I thought I might take next week off," said Harry King casually as he buttoned up his raincoat. "I thought we might visit a few estate agents and ask for keys of cottages. Remote country cottages without telephones."

"You really mean it?" said Maeve, hugging him. He swung her round the cramped hall to the delight of the twins in the doorway. "A

171

second home in keeping with our new station in life."

"And no more late nights," she said joyfully.

"No more very late nights," he corrected her. "And every other weekend a long one."

"I can't wait," she said. "Come on, kids. Neither can your father if he's to get that train. Early tonight?"

"Should be," he said, standing back as she helped the twins with their coats. He felt vaguely uneasy, not telling her about the river trip. There had been no sense in alarming her with Tom Baxter's extravagant final fling of fantasy. Baxter. Poor bugger. He hated the thought of kicking him in the goolies. "Right, then you two," he said. "Let's be having you."

It had been a pleasant enough way to see London, Franklin admitted to himself. Dave and Myra had talked endlessly about taking such a trip. They were great armchair travellers and Myra had also enjoyed every Queen Elizabeth on the screen from Bette Davis to Glenda Jackson and read a thousand romantic novels set in the age besides. Tales of Drake and Raleigh, Leicester and Essex and their loves for the Virgin Queen littered the shelves of her bedroom when she was fifteen and whenever he came in from a ball game in the back yard she was sprawled across the sofa reading another. *The River Queen* was one of her early favourites and Dave had wryly accepted from the very first idea of this European trip that a voyage down river to Greenwich, birth of the great queen, was unavoidable.

The Thames must have been broader and cleaner then, though, he thought. Salmon and swans, state barges and open fields—but it had been a nice trip, for all the spinning jumble of historical facts fed over the PA by the guide on the *Good Queen Bess* as she chugged downtide through the city, past the great dome of St Paul's and a heavy crop of other Wren churches, slender spires peeping through the great glass tower blocks around Tower Hill. The Tower of London, Traitors' Gate, All Hallows by the Tower, or what remained of it after Hitler's blitz, Roman pavement, Boadicea's ashes, a spire added since the war to fill in the sad skyline, and, in deference to the many Americans craning through binoculars and camera viewfinders, the guide added a quick mention that the register records the marriage of John Quincy Adams, sixth President of the United States, and William Penn, too, what do you know, honey, was baptized here in 1644.

Yes, but Myra would have enjoyed it all. And the site of

172

Shakespeare's Bankside Globe Theatre, Chaucer's Tabard Inn, Dickens's riverside London, Dr Johnson's George Inn. She had studied the literary side for months before the trip. And, God, how she would have loved Greenwich—the approach by water, the twin domes of the Royal Naval College, Wren again surely, and beyond them the Queen's House. And down on the waterfront the old tea and wool clipper *Cutty Sark*, honourably retired in dry dock now, and snug beside her little *Gipsy Moth IV*, the craft of Chichester, a modern sea-faring Sir Francis knighted by his own Queen Elizabeth on this very spot. Myra would have loved that, all right. And so would Dave, for all his chuckling protests.

And no better place for a picnic than Greenwich Park, rising behind the Old Royal Observatory on the Greenwich Meridian, not three hundred yards from the Queen's Oak where the young Elizabeth played with her sister Mary. Oh yes, he was glad he made the trip for Myra and, one day, back home, they would share it together in Dave's memory.

He held his paper cup out absently as Harry King offered the last of the Chablis.

"All very pleasant," said King, "but it hardly seems to bring the promise of action."

"Action?"

"Action. You know, like our crazy killer friend tracking us down river and foully doing us to death here on the wooded slopes of Greenwich Park watched by Master Sleuth Baxter from behind the Queen's Oak."

"Oh," said Franklin comfortably as he gazed out over the distant Isle of Dogs on the other side of the river. "So that's what's supposed to happen."

"I did get that general impression," said King, "and having spotted Tom Baxter at least seven times this morning between Westminster Pier and the Maritime Museum I don't think I was barking up the wrong tree. And talking of trees, I must see if I can find one without a flatfoot lurking behind it. Too much wine. Back in a minute."

It was too open for a quick pee behind a tree, though, he discovered as he crested the ridge behind their picnic spot. Beyond the statue of General Wolfe gazing steadily out over the river, he was thankful to see two toilet blocks beside a shuttered refreshment kiosk. He hurried towards the Gents.

That was better. He pulled his zip closed again, turned, slipped slightly on wet leaves on the greasy stone floor and skidded to recover his balance as something with matted hair and a wild stare fell upon him with a savage snarl.

Oh God, he thought as darkness closed in, no cottage for Maeve and the children now.

"And when did you last have a holiday there?"

"Four years, must be," said Jim Dunn, bewildered and tired over the crackling phone line.

"Sunnyside Camp."

"That's right. Have you heard anything?"

"I'll be in touch later today, Mr Dunn. I promise." He rang off.

As he crossed the road from the telephone-box and walked back through the side entrance of the park he could see King and Franklin together at the top of the slope. King scrambled to his feet and wandered up to the top of the hill. Baxter hurried up towards them.

"Hi," said Franklin. "Breaking your cover then?"

"It was worth a try," he said. "And now we'll try it your way. Where's King gone?"

"Just taking a leak. My way?"

"Yes, you were right. There is a place. They couldn't afford many holidays, just the odd week on the Isle of Sheppey down in Kent. A holiday camp near a resort called Leysdown."

"And the kid liked it?"

"Apparently. Only place he knew outside London. Never even went on an away football trip."

"Far from here?"

"About an hour. Taking a leak where?"

"What? Oh, King. Behind a tree, he said. If he could find one without a flatfoot, since one of your guys has been watching us have lunch from those trees on the ridge."

Baxter stared at him. "One of my guys?"

"Why yes, you do have a guy up there?"

"No, I don't. I'm on my own. I told you I would be. He'll not need a tree to take a leak. There's a Gents behind the statue. And Sidney's struck in a park loo before."

Sidney was flustered. There was no getting away from it—things were not going to plan. He would have liked to go back to yesterday morning. Start again without the muddles. Too many people getting

174

in the way. In the beginning it was all beautifully simple, specially when he had the Scotch to keep his brain well oiled and working clearly. Still, adapt. Like before. And at least he had timed the train a treat, through the booking-hall and over the bridge and into the nearest carriage door sliding past him. Seen by nobody. He was sure of that. And that was the plan for the rest of the winter. Lie low. Then back to London one day, maybe to this south side. It was all London, after all. And there was plenty of tourists. He had quite enjoyed his own tour of the park with Franklin and his friend. Bloody shame about Franklin, though. He should have made sure he had followed the right one into the bog before he made his move. Christ, if he had waited in the trees it could have been perfect. Mystery geezer goes off to the bog and Franklin's all alone on the slope. Pad up behind, one thrust and away.

Never mind, never mind. He was going on his holidays. He laughed to himself. He always loved it there. They had the same chalet three years out of five. He had to change at Gillingham, he was sure of that. These Greenwich trains went no further than Dartford or Gillingham. But he could pick up a coast train at Gillingham and hop off at Sittingbourne. No bother. Then change trains, same island platform for Sheerness on Sea as the destination board always grandly announced. He had always loved seeing that board. It meant they were nearly there.

Then he must find food, maybe a transistor radio for music at nights through the winter, probably find some booze, too. That was important. And he knew a nice snug hidey-hole miles from anywhere. Oh yes, a very cosy winter there and no mistake. And Baxter combing the country for him all the time. He laughed again. Tough luck, Baxter.

"I said stay together at all times," said Baxter furiously.

"I didn't realize I had to take him with me when I wanted a pee," said Harry King, rubbing the back of his head ruefully. "I didn't half fetch my head a wallop on that floor."

"You reckon he thought Harry was me," said Franklin.

Baxter nodded. "When he followed him in—yes. Understandable error. Same light mac, same build. Just as well he doesn't know what Harry looks like—after some of that peerless prose in the *Globe* he might have decided to take him out anyway."

"I thought he was going to," said King shakily, settling himself gingerly on the park bench beside the statue. "I do feel queer. What now?"

"Hospital for you," said Baxter firmly. "And I've rung the local nick from the keeper's lodge."

"You made that other call earlier," said Franklin. "You're going?" He nodded.

"What other call?" said King. "And going where?"

"Tell you later," said Baxter briefly. "Meanwhile, you're going to have to sit on this one, Harry—for the next few hours anyway."

"Don't you worry," said King. "Falling over and banging my head on the bog wall when I come face to face with the Scoop of the Year doesn't leave me covered in glory as I move into the executive washroom stakes. The lads would never let me forget it. Besides, I've a nasty feeling I'm about to go into shock. I really thought I was about to meet my maker back there."

"Leave him with me," said Franklin. "You think he's on his way then?"

"Yes," said Baxter. "Cursing his luck at missing out on you, very probably."

"That could really burn away at him, you know?" said Franklin. "The one loose end he didn't tie up."

"I don't think he'll think of anything but going to ground now," said Baxter. "Listen, Frank Armstrong'll be here within the half hour. I've told the local boys. Tell them what you can until he comes."

"You're going on your own?"

"We don't flush him out with posses," said Baxter with a faint smile. "Not down there. Look out, I think your friend is going to faint."

Sidney was pleased with his journey. No bother. No ticket yet, either, with the change as quick and easy each time as he had remembered. Sittingbourne was slipping behind now as the train headed over the marshes towards the murky, swirling waters of the Swale. He wiped the condensation from the window. The tide was out, the mud-flats grey and sinister. It had looked a bloody sight more inviting when the water was up on a high August Saturday morning with a week of sun, sand and sea ahead and as may ice-creams, potato crisps and bottles of pop as he could consume in a day before fish and chips in the evening. He rubbed the stubble on his chin thoughtfully. Grow a beard, that was the thing. No one would know him when the summer came, not with a thick growth of black beard. Might stay down here. Get a job doing the deck-chairs maybe, or on the boats, even. There was docks at Sheerness. Cars from the continent, timber, steel, that sort of caper. Yes, he'd get a job there, all right. All-the-year-round job, maybe. Maybe even buy a new bike. He felt sad at the thought of his bike in the yard back home. And Mum and Dad. He bit back a sob. He was not going to think about Mum and Dad. That was bad. That was much worse than the bike.

The train passed on through Swale Station without stopping and rumbled over Kingsferry Bridge across the river and on to the island. Sid flopped back into his seat as Minster Marshes passed. Plan of campaign, that was the thing, son. Could go into Sheerness, all the way. He remembered the pie shop, everything from cheese and onion, piping hot, to strawberry and apple, sweet and sugary, all fresh-made in the bakery behind, scalding in the hand. But tickets to be collected at the end of the line. Station men to remember faces. Then there was Queenborough. Industrial town, glass works and foundries, he remembered from the bus trips through the island. Chemical works and scruffy shops. Even his mum had sniffed at that lot through the bus window and it had to be tatty for her to sniff at it. The times she dreamed aloud for a little house and never showed the slightest inclination to leave the grim flat in the buildings. He was doing it again. He shook his head fiercely and gazed out through a mist of tears at the oozy mud channels through the marshes. The train was sliding into Queenborough. He lowered the window and peered out. The platform was deserted as the guard climbed back in. The buzzer sounded and he opened the door, dropped down and pushed it shut as the train gathered speed, snaking away through the gloom towards Sheerness. The little station was deserted.

In the road outside he hesitated. The signpost pointed right to Eastchurch. He followed. He had hardly tramped two hundred yards when a bright red Ford Fiesta pulled up beside him and a genial, burly, scarlet-faced man in his fifties called across the road to him: "How far you going, son?"

He licked his lips nervously. "Leysdown," he said hoarsely. "Just going to Leysdown."

"Then hop in," said the man.

"No, it's all right, ta," he said.

"Hop in," said the man again. "There's no bus. I can run you as far

177

as Eastchurch. It's going to piss down in a minute or two, you see if it doesn't. Come on."

Sidney cursed under his breath and crossed the road and the man leaned across and opened the front nearside door. He climbed in and did the seat-belt up with difficulty. He wasn't used to cars. You didn't need a car in London. The man looked at him curiously. "Not used to seat-belts?" he said.

"I live in London," said Sidney shortly. "Motors are too much bother up London."

"Ah," said the man. "So they are. Can't get far without one down here though. What brings you to these parts?" The car moved off.

"I'm staying with my gran," said Sidney. "In Queenborough. I been ill. Got a few weeks off."

The man chuckled. "Bloody hell," he said. "Good place to come for a health cure, Sheppey, specially at this time of year!" He laughed gently for a few seconds. "Finding it hard to fill your days, I bet."

"Yes," said Sid. "I was just going walking."

"Sorry to spoil your exercise," said the man. "I thought you were maybe on your way home. Hitching back from the docks, like. Still, walking back to Queenborough will give you an appetite for your tea. Do a good tea, your gran, does she?"

"Not bad," said Sid, desperately seeking invention. "Crumpets sometimes."

"Nothing like a nice piece of crumpet," said the man solemnly. They laughed together, men of the world.

"What you doing here then?" said Sid, emboldened by this exchange.

"I'm a prison officer at Eastchurch," said the man."

Sid trembled. "Oh yeah?" he said. His voice sounded strangled, high-pitched. He knew it.

The man glanced at him sideways. "Yes, a screw," he said. "And why not? I like the life. It's not a hard nick, Eastchurch. I know worse. Whereabouts in London you from?"

"Peckham," said Sid, thinking in sudden inspiration of his Auntie Ida.

"Know it well. Used to drive to Brixton from there last tour," said the man. "Where exactly?"

"Manville Road," said Sid, thanking the Lord for Aunt Ida and Uncle Percy. "Just opposite the Coach and Horses."

"Bloody hell, only my boozer for two years," said the man, shaking his head in wonder. "Small world. Not a bad pint neither. I can't take to these Kentish ales. Here suit you?"

"Anywhere. Great. Ta," said Sid.

"You're very welcome. Give my love to Peckham and the Coach and Horses," said the man. "And enjoy the rest of your health cure." He laughed again. Sid unbelted himself and clambered awkwardly out. He slammed the door and the little red car roared off round the bend.

He stood in the middle of Eastchurch and scratched his head. Straight on for Leysdown then. Prison officer. Bloody hell. Nothing given away, though, thanks to Auntie Ida. The thought of his fat old auntie gave him the same tremor as his earlier recollections of his mother. He shuddered, and pictured Wayne and little Kenny, cod and chips before the match, the body in the doorway and more bodies. Bodies everywhere and blood in the office. Blood all over the office. Julie and Swain. No, that was not him. That could never have been him. No way. Bloody hell, he needed a drink. A bottle of the stuff. And quick. Hopefully he started to run down the road towards Leysdown. The rain started to pour with renewed vigour.

As he ran he saw the desolate landscape of fields and sheep was gradually being broken by the odd wooden chalet bungalow, paint-peeling shutters banging idly in the winter wind. Then the first of the caravans, soon twenty in a field, then thirty, until the fields themselves opened up to reveal great prairie crops of caravans, row after row stretching as far as the eye could see. The Argosy Caravan Park. Seaview Holiday Homes, Golden Sands Chalets. Bingo Haven stood boarded up and desolate on the other side of the road. Gift shops and ice-cream parlours, cafés and amusement arcades all asleep in silent hibernation in the cold greyness of the winter day. He recognized one, the Jolly Roger Amusement Hall, but most of the others seemed to have changed hands since the Space Invasion. But there was the chip shop they always used and beyond lay Sunnyside Holiday Camp. "Stay on the Sunny Side!"

He crossed the road and stood before the barred gates. The chalets looked more like army camp huts in an old wartime newsreel shown on the telly than the fun centre he remembered, but this was the one all right. And, Christ, man, the deader the better. This was going to be his supply depot for the winter, wasn't it? He trotted down a rough lane flanking the high wire fencing round the camp. Breach the defences and then make a recce, like they did in the pictures.

There must be a gap round the back somewhere and if not he would have to climb over. This must be the best bleeding place in the world to hole up for the winter. More peaceful than the North Pole—and about as bloody cold when that wind swung east, too. He would have to dig out some clothing from somewhere. He would find it.

There was a narrow opening in the wire beside the first side entrance and he slipped through carefully to find himself between two rows of trim wooden chalets in faded pastel shades of pink and pale blue. The bar and buttery was round the front. He didn't know why it was called the buttery. It was just a great barn of a self-service café really, but that was the place to be right now, out of this sodding wind and rain. It was beginning to come down with more persistence now, fairly hammering on the roofs of the chalets and beating through the cloth of his turned-up jacket. The cafeteria was at the end of the rows of chalets and he worked his way round to the far side.

The sea appeared beyond the point, grey and heaving, with crests of white whipped by the wind off the waves. A small coaster plunged and rose as it headed round the mouth of the Medway Estuary, ready to run in on the tide to Rochester. Farther out, a heavy tanker ploughed on in a long four-mile curve of a turn, bound for the Thames Estuary, way beyond Grain. Crude for Canvey Island and the refineries beyond. An Olau Line ferry from Holland was coming in fast, making for Sheerness Docks within the half hour. Christ, he hadn't seen the sea for four years. He moved on down the seaward side of the café block, hunting for a loose shutter well out of sight from the road.

He found one at last, eased the wood back and slammed his elbow into the middle pane of the sash window. The glass tinkled in and he reached carefully through to push the catch open. The wood was warped and crudely painted over the lock so it took a good hard shove with both hands to send the bottom half of the sash skidding upwards until it jammed. He wriggled through the gap, falling on the floor with a grunt. He picked himself up, pulled the shutter closed again and tugged the window back down with difficulty. There was still a pale gleam of light through the loose shutter, but it was too gloomy to see across the room. He shut his eyes for a moment to try and get used to the darkness. He peered about him. It was apparently some sort of store-room, full of wooden crates, cardboard boxes, two shelves stacked high with old white overalls. He moved cautiously forward in the gloom towards the far wall and found a door handle. It turned stiffly and he found himself in a long corridor. He knew where he was at once. Snooker and table tennis were off down there to the left so the main dining-room and kitchens were to the right.

The dining-hall echoed to his footfalls. Here, too, the windows were shuttered and barred against the ravages of winter winds and any vandals eccentric enough to track the place down in winter weather. He peered through a crack in one shutter. The tanker was still making its long slow sweep round in the heaving seas. His eyes were finding the darkness easier to cope with now and he crossed the hall more confidently, boots ringing out. He knew the passage at the far end led past the kitchens to the store-rooms opposite the bars. And he struck treasure in the very first store-room.

It was Scotch. Several cases of the stuff. John Grant's Standfast Off the back of a lorry maybe, or a shady deal carried out in the winter, ready for the season ahead. Maybe just old stock lying in store for better prices the following summer. But suppose it was paint or paraffin parcelled up in old Scotch boxes? He ripped the top of the first box open. His anxious grasping fingers found the seals and tops easily enough. He tugged a bottle out, heavy and cold to the touch. He opened the seal, unscrewed the cap, took a cautious slug. Christ! His eyes watered as he spluttered. Powerful stuff. Still, before the week was out he would be able to track down some mixers from the back of the bar stores, he was sure of that. Some American ginger, maybe. There must be a room full of glasses somewhere too. He took another slug and wandered out into the corridor to explore the next room. There were more chests and crates on the floor and two low shelves along the wall. Hundreds of plastic cruet sets, egg-cups, plastic crockery to supply an army and more. No sign of glasses. Who needed glasses? He took another pull at the bottle. Glub, glug, smack of the lips. Lovely stuff. That was better. He went on through to the next room. Kitchen supplies again. Drums of washing-up liquid, scouring pads and dish cloths, cleansers and detergents, scrubbing-brushes and mops. Not much future there.

It was the fifth and final store-room that yielded the harvest he was hoping for—food. He bent to explore the heavy cartons stacked round the room. The sticky seal peeled away from the first and he pulled one flap open. There was a heavy metallic thump as its contents slid sideways out on to the floor in the gloom. Tins, hundreds of them. He held one in front of his nose in the darkness. Baked beans. He pushed the door open with one foot and a pale light shone through from a shutterless window in the corridor. Yes, the boxes were all identical. All baked beans. Well, that wasn't bloody bad, was it? You could live on baked beans all right. Be a windy old winter, no doubt about that. He sniggered and took another slug of Scotch. Be a tin-opener among all that cutlery next door, too.

Back to the plan of action then. The Scotch was bloody welcome all right, but it made him uneasy, too. If there was Scotch here there might be other booze, too. Worth hundreds. So they wouldn't leave it unattended for eight long months of winter. No question, the thing was to move on to that snug hideaway, move in as much food and booze as he could, travelling by night, and then lie low, well away from the camps. They would hardly notice the odd box of this and that missing until they took stock in the spring. But first, a few drinks, something to eat and a kip, then out by moonlight, chaps, and over the top. He sniggered again. He was in command. Drink up. Cheers, everyone. Glug glug.

The assistant governor inspected his warrant card with interest. "And what brings you out here, Mr Baxter? The need for a chat with one of our guests? You're not expecting anyone to break in, I trust?" He laughed gently.

"I'm looking for a young lad on the run and I believe he may have come back to the island to lie low. It was one of the few places he knew outside London in his childhood, indeed the only one."

"Yes, but why us? Is he an ex-prisoner?"

"No, it just occurred to me on the way down that anyone seeing a rough lad on the move, possibly over open ground or remote roads on the island, might assume he had, in fact, broken out from here, and phone you to ask. Have you had any enquiries during the last few hours?"

"No," the assistant governor said thoughtfully. He picked up his pipe and started to polish the bowl with his thumb. "The island's an inhospitable place at this time of year, but there's plenty of chalets and caravans a man might find to hide in. He'd be hard pushed for food and drink, maybe, but there are remote holiday bungalows where there would still be provisions in the larder, I dare say. He'd certainly find few enough inhabited places to burgle on the east side of the island, although there's a modern estate at Warden Bay."

"Excuse me, sir." The red-faced officer who had shown Baxter to the office was chewing his lower lip nervously.

182

"Yes, Webb?"

"Well, as a matter of fact, on my way back from Sheerness before I came on, sir, I picked up a lad at Queenborough Said he was staying with his gran after being ill. Didn't exactly look a delicate flower, though, sir, and when I said I was a prison officer he looked very jumpy. I wasn't in uniform, you see, sir, being back on my way to the house first."

"Jumpy?" said Baxter.

"Well, a bit startled, like," said the officer. "I didn't think anything of it. Lads do jump a bit sometimes when they hear what you do. I've known it in pubs. And this one had never done time, no Borstal nor nothing. I can always tell. Never been in an institution. Big, strong, rough maybe, but not hard, I'd have said. So I dropped him off and thought no more of it."

"That him?" said Baxter.

The officer looked at the newspaper picture doubtfully. "Not much of a likeness, if so. Could be, I suppose. Hair longer. I assumed he'd be walking back to Queenborough so I didn't look to see where he went after I left him. I told him it was going to piss down, sorry, pour down with rain, though."

"Does that help, Mr Baxter?" said the assistant governor.

"I think so," said Baxter. "I was brought up just up the creek from here, but I haven't been back in years. How many caravans and chalets would you say there are at Leysdown?"

The assistant governor considered.

"If you'll pardon me, sir," said Webb. "I'd say a dozen men could search for a month. There's thousands, sir. Hundreds and bloody thousands of them."

And the words were still ringing in his ears as he drove away from the main gate. He had never been a gambling man, professionally speaking. Chanced his arm occasionally, even cheated and cut off the odd corner or two, but police work had been playing the percentages again and again. Patterns were predictable and that was what brought villains down so often. But this was different. And he was going out with a bang, not a whimper. He had promised himself that much. He ought to be on the blower to Kent Police right now. But the warder was right. Sidney was not a Borstal boy or an old lag. He was not like the others. All the same, Baxter recognized with a grim smile in his eyes as he adjusted the driving mirror, that was not the reason he was driving slowly down the road to Leysdown on his own, through

183

deserted bungalows and bingo halls, holiday camps and shuttered cafés. He wanted to take Sidney back, by himself.

There was a chapel on the south side of the road, away to his right. He glanced at it casually as he approached another sprawling expanse of caravan sites and holiday camps. A path began beside the chapel, heading off over wild and desolate land studded only with occasioal sheep and humps in the ground. And the figure that passed beyond the chapel and headed away over the path through the sweeping rain could have been a farmer hunting for a sick sheep, or a keen bird-watcher seeking Brent Geese stopping over until their return to Russia in the spring.

But Baxter knew it was neither. The figure hunched into the driving rain had the painful, plodding gait of the townsman ill at ease in such a landscape, constantly shifting a heavy and ill-balanced sack from shoulder to shoulder and travelling too fast. The countryman's steady stroll would have been better suited to such a rough path. The figure plunged into a dip and emerged again, almost losing his footing as he scrambled up the other side.

Baxter switched off the engine, climbed out of the car and locked it deliberately. There was no hurry. He pulled his collar up about his ears and crossed the road. The grey sky was turning to purple behind the new buildings on the distant skyline. The lonely figure was trudging off along the path towards the first of the buildings. He disappeared into yet another dip to appear again as Baxter in turn crested a steep mound. The prominent hump of Harty Island was in view ahead now. Oh dear, oh dear, your luck has turned now, Sidney old son, and no mistake, he thought almost fondly. Another ten minutes and you might have been clear and away to lie low for God knows how long in such a desolate landscape. Might even have made it back to the mainland over Harty in time and then away, but not forgotten. We would never have chosen this wild track to follow you. You were supposed to stay in the comforting sprawl of chalets and bungalows, caravans and cafés. But you didn't and I saw you and I know this landscape, Sidney, because very many years ago on grey Thursday afternoons when the football pitches at school were water-logged, I would come down on the mainland side of Faversham Creek and shout for old Jim Wedge the ferryman to come out from the island for a late afternoon on the Swale, watching with Jim the high wheeling kestrel, the timorous, scattering oyster-catchers, scuttling across the Sheppey shores at one moment and wheeling in

184

great clouds of alarmed chatter the next, redshank, dunlin and turnstones all busily scampering and complaining along shingle, shell and sand. And always Jim Wedge talking, tales of birds and of fishing exploits and wildfowling by moonlight with his little old boy, Kentish for his son who was every day of fifty.

He crested another mound. They were everywhere this side of Sheppey, burial chambers from bloody battles waged by Saxons and Danes according to Porker Crump, his history master, but just refuges for sheep in time of flooding according to a scornful Jim Wedge and his little old boy. And round Harty Island wound the waters of the Capel Fleet, once a natural defence linked to the sea at either end, now a canal of a river after reclamation had sealed off both entrances, but tidal and alive with duck at this time of year, wigeon, teal, mallard, pintail, shoveller, shelduck, black and white tufted by the hundred.

The figure ahead had found a hard road now and was heading south along it. He never looked back, although he stopped often enough to shift the cumbersome load again from shoulder to shoulder. Supplies for a winter lying low, perhaps. God alive knew where he proposed to spend it, though. Baxter hurried now, gaining fast on the quarry every time he stopped to shift his load. They passed a windpump and reached the entrance to a farm called Elliots. It had always been Elliots. It was even marked on the map. And they passed through the farm and headed on due south towards the Swale.

Sidney, you fool, where the hell do you think you are going? On a mount overlooking the river entrance stood St Thomas's church, the loneliest of all the lonely churches he explored in his Kent childhood, with a sparse scattering of gravestones in the grass and to the right an empty house, stark against the glowering evening sky. Behind the house a small moated island. Saxon defence, said Porker Crump. Roman, too, said his Latin master, commanding the entrance of the river.

This was the site of Sayes Court, fortified for centuries, but if a fleeing man could have found refuge here from invaders in ages gone by, it was unavailing to a lad from the Edgware Road with the stitch in his side and one boot sole flapping, fast running out of wind and warmth, and a figure closing on him from behind.

Sidney paused and considered, bent over tight with pain. He could not seem to think straight any more. It had happened too quickly.

The security men arriving in the van to check out the camp with their Alsatian. He shouldn't have panicked and run. He should have kept cool and waited. They would never have found him in the store-room. And the bungalow he had planned to find for a hideaway was at Warden Bay, in the opposite direction. He had been too keen to slip out of the camp before they spotted him and he had taken the first path by the chapel. But this was not like Warden Bay. It was wild and windy and chilled the warm glow of the Scotch out of him. The distant buildings seemed a possibility when he left the chapel and that old house might have done, only there was someone here, close behind him, coming on all the time. His chest heaved as he fought for breath. The wind and rain seemed stronger by the second and darkness was closing in. There was no route ahead across the lower salt-marsh where fat geese gorged themselves contentedly, oblivious of the weather. A path ran beside some old farmworkers' cottages ahead. He splashed hopelessly on. Ducks called and quarrelled from the dyke beyond the sea wall. He seemed to have reached the end of the world. But the figure behind him kept on coming. He knew it was no casual stranger. But he wasn't going back.

Baxter knew he must not stop now. He plodded steadily on past the farmworkers' cottages and on beside the sea wall, watched warily by the nearest ducks. The figure ahead stopped again. And with a great heavy windmilling whirl of his arms he swung his bundle away through the air in a slow curve. It landed in one of the long ponds beside the sea-wall with a splash that set families of ducks rising with squawks of terror and indignation. The two men on the wall, not twenty yards apart now, watched the heavy sack sink into the muddy water. It was deep. And the first figure seemed satisfied and moved to the edge of the wall as the second started running towards him in sudden alarm.

Sidney fell sideways in the same semi-cartwheel that the bag had described when he threw it a few seconds earlier. And the murky water accepted him with a similar splash and more ducks screamed in rage and took to the air, wing-beating away across the desolate scene as the second man came running and dived deep into the water.

Baxter rose from the water for the third time with a superhuman effort, took one final great gasping gulp of air and coiled and curved back down into the black depths in a final despairing dive. And this time the body did come free as he tugged. It rose with him, slowly and

186

reluctantly, and he dragged it the final feet to the surface. They broke water together. It gushed from their noses, their mouths and their hair. He heaved and gasped, thrust an arm under the youth's jaw and paddled sideways and slowly to the sea wall. It took another effort of strength he thought beyond him to land Sidney like a huge catch from the deep on the corner of the wall. As he turned the body over and clambered out he noticed the pockets were crammed with tins. Tins of baked beans, the weight which had taken him so swiftly to the weeds at the bottom.

He started to pump the water from the lungs, pressing and thrusting, straight from the manual he had studied as a young copper thirty years before. And the water came out and he blew air in. In and out he pumped and then he blew, but through the mud he could smell the Scotch and he knew it was hopeless if the boy had been drunk, but he would not give in.

There were no dying words from Sidney, no tremor of life at all. So Baxter took him to the lonely inn above the saltings. He made three telephone calls and he drank three brandies and he and the landlord kept the murderer warm and dry. But they could not bring him back to life.

The coroner, who had a nasty cold, blew his nose loudly and replaced his handkerchief with great deliberation before continuing. "Whether this unfortunate youth intended to take his own life or not we shall never know and in view of the large quantity of alcohol which he had consumed in the hours immediately preceding his death, it is doubtful whether he himself knew exactly what he was doing when he plunged from that sea wall. The hideous and appalling tragedies leading to his flight and attempted arrest are matters for inquiry by other coroners' courts and it is not for me to comment upon them. But it is clearly right that I should record this verdict as an open one and I would only add two comments.

"I commend the officer, Mr Baxter, for his devoted efforts to save the youth's life and I offer my most profound sympathy to the boy's parents for the dreadful ordeals they have suffered these past days."

"Stand please!" called the coroner's officer pompously.

Baxter turned and made his way to the back of the room.

"Fancy a drink, guv?" said Armstrong at his elbow.

"Yes, I do," he said, pushing his way through the throng in the lobby and out down the steps into the street.

"There's a nice little boozer down on the right," said Armstrong, leading the way. "I sussed it out last night. Bit poky, but it's not a press pub."

Baxter followed. "Did you have someone run Steve Franklin out to the airport this morning?" he said.

"He wouldn't have it," said Armstrong. "Said he'd take a bus from the air terminal. He just seemed glad it was all over. Nice feller."

"Yes," said Baxter thoughtfully, "if it hadn't been for him I would never have thought of asking the Dunns if they had an old holiday haunt Sidney loved. Franklin had a case just like it back home apparently. He had to shoot the guy in the end."

"We don't like shooters," said Armstrong.

"No. Still, didn't make much difference to Dunn in the end, did it? He's in the mortuary."

"That verdict might just as well have been suicide," said Armstrong, leading the way into the tiny pub. "It wouldn't have made it any worse for the parents. I mean, the bugger had murdered six other poor bastards."

"And it could have been seven," said Baxter. "Harry King was lucky."

"So were you, with respect, guv," said Armstrong, as they reached the bar. "That caper in the park . . ." He shook his head.

"Pint of bitter please and a large Glenfiddich. Nearly came off, though, didn't it? Sidney was a smart boy. I knew he'd turn up on the outing if we didn't frighten him off. What a weird one to finish on."

"Mind made up?"

"Oh yes. I don't think I'd have had a lot of choice anyway. But it's a good pension and the new job's a nice number. Diana's delirious at the idea of my coming home at six every night."

"Hullo, Mr Baxter," said a cheerful young voice behind him. It was young Kevin Toomey from the *Globe*.

He groaned. "What the hell do you want?" he said.

"I tracked you here from a discreet distance," said Toomey. "One of your specialities, I seem to recall. Large gin and tonic please, love. I heard this was your last case, Mr Baxter."

"So?" he growled, sipping his Scotch.

"Might make a nice line, specially if you were going—reluctantly, shall we say?"

"I think I can manage without any publicity from now on, thanks all the same."

"Nothing knocking, mind. And we did give you a good spread on the arrest. Sorry, attempted arrest."

"You did," said Baxter. "And if you check with Harry King, who I understand is now your boss on the news desk, I think you'll find he is quite happy to leave me in peace."

"Yes, it's funny, that," said Kevin reflectively as he paid for his drink. "Can I get you both fresh ones? No? Thanks, love, and a packet of peanuts, please. I mean, Harry had some set-up with the American, Steve Franklin. Then the next thing we know he's had some sort of tumble and cracked his head. He comes into the office looking like death, clears out his old desk and pisses off for a week's holiday with his family. Oh, he's back now and chirpy as ever, as well he might on his new salary, but I saw his face that afternoon and he looked as if he'd come face to face with something very nasty indeed and wanted to forget it in a hurry."

"I wouldn't say that day was one I want to recall particularly fondly," said Baxter. "Yes, a quick one, then, Frank. I'm meeting Di for lunch. She's going to buy me a pin-stripe suit." He leaned on the counter and stared ruminatively through the hatch into the public bar. A couple of young lads at the front looked vaguely familiar. He frowned. He had clocked those faces before, right enough. Christ, it was going to be hard to switch off old habits.

"Bloody hell, that's him, that Baxter," said Kenny, muttering into his pint. "No, through the hatch there, glaring."

"So what?" said Wayne. "We done nothing. We're entitled to go to an inquest."

"Yes, I know," said Kenny. "Creepy, though, wasn't it? Hearing them talking about him like that. You reckon he was going to make a swim for it when he went in off that sea-wall?"

"No!" said Wayne scornfully. "He hardly ever went down the baths, did he? Well, only for a bath. I mean, in the pool he was a bloody dead loss. He used to sink after two yards. No, I reckon he just went potty weeks ago, old Sid."

"He always was a bit potty," Kenny agreed. "Specially about tourists. He couldn't stand them, could he? That last Saturday, down the market. Going on and on about it."

"It's the thought of that Wednesday night still gives me nightmares," said Wayne. "Bloody hell, it's only a week ago! Old Agger was saying last night, it could have been us lot, stabbed in the guts in

189

the middle of the Fulham Road."

Kenny shivered and then brightened as he drained his glass. "Here," he said, "my old man said he'd run us over to Charlton to see the lads on Saturday."

"What, to the Valley? Great!" said Wayne. "We owe them a right thrashing this season. Tell you what, we'll win three nought. Clive two, Davie one, diving header!"

"Super Blues!" said Kenny. "That Agger'll be sick missing out on one of his precious away games. He's got to go to a family wedding." They paused to consider the prospect, cackling with laughter.

"Anyway, Mr and Mrs Dunn, we would be prepared to pay up to fifty thousand for the full story of Sidney's life and all the family snapshots and any papers or diaries which perhaps he might have had in his room. It's a lot of money. The buildings are rather spartan, I know. You could move out of the area, perhaps retire to the coast and take a bungalow, Margate or Cliftonville, perhaps. You have your own lives to lead again and dwelling on this tragedy won't help. I'm sure you have many happy memories of Sidney you would like to share with our readers."

Elsie Dunn sipped her port and lemon cautiously and looked round the hotel lounge with wide-eyed awe. "Fifty thousand pounds?" she said. "That much for our Sidney's story?"

"It's easy for you to say it," said her husband gruffly, equally ill at ease in his best blue suit. "But who says you'd pay it?"

"Oh, I have full executive authority to make the payment to you," said Harry King smoothly. "Don't you worry about that. I can let you have a cheque this very afternoon. Then you'd come away to a nice hotel like this one, only quieter in the country. I'd chat with you for a day or so and one of our reporters would take it all down on paper and everyone would see that young Sidney was just a normal boy, with his records, his bike and his football, who was sadly taken ill. You could explain all that to our readers, you see. And then you could start a new life. Your railway pension is due soon, too, I believe, Mr Dunn."

"Eight months' time," he said. "God, Elsie, who'd have thought our Sidney could have bought us all that?"

She nodded. "Ramsgate," she said.

"I'm sorry?" said King.

"Ramsgate's nicer than Margate or Cliftonville, they say," she said. And she started to cry.

Back in Giles Buildings old Mrs. Roberts peeped out through her net curtains at the gleaming motor-cycle in the corner of the yard. It looked as if it might rain. Sidney always kept his bike well covered up against the wet weather. He wouldn't have wanted it to get rusty. He seemed a nice boy at heart. Always gave her a name, although she could not deny the Buildings would be quieter without him. She twitched the curtain back into place and went to make a cup of tea in the dark kitchen.

Out in the yard the weather proved her forecast accurate. It started to drizzle and then to rain with a steadier beat. The water splashed off the handlebars of the motor bike. High on the flyover opposite, traffic sped above the Edgware Road with a wet, slick rhythm.

Steve Franklin's flight bus rolled past on its way to the airport. If he had looked up from his newspaper and over to his left he would have seen the inscription at eye-level on the side of the block: 'Giles Buildings, erected 1880 by the Cornworthy Trust".

But he didn't look up, which was really just as well, for the story was over for him, too.